VILLAIN
IN THE
VINEYARD

VILLAIN
IN THE
VINEYARD

A Chesapeake Bay Mystery

Judy L. Murray

LEVEL
BEST BOOKS

Author Photo Credit: Malgorzata Baker Photography

First edition

ISBN: 978-1-68512-928-6

Cover art by Level Best Designs

This book was professionally typeset on Reedsy.
Find out more at reedsy.com

To my very talented children, Meghan and John.

"A house is bricks and mortar. If there is evil, it's in somebody's heart."

—MISS JANE MARPLE,
THE SITTAFORD MYSTERY

Praise for Judy L. Murray and her Chesapeake Bay Mystery Series

"I've loved all Judy L. Murray's Chesapeake Bay Mysteries, but I think this one may be my favorite. With a richly layered plot, a brilliant cast of characters, and an authentic feel for both policing and sleuthing, *Villain in the Vineyard* is a gem."—*Connie Berry, USA Today* bestselling author

"My first time reading a book from the Chesapeake Bay Mystery Series and I did not put it down until finished. Between the fast-paced mystery and the extremely likable characters, I was enthralled with *Villain in the Vineyard*. Helen Morrisey is the sassy sort of true-blue friend you would want. ...Thoroughly enjoyable. Looking forward to getting caught up by reading the first three in the series with a glass of wine and some of Helen's Twizzlers."—*Kings River Life Magazine* review

"Award-winning author Judy L. Murray is a master of mystery suspense laced with a bit of humor and romance."—*PenCraft,* First Place Annual Award

"A gruesome discovery turns a Maryland realtor into a sleuth in Murray's series-starting mystery. *Murder in the Maste...*with plenty of romance, surprises, and a climax that's quite the cliffhanger. ...A strong debut whodunit with a memorable main character."—*Kirkus Reviews*

"Mystery fans will delight in following Maryland Realtor Helen Morrisey as she solves a double murder in *Peril in the Pool House* with the assistance of the vintage detectives populating her imagination."—Lucy Burdette, *USA Today* bestselling author

"A master of mystery suspense, Judy L. Murray is an author to watch... Plenty of red herrings, well-plotted mysteries, and a couple of hints of romance will keep the reader guessing in *Killer in the Kitchen*. With a confident voice, the author has created an indelible heroine and a dazzling cast of supporting characters that are as original and vibrant as the protagonist."—AuthorsReading.com

"*Peril in the Pool House* is smart, fast-paced, beautifully written, and utterly charming. Five stars!"—Connie Berry, *USA Today* bestselling author

"Murray layers lots of suspects in *Peril in the Pool House*...The plot is fast-moving, the relationships among the characters are believable and endearing, and the up-and-down lives of Helen and Joe are once again involved in a murder. I love the way Murray wrapped up the mystery. I highly recommend it."—Susan Van Kirk, author of the Art Center Mysteries

Chapter One

Real Estate Rule #4: Beware a house covered in tangled vines, for they conceal deceit.

Dwarfed by a half-ton red snow plow, Helen Morrisey tapped the brakes of her navy-blue Mini Cooper and followed it down the narrow main street of the flourishing little water town of Port Anne, Maryland, toward her real estate office and second home. Port Anne sat at the very top of the enormous Chesapeake Bay, its watershed stretching over five hundred miles and six states from New York to Virginia before spilling into the Atlantic Ocean. Helen never got tired, winter or summer, of gazing across its endless expanse of moving water. This February, it was mostly blue, gray, and white ice. It was the coldest winter in twelve years.

Her windshield wipers scraped across her window as the winter sun struggled to announce morning. Helen didn't notice. She'd reached what she considered a momentous decision. She was excited.

Her cell rang. She smiled. Perfect timing. It was Joe, man of the hour. She punched the Bluetooth call button on her dashboard.

"Good morning, Detective McAlister. I was thinking about you."

"Hi. Got a minute?" Joe sounded tense, distracted.

She frowned. "Sure." Helen could hear Joe's car radio squawking in the background. "Hold on. I'm sitting at the red light coming into Port Anne." She gave a wave to a pedestrian on the sidewalk and stopped in a nearby lot. "Okay, what's up? Need to cancel dinner tonight?"

1

"Most likely." The detective hesitated. "Do you know a Bill Elison?"

"Yes, I know Bill. He's a client of mine and a friend. We're meeting this afternoon. He lives outside of Port Anne off Lara Cove Road, not far from Captain's Watch B&B. He's the owner of Bayworks Cleaning Services in town. Why?"

Joe cleared his throat. His voice dropped. "I'm sorry, hon. There's no easy way to say this. He's had an accident. He fell down his basement stairs. Might have broken his neck. Coroner is on his way."

"Oh, no." Helen choked on her words. "I've known Bill for years. He is the nicest man." She bit her tongue. *"Was.* Why did you think to call me?"

"We found your Safe Harbor Realtors business card in his shirt pocket."

Silence. Helen tugged her coat up around her ears. The first of February on the Chesapeake Bay could be cold. Today was bitter, a record breaker. She cranked up the heat in her coupe, her nod to the tenacious Nancy Drew. Hot air blew across the dashboard and onto her face. She pushed her short, dark hair out of large green eyes and stared with blurry eyes at the narrow street coated in salt mix in front of her.

"Helen, are you there?"

She blinked. "Yes, I, I'm in shock. I can't believe what I'm hearing."

"When did you last see him? And where?"

"Geez, we met at his house on Tuesday. Two days ago. About three o'clock. He wanted to sell his house. We were meeting again this afternoon to go over my numbers and decide on the price." She tugged off her leather gloves and blew on stiff fingers.

"Does he have family nearby? I need his next of kin."

"I'll send you his daughter's number."

"If you could come right now, I'd like you to walk through the house before more people trample through it. You can tell me if you notice anything different since you were here. Can you do that?"

"Of course. Let me make a call and put off my eleven am appointment. I'll be there in about ten minutes. This is so sad."

"I know. I'm sorry." Joe hung up.

Port Anne was home to Helen. College years in Washington D.C. to earn undergrad and master's degrees were exciting, but big cities could never replace her little town on the bay. She felt lost when she couldn't see the water. In her late twenties, she came back and nursed her mother until she passed away. Down on the docks of Port Anne Yacht Club, she met her true love, Andy Morrisey. With his background in site engineering and her fascination with rehabbing old houses, they became inseparable until he died five years ago.

Over the past ten years, Port Anne began morphing from a tiny, one-light crossroads to a newfound tourist destination with fancier pocketbooks discovering its charm. McMansions started popping up along the Bay's shorelines, razing summer cottages. Old timers often resented these newbies. It was an ongoing tug of war between those who resisted any change and newcomers with new money and new ideas. Slowly, slowly, some of Port Anne's young people were heading to colleges, while others stepped off the crab boats of past generations for new technical skills. It wasn't an easy transition for anyone who'd grown up on the Chesapeake.

The scent of crab cakes wafted down the street from The Blue Crab as she passed two sandwich boards sitting on the sidewalk. Port Anne's shops sold goods ranging from sweatshirts to luxury handbags. Store owners and restaurants depended on loyalists seeking local delicacies rather than discounts. Water Street Market, a gourmet mini grocery store, had revamped a sixties era abandoned gas station and sat catty-corner to the only intersection with a traffic light. Their fresh seafood and Italian specialties were to die for. A foodie who hated to cook, Helen made a regular stop to pick up premade dinners she could pop in her oven. She pretended they were homemade.

Winter months, after the holidays and before the spring arrivals of boaters, caused Port Anne businesses to struggle. Herb's Bait Shop, quieter in February, would be bustling with fishing enthusiasts from miles around in a couple months. It wasn't his amazing array of gear that pulled visitors inside.

It was Herb's advice on fishing that came from generations of experience. Advice a chain store could never match. A full-scale cardboard President George Walker Bush holding a fishing rod stood sentry on the sidewalk and drew you inside. Across from a utilitarian brick post office, St. Mary's Church protected precious graveyards that went back to the 1700s.

She slowed and studied Calli's Tomes and Treasures colorful windows, chocked with hand-designed jewelry, candles, and charcuterie boards, Port Anne t-shirts, and seasonal pillows. It was the unofficial bookstore for the area. Book signings ran from early spring up through Christmas. Tomes and Treasures was a shop plucked from a Hallmark movie.

* * *

Helen hit Tammi's direct dial on her phone. She hated to tell Tammi her news. They'd worked together with Bill for years.

"Good morning." Tammi picked up, her voice its usual booming, cheery self. "Helen Morrisey's office. This is her Assistant Extraordinaire Tammi Damon speaking."

Helen couldn't help but feel better. "Hello Assistant Extraordinaire. I need to rearrange my schedule today. Can you make a couple calls for me?"

"Sure. What's up? Had a late night with your favorite detective?" Tammi's bangles clinked on her keyboard. "Okay. Got your calendar open. What's happening?"

Helen inhaled. "Joe just called me. He's at Bill Elison's house. Bill fell down his basement stairs." She cleared her throat. "He's dead."

Tammi's voice dropped to a broken protest. "No, that can't be. I texted him yesterday morning to confirm your appointment for today."

"Did he sound all right?"

"He gave me a thumbs-up."

"Bill couldn't be much more than sixty."

"A lesson for you. Not good to live alone. You should let Joe move in with you."

Helen made a face. "Let me remind you, I'm about to turn fifty-four and have plenty of company already."

"You live with an imaginary Detection Club. Your crew of consultants doesn't constitute a personal relationship. They don't keep you warm at night," Tammi objected.

"I'm ignoring you. Besides, I've got two cats. Can you catch Calli? She's expecting a Zoom call from me at eleven. I'm walking her through her offer online, and then she'll sign electronically. Push her back to this afternoon if you can. Joe wants me to check on Bill's house. See if I notice any changes since Tuesday." Helen scrolled down her calendar. "I'm not sure how long I'll be. Try to make two o'clock work. Don't mention Bill until we know more."

"Sounds like he's inviting your Detection Club to help solve a case."

"Don't be ridiculous. The last thing he wants is me quoting the wisdom of five amateur sleuths. I'm lucky he tolerates them as much as he does. Besides, this is an accident, not murder."

Tammi hmphed. "Was Bill married? I don't remember."

"He's divorced. His kids ran the business with him." Helen hesitated. "Do you remember Alicia Jarrett? Young widow, two grade school children."

"Of course. You've checked on her for years. Isn't she in remission for colon cancer?"

"Thank goodness. Her husband died about three years before she was diagnosed. I called Bill and told him about Alicia. Asked if he'd consider reducing the fee to clean her apartment once a month until she was back on her feet, and I'd cover the bill. Bill didn't hesitate. The very next day, Bayworks was at Alicia's door. They scrubbed her house from stem to stern. It's been almost two years now. Bill sent his crew every month, no questions asked. Whenever I asked for an invoice, he refused to send it."

"He was such a teddy bear. A lot of people in town will miss him." Tammi gulped.

"That's for sure." Helen sighed. "Do me a favor. Forward Bill's thumbs up text he sent to you, and the time you received it. It might help Joe."

"Will do."

* * *

Just before she reached the border of Osprey Point State Park, she turned onto Lara Cove Road, bumping along the long, twisty, narrow road in the winter gloom. Her coupe skirted around uneven pockets of ice water toward the brink of the Chesapeake Bay facing Ferry Point. She spotted Joe's black unmarked Ford Explorer, its lights flashing, in front of a long, low ranch. A volunteer ambulance service from town, along with two marked police cars, were parked at Bill's front door.

A deputy halted her approach.

She held up her ID and a business card. "Detective McAlister asked me to come." The uniform stepped aside.

She could hear Joe's deep voice from the living room and followed it. His broad back was turned to her, a young officer next to him taking notes.

"Joe?"

"Hi. Thanks for coming over. I know this will be hard." He handed her blue foot coverings and plastic gloves and gestured toward the basement stairs. Bill Elison's bulky body was sprawled out on the concrete floor below, blood pooled around his head. A shipping box lay on its side near him. Two EMTs were packing up their medical equipment.

Helen gulped and covered her eyes. "I'm usually the one who calls you to a death scene."

"Don't remind me."

"Who found him?"

"His house cleaner. She works for his company and cleans his house Tuesday mornings. She has a key. She came by today because she'd forgotten her eyeglasses. The last job she did was fold towels in his basement laundry room. The basement door was open, and the lights were off. When she flipped on the switch, she spotted Bill at the bottom of the stairs. She could barely speak; she's so distraught. I sent her home. We'll interview her later."

"How can I help?" she asked, her voice low, her face bleak.

"Everything indicates an accident. I'm being cautious. Coroner should be here any minute to confirm. I'm hoping the office sends Ed. The EMTs

6

think Mr. Elison has been dead a while, maybe as much as two days. You may be the last person to have seen him alive."

"Two days is a long time not to be missed. I'm sure Ed can narrow the time down. He's the best coroner around."

"How well did you know Bill?"

"A mix of business and pleasure. He was a Port Anne Yacht Club member. He started Bayworks, a residential cleaning service, years ago. Built it into a successful family business. I hire them to clean houses before we put them on the market. They do an excellent job. He has a daughter, Georgia. Her husband's name is Todd Myers. Tammi and I have worked with Georgia a lot more often than Todd because she processes our requests for service. I think they have one child about fourteen. I'd spot them out on their boat. Do they know yet?"

"No. I called Georgia before you. She's on her way."

"I got the idea they were all close. This news will be devastating."

"Wife?"

"Ex. I never met her. He told me they divorced about six years ago."

Joe jotted down another note in a pocket-sized spiral pad. "Why was he selling his house? Any problems?"

"I don't think so. Bill wanted to buy a townhouse in Port Anne Isle. He wanted a dock for his boat, but a smaller house with less maintenance. Such happy plans." She covered her eyes and swallowed.

"Girlfriend?"

"Not that he mentioned. I didn't ask."

"Let's inspect all the rooms. Take your time. Tell me if anything appears different since you were here. What time did you meet?"

"Today's Thursday. We met Tuesday at three. Finished up about five-thirty. I headed for home after that. Wouldn't he have gone into his office Wednesday morning?"

"You would assume." Joe ran strong hands through his Marine cut of thick brown hair, his sideburns touched with grey. They both turned toward the sound of heavy footsteps at the front door. County Coroner Ed Tarlone, followed by two assistants, bustled in.

Joe offered his hand. "Ed, thanks for getting here so fast. You remember Helen?"

The short, stocky man with thick horn-rimmed glasses set, as was usual, on the top of a thinning crown, eyed Helen. Dressed in a white bunny suit, he gave her a startled blink. He dropped a bulky medical case on the floor with a weary thud. "You again? Remind me to never hire you to sell my house. You're a bad penny. Keep turning up whenever there's a body."

Helen returned his tight smile. "Don't blame it on me. Joe called *me* this time."

Ed grunted. "What have we got?"

Chapter Two

J oe led the way through the kitchen to the basement doorway. "The victim is Bill Elison, homeowner. It appears as if he fell down his basement steps. EMTs think he's been gone at least twelve hours. Could have been as many as thirty. I asked Helen to walk through the house with me. She met Mr. Elison here Tuesday until about five-thirty pm."

"Let's take a look." Resignedly, Ed lowered his glasses down over a wide nose and trundled down the stairs, his forensic assistants at his heels.

Joe took Helen's arm. "Let's start in the kitchen. Everything seem the same?"

Helen's eyes roved the countertops. "Those dishes weren't in the sink. He must have eaten dinner and didn't clean up afterwards. Then again, we don't know if it was Tuesday night's meal or Wednesday's, do we?"

She circled the room. "We sat at the table. He took me through the house while I made notes." She picked up an orange and blue ballpoint pen in the center of the table. "One of my freebies. Give them to clients all the time." She picked up a silver one and squinted at the imprint. "Vince Caffrey, Insurance Broker. He must be Bill's insurance agent. Don't remember that being here, but I may not have noticed." She set it back.

"He offered me a glass of wine, but I turned him down. I wonder if he'd be alive today if I'd stayed for that drink. We walked over to his garage. Didn't last outside because it was so darn cold." She choked. "You know I hate the cold. Hurts my fingers and my feet."

"Anyone aware you were meeting?"

"Other than Tammi? She's got a GPS on me twenty-four seven. Yesterday, she confirmed my appointment for this afternoon."

"That's helpful."

Helen scrolled through her texts, then held her phone up to Joe. "Here, I'll show you. At eleven thirty-one, Wednesday, Bill gave Tammi a 'thumbs up'." She frowned. "Is there a chance he didn't send the message?"

Joe squinted at her screen. "Copy that text and send it to me. We haven't found his phone yet, but we'll run DNA on his case as soon as we find it."

"If he were anything like me, a dozen people could have touched his phone. I hand my phone to other people all the time." She grimaced. "I'd think they would have talked with him in the past twenty-four hours."

"I do too. I'll talk to Georgia. Follow me." Joe led her back to the stairs. "Did you go into the basement with him?"

"Absolutely. I took notes on the house systems, water leaks, all that."

They watched as Ed, on his hands and knees, crawling around Bill, taking photos from every angle with a Nikon. "See anything from here? I can't take you down right now. Let's go this way." Joe pointed toward the hall.

Helen hesitated. Jessica Fletcher was murmuring in her ear. "Did you say he might have tripped?"

"We're guessing he was carrying that box and lost his step."

She kneeled down, put her left cheek to the floor, and squinted. She brushed her fingers along the edge of a thin strip of metal threshold running between the wooden kitchen floor and the carpet at the top of the stairs. "This is odd. The strip is raised, and the carpet is torn. I would have spotted that when Bill took me downstairs. It's the kind of hazard homeowners ignore, and I warn them to fix before we have buyers touring the house. Lawsuit in the making."

Joe bent next to her and snapped photos. "Someone wouldn't notice it until they caught their toe. By then, it might be too late." He gestured at the step to forensics.

"Exactly."

He sat back on his heels. "Good catch, Nancy Drew. That's why I asked you here."

"Thank Jessica Fletcher this time. She taught me to assume the most unlikely, especially if it could be murder. I checked because she's rarely wrong."

"I didn't invite her," Joe protested. "Or any of your Detection Club sleuths, for that matter."

She waved him away. "Like it or not, they're all here, with antennae up." She stopped and reached for the light switch at the top of the stairs. "Did you say the light switch to the basement stairs was off?"

"It was when we arrived. The cleaning person said she flipped on the light to vacuum the stair carpet and use the laundry room. She turned the light off before leaving. The switch was off when she came back to get her glasses and found Bill on the floor."

"Doesn't it strike you as odd to find the light switch off? I remember he flipped on the light before he led me down. These stairs are dark. Wouldn't Bill's first instinct be to turn on the light before he starts down the stairs? Then he trips, drops the box, and falls all the way." She reenacted Bill's moves. "If this was an accident, why did the cleaner find the light off?" Helen pointed. "What about this switch for the oil burner? Was it on or off? Up or down?"

"It was off when we arrived," Joe responded. "Why?"

"Bill pointed it out because it's next to the light switch. I suggested he replace this white cover with a red one to identify the oil burner. I told him I had a tenant who complained their heat wasn't working. They kept turning off the oil burner switch instead of the light until I changed the cover to red. If someone pushed him, then turned off the stairs' light as they left, it's a good bet they flipped the oil burner off along with the light. Bill would never turn off the heat in the middle of February."

"Explains why the house is cold. I'll have a deputy check with the cleaner. Let's look around Bill's office."

Helen eyed the rear door. "Any sign of forced entry?"

"No. If someone did harm him, Bill either knew them and invited them inside or they had a key."

"Which would probably be his family or the cleaning staff."

"Agreed. This wasn't a break-in."

They stopped.

"Joe?" Ed climbed the stairs.

"What do you see?"

Ed glanced at Helen. "There's a severe bruise on the left side of the skull. It's likely a result of his fall along the rail. The right side is different. The angle and impact suggests one thing. Someone deliberately slammed Mr. Elison's head against the concrete."

Joe glanced up at Helen. Her face was white.

"How confident are you?" Joe asked.

"Very. I'll confirm after the autopsy, of course."

"What we need to decide is if this was an accident that led to murder, or murder a killer staged as an accident." Joe touched Helen's shoulder. "Either way, we've got a murder on our hands. Let's check the other rooms."

Bill's office was long and narrow, running across the back of the house. A black desk faced tall windows offering a broad view of the Chesapeake. Two Bald Eagles, talons out, skimmed along the water's edge searching for breakfast. It was a peaceful room. The sun had begun to brighten as the morning fog lifted, but the waves were frozen in motion. Plaques on the wall, awarded by the Kent County Business Association, hung on the east wall.

Helen studied the collection of family photos on his desk next to a computer monitor. "Grandchildren," she pointed out. "He told me they'd come back from a trip last week to Disney World." She spun around. "The desk is messier than when I saw it, but he could have been working after I left."

Joe shifted papers. "Ahah! Bill's cell phone." He reached into his jacket pocket, took out a plastic baggie, and dropped the phone inside.

Helen pointed at an empty rock glass on Bill's desk. "He had a nightcap. We parted about six or so on Tuesday. Makes me think he walked around the room with a drink in his hand either Tuesday or Wednesday night."

She wandered around the room. "Here's his liquor cabinet. Typical choices. Must have been a fan of Blue Heron Vineyard down the road. There's three bottles of their cabernet. Do you think anything in the house was stolen?"

"No sign of it so far."

"Bill showed me his wine collection in a temperature-controlled cabinet in the basement. Nothing fancy. Holds about fifty bottles."

She set aside a flyer describing Bill's new townhouse and lifted the lid on his copier. "This is interesting." She flipped through a stack of papers from the tray. "This is his purchase agreement for his new house. His signature is dated Wednesday, January thirty-first. The cover sheet says he scanned it at eight eleven am."

Joe peered over her shoulder. "Proves he was alive Wednesday morning. He texted Tammi the thumbs up later, unless someone tampered with his phone." Joe tucked the sales agreement into an envelope and sealed it. "Let's check the second floor."

Upstairs, Helen pushed back the door to Bill's bedroom. "He was wearing that mauve sweater on that chair Tuesday night. I remember because I really don't like purplish colors on a man."

"Note to self. But no law against changing his clothes. Maybe he didn't like purple either."

"Don't be smart," she retorted.

Joe grunted.

She fingered a blanket. "The bed is neat. He either never slept in his bed Wednesday night or was still alive Thursday morning after he made it."

"Agree. Time of death is later Wednesday or early this morning."

"Joe, I've had three clients' houses defaced since early January. Two other clients canceled working with me in just the past week because these attacks are circulating around Port Anne. Maybe they're right to be worried. Is there a chance Bill walked in on my vandal, the vandal panicked, and pushed him down the stairs?"

"At this stage, anything is possible, but I think it's unlikely."

Helen bit her lip. "This could be my fault."

"That's ridiculous. None of this is your fault, even if it is the same perpetrator."

"Dad? Detective? What's going on?" A woman's frantic voice called up the main stairs.

"Must be Georgia Myers," Joe muttered and headed back down the stairs with Helen behind him. A woman in jeans, a zippered jacket with Port Anne High School across the back, and navy sneakers, spun around at the sound of their footsteps.

"Mrs. Myers? I'm Detective McAlister. This is Helen Morrisey with Safe Harbor Realtors. She was supposed to meet your father later today."

"We've worked together," Georgia nodded.

Joe steered her toward a couch. He drew up a chair and faced her, his dark brown eyes gentle. "His cleaner found your father this morning and called for help. I'm afraid your father is gone. I'm very sorry."

Georgia went white. She trembled, hugging herself. "I don't understand. How? Did he have an accident? My dad was as strong as an ox."

"Our coroner is with him now. He's reviewing the scene. There's a bent piece of stair trim and a tear in the carpet. A large box is upended at the bottom. At this point, we're not sure how it happened. Someone may have pushed him down his basement stairs or hurt him after he fell. The basement lights were off when we arrived." His voice dropped. "I'm sorry."

"Are you suggesting someone was in his house and deliberately hurt him?"

"It's definitely a possibility. There are signs he suffered a blow to the back of his head."

Helen tucked an arm over Georgia's shoulders. "Did you call your husband?"

The younger woman glanced at her phone. "Todd? I called and texted. He didn't pick up. He's at the county sports arena with my son, Matthew, and his baseball team. They use the indoor practice field in the winter. It's almost impossible to hear a phone ring inside the building." Her hands shook.

"I'll send a deputy to the arena and inform your husband."

"Thank you." She struggled to get the words out. "Can you be sure my son doesn't come here? He loved his grandpa." Georgia started to cry.

"Can someone be with Matthew for a few hours?" asked Helen, handing her a tissue.

She wiped her cheeks. "Vince Caffrey can take him home. He's our youth league baseball coach."

"Good. If Matthew needs a children's grief counselor later, you tell any of our deputies." Joe studied the young mother. "We're trying to ascertain your father's time of death. Helen was here late Tuesday. Did you speak to him since?"

Georgia gestured to Helen. "He told me he was meeting you here when he left our office Tuesday afternoon. He was excited, and I was glad. I told him you were the best Realtor around. He always liked working with you. I didn't care for the agent who sold him the new townhouse." She caught a jagged breath. "We didn't talk afterwards. He needed time to sort through his paperwork. I thought I'd give him some alone time."

"Any chance your husband talked with him?"

"I doubt it. They don't talk."

Joe eyed Helen. "Do you mind staying with Georgia until Todd arrives?"

"Of course not. Whatever I can do."

Chapter Three

J ust before noon, Helen trudged up Safe Harbor's wide planked steps
and across its wooden porch. She scraped the salt off the soles of her
boots on a mat in front of the Victorian's massive old door. A captain's
bell jingled, and she inhaled the normal, cheerful chatter. It was a warm
blanket on a cold, sad day. When her husband, Andy, died, they proved they
were her second family.

The receptionist gave her a friendly wave as she headed down the hall.
Their office administrator, Stella Perdue, with a round face and a cap of
short grey hair, glanced up from a file. Stella directed sales agents' comings
and goings like a traffic cop during a Port Anne parade.

Tammi Damon, her assistant, was holding court as only she did. With
her thousand-watt smile, smooth dark skin, and dangling earrings that
matched the weather or her mood, people might think she was Helen's
personal publicity agent. She was also her drill sergeant and her best friend
in disguise. Tammi followed Helen into her private office and took a seat
across from her.

"How are you doing?"

Helen tossed her orange leather tote onto her desk and collapsed into her
chair.

"The police believe Bill was murdered. Joe asked me to walk through
the house in case anything seemed different." She rubbed her forehead. "I
helped Joe break the news to Bill's daughter, Georgia." Helen's voice trailed
off. "I may have been the last person to see him alive other than his killer. He
was a good man. He was a volunteer firefighter and on our school board. He

did a lot for Port Anne. It's so sad for someone to work to build a business for his family and never get to reap the rewards later in life. When we talked Tuesday, he was ready to start enjoying himself. New house, less work. He was planning a cruise." She opened her desk drawer and took out an open bag of Twizzlers. She offered them to Tammi, who wrinkled her nose. "Lunch," Helen declared.

Tammi's sparkly snowflake earrings swung back and forth. "I have a salad on my desk."

"Aren't you the perfect picture of health?" Helen sniffed. "Did you reach Calli about rescheduling our Zoom call to this afternoon?"

"I did. She'd much prefer to meet you in person. She's willing to come here if that's more convenient for you."

"Why is she insisting she sign her offer in person?"

"Some people appreciate face-to-face meetings. Buying a house is an important moment for her."

Helen walked to the window and stared out at the little main street. A single line of traffic crawled along, bumper to bumper. She listened to the concern in Tammi's voice. "Good advice. Give me a sec." She picked up her phone.

"Calli? It's Helen. Instead of coming over to my office, why don't I stop by your shop at two? We can go over your offer there." She heard the relief in Calli's voice.

She smiled at Tammi. "Better?"

"Much better. She's nervous. You complete these contracts all the time. She does this once or twice a lifetime."

"Thanks for reminding me." Helen waved another Twizzler at Tammi. "Now, don't you have other work to do besides keeping me in line?"

* * *

The Port Anne Volunteer Fire Company's digital sign flashed twenty-two degrees. Shivering, Helen pulled up the hood on her long down coat as she scooted along the sidewalk toward Calli's Tomes and Treasures, two blocks down. Pulling on Calli's aqua-painted door, she stepped inside and slammed it shut to keep out a chilly blast. "Phew!"

Calli's assistant, Viv, raised her eyes from the register. "Hi, Helen. I heard you were on your way."

"I'm sure it'll cost me money," Helen laughed. "Do I ever leave this store without buying?"

"Hopefully not. Business has been quiet since the holidays."

"Everyone is claustrophobic by St. Patrick's Day. You'll pick up as soon as April starts to tease us with a taste of warmer days. Is Calli in the back?"

"Doing paperwork. Want me to get her?" Viv leaned across the wooden check-out desk, a hand cupped to her mouth. "She's kind of nervous about moving."

"I'll find her." Helen squeezed between the rows of displays to reach a rear room lined with candles, sweatshirts, tote bags, and wooden signs.

A tall, regal woman in her early seventies sat at an old desk surrounded by new orders. Her grey eyes lit up. "Hi! Thank you for coming into the store." She set down her readers, her face pale. "Are you sure I'm making the right decision? I've lived in the same house over forty years."

Helen opened her tote. "I wouldn't encourage you if I thought this wasn't perfect. I'd rather lose a sale than a good friend." Her voice was warm with encouragement. "You won't have to worry about house maintenance anymore, and you'll be minutes from the shop."

Calli smiled. "They'll have to carry me out in a box before I sell this shop." She leaned back after her last signature, excited yet more relaxed. She set down her pen. "Well, Nancy Drew, I hear you were at Bill Elison's house this morning." Her face darkened. "Did he really fall down his basement steps?"

"Bad news travels fast, doesn't it? The police suspect murder. Joe McAlister asked me to walk through the house with him. I may be the last person to see him in person." She studied Calli's worried face. "Do you have something to tell me? Spill it."

Calli's chin dropped, and her eyes clouded. "Bill and I grew up together, and I'll really miss him. I was thinking of his type of job. He saw the inside of how people lived every day. I'm sure he was used to keeping their secrets.

Reminds me of you and your job."

Helen's green eyes widened. "Good thought, and you're right. I can tell you who sleeps with whom in whose bed. Who hides candy in the bathroom drawers? Who has maxed out credit cards? Who is a hoarder, and who is OCD? It's amazing what clients leave out on display for someone they assume won't notice. They're careless. Unless their habits could impact their sale or are illegal, I have to look away. Are you suggesting he may have seen something he shouldn't? That he might have been silenced?"

Calli only shrugged. "You're the one who consults your own Detection Club."

Helen put a finger to her lips. "Shush. Don't let Joe McAlister hear you." Helen's cell rang. "Sorry, I need to take this." She squeezed the shop owner's arm and rose. "Thanks for your insight on Bill. I'll keep you posted on your offer." She crossed her fingers.

* * *

She stepped onto the sidewalk to answer Joe's call. "Hi. Any news on Bill?"

"Waiting for Ed's autopsy report."

"I'm trying to come up with a list of possible suspects if Ed confirms Bill was murder. So far, I'm at zero." She slowed in front of Prime and Claw Restaurant. "Did you decide if you need to cancel dinner?"

"I'm definitely working late."

"After today, I'd just as soon go home and crawl into bed early. How's tomorrow night? I have to meet Oscar Banyon, the owner of Blue Heron Vineyard, at four. He's finally ready to put twenty acres of his property on the market."

"I thought you had a board meeting for the yacht club at six."

"I do. We both do. Oscar's our commodore. Marketing his land will make working with him a bit sticky. He and our buildings and grounds chair, Vince Caffrey, are butting heads. The Board operates on a shoestring budget, like most small yacht clubs, and the rest of us are trying to prevent a dog fight. Unfortunately, Oscar tends to enjoy creating a scene."

"You're always complaining that those board meetings are long and boring. Sounds like this one could be entertaining," Joe commented.

"Very funny. Meet me about seven-thirty in the Burgee Lounge. Thirst usually encourages everyone to wrap up their discussions no matter how heated."

"That works. Why does the name Vince Caffrey sound familiar? Have I met him?"

"He's good friends with Georgia and Todd Myers. Coaches their son Matthew's baseball team and took him home today."

"Ah, yes, Georgia mentioned him."

She wiggled her fingers in the cold. "I'm walking back to my car. See you tomorrow night."

"I'll be leaning on the bar with a bourbon in my hand. Any chance we can finalize our trip to Italy for May? We've only got a week to meet Howard Travel's deadline."

"Hmm. I suppose we could. Can you have a cabernet waiting for me?"

"I'm surprised you don't want a Nora Charles Sidecar."

"That's a great suggestion. Nothing like a brandy cocktail in this weather. Nora sure knows how to pick them, doesn't she?"

Chapter Four

Friday late afternoon, Helen's Mini bumped up the long twisty private drive in the winter's gloom. Rolling fields led to neat rows of round bales of hay and two beautiful horse stables beyond. Miles and miles of steel-gray water splayed out before her. A long white wooden fence along one side of the drive parceled off a neighboring farm. It ended at a black gate with elaborate scrolled iron forming an overhead arch. She stopped and flashed on her high beams to study a carved, burgundy and gold painted sign. "Blue Heron Vineyard. Welcome," she read out loud. Underneath, smaller script stated, "Tasting Room, Private Events Year-Round." Her dashboard read four o'clock. "Right on time," she muttered and pressed on the gas.

About another half mile further, a wide stone courtyard led to a sprawling three-story bluestone and frame house looming near the top of the hill. A wooden arrow pointed to an impressive, gray-framed wooden barn housing the tasting room and much of the wine fermentation equipment. The Realtor in her was excited. Representing land as renowned as Oscar Banyon's was a major coup. She'd beaten two other top agents, one a wine connoisseur from the Carolinas, to get this listing. She'd worried Oscar would be wooed by the cachet of an out-of-town luxury broker. She parked at the entry's sliding barn door and switched off the Mini.

Her driver's side handle clicked, and her door swung open. A man stood in the dusk.

"Helen?"

She jumped. "Oscar! I didn't see you!" She pushed her hair off her face with gloved hands as she faked a heart attack.

In the shadows, the man was about five eight with neat front teeth and jowls. His nose was long and beaked, accented by a short gray beard. He wore a cashmere fringed scarf. Helen had never seen him without a wool beret, one side draped toward his right earlobe and settled low over his forehead, barely an inch above groomed eyebrows. His style was a throwback to the forties. On the other hand, his thick, dark hair and bronzed skin in the midst of winter exuded a kind of charm. Oscar delighted in his public persona.

His light eyes reflected in the dim light of her car dome. "Sorry I startled you. Leave your car here and let's get inside. It's freezing." Crossing his arms, he clapped his shoulders.

The Mini had chilled in seconds. She grabbed her laptop and darted behind him to the entrance. They ducked inside.

"My Lord, it's cold. I guess we're not going to see Punxsutawney Phil's shadow early this year." She tugged off her gloves and rubbed her hands together.

"That we will not," Oscar agreed. "Come." He tossed off an insulated vest with a Louis Vuitton logo on a breast pocket and reached under the bar. "I've got a special cabernet we're releasing next month as an American Bordeaux-style blend. It's similar to a French Bordeaux but with a bit more blackberry. It'll warm you up."

"I'm honored to enjoy an advanced taste." Helen climbed onto a red leather bar stool and set her tote onto the glossy wood countertop. Oscar handed her a tall, glistening glass of deep red fluid.

"Umm. This smells delicious. Do I detect a hint of cherry?"

Oscar's eyes gleamed in pleasure. "And it tastes even better. Cheers." The two clinked glasses.

"Just what I need. It's been a rough couple of days."

He raised his eyebrows.

"I'm sure you've heard by now about Bill Elison's death. It's rocked me. The police think I may have been the last person to talk to him before he died."

Oscar sat back, surprised. "The rumor I heard was he fell."

Helen's voice dropped. "He did, but there's signs someone attacked him."

22

He startled. "Terrible, terrible shame. Bayworks did all the sanitizing of this wine room and our equipment. Our house, too, come to think of it."

"Did he have any reason to stop by in the past few days?" Helen asked.

"Hmmm. He stopped in about ten days ago. Checking on his crew. His son-in-law didn't show up, so Bill took his place. Bill loved to pick my brains about the best wines. We'd joke together that he couldn't afford any of the ones I recommended." Oscar studied his wine through his glass, his voice dropping. "I don't look forward to dealing with his son-in-law."

Helen stroked the bar. "I've never seen a wood grain in this color. It's stunning. What is it?"

Oscar tapped the wood. "It's called Alder. Comes from the Pacific Northwest. I admired it in a restaurant years ago and swore I'd use it someday." His cell rang with a flourish of French aria. He ignored the call.

Helen drew her eyebrows together. "That song sounds familiar."

"It's 'Dernière danse' and sung by French songwriter Indila."

"You say that so beautifully. What region were you from? I studied French in college but never had the tongue for it."

"I've been in the States too long. My English has influenced my French dialect."

She gestured at the photographs of vineyards around the room. "Those are beautifully matted. Is that your family's home? Do you visit often?"

"Aren't they lovely?" He made a remorseful scrunch of his lips. "I'm afraid my family never forgave me for leaving our vineyard to come here. I haven't been back in years."

"Do you regret it?"

He waved a hand. "I was a young man intent upon making my own way. My father refused to understand."

"Carving your own path when your family owns a business is never easy." She sipped again. "I'm guessing that suntan came from traveling south."

"Not often enough. If we're lucky, Paula and I will hop on a quick flight down to Boca for a few days."

"Nice choice," Helen laughed. "Does your daughter like to go with you?"

23

"She's my stepdaughter, Billie." He wrinkled his nose. "I leave her at home. Makes Paula furious, but I don't care. I told them both it was time she got off my credit cards and got a job." He made a low, sadistic chuckle.

A rear barn door on the opposite wall slid open.

"Oh, Oscar, I apologize. I didn't realize you had a guest." A woman about thirty years old stepped inside. With olive skin, full, cloudy, dark hair, and beautiful teeth, she reminded Helen of a Kardashian.

"Michele," Oscar beamed, "come meet Helen Morrisey. She's representing me in the sale of my extra lots. Helen, this is Michele Mancuso, my winemaker. Come join us."

"So glad to meet you." The two shook hands. "Why does your name sound familiar?"

Michele made a modest tilt of her head. "My father and grandfather own the Mancuso Wineries in Napa, California." She tossed her down jacket onto a nearby chair.

"Really! That's an impressive legacy. I was in Napa years ago. It's beautiful countryside. How is it you aren't working with your family?"

Michele inched over on her stool to sit closer to Helen. "I'm proud of my family, but I reached a stage where I wanted to establish my own name. Get out from under their supervision. Oscar told me he did the same when he left France. We're kindred spirits." She flashed an affectionate eye at her boss.

"Is this new red your creation? It's delicious."

The winemaker smiled. "It is. We are extremely excited about it."

Helen's sharp eyes traveled around the cavernous room trimmed in stained, rough barnwood. Shafts of dwindling light picked up the mahogany bar's brass edge running at least twenty feet along the rear wall. Twelve tall, round wooden casks were stationed down the center with burnished iron lamps on each one.

"This building is impressive. It does your wines justice. Are you ready for the library fundraiser in three weeks?"

Oscar's eyes glistened. "Of course. I've held events here ever since I started twenty-five years ago. This isn't my first soirée." He settled himself on a stool and fondled his tall wine glass. A fleur-de-lis pattern set in a gold signet ring twinkled on his left hand in the dim light. "It's a perfect excuse to bring new visitors to the vineyard."

"No regrets about selling those twenty acres?"

"We've got plenty of acreage for growing grapes, and the slope of those lots makes planting more difficult. Vineyard events are big business year-round. I'd like Blue Heron to diversify. Right now we're missing out."

Helen took another appreciative sip of their new blend. "I admit, I'm a bit surprised you decided to hire a local Realtor instead of a national vineyard specialist."

"I weighed my options. I decided I wanted someone who would focus on my property and not get diverted by other vineyards on the West Coast." He paused. "The question is, are *you* ready?"

"Oh, we're ready. After twenty-six years in the real estate business, this isn't *my* first soirée either. I love having a captive audience. It's a beautiful piece of land. I don't know much about wine, but I know a lot about the Chesapeake."

Oscar topped off her glass. "That's exactly why I chose you." He pointed at her phone. "Jot this number down under my name. Our rear door has a digitally programmed lock. Helps my core staff get in and out. Our security system shuts off when the doors unlock. Be sure to show potential buyers who their neighbor would be. The tasting room and facilities will impress them."

"Thank you." She repeated the code numbers.

"Let's make a toast. To top dollar."

"Maybe we should wait and toast after the lots are sold," Helen said.

"I'm not worried. And I'm not in a hurry. We'll get my price."

Helen's eyebrows raised. "Speaking of price, what have you decided? All I need is a number and I'm ready to go to work." She handed him a pen.

Oscar glanced at his watch. "We both need to leave for the club board meeting. Let me review your numbers again in the morning. Can you stop by about four, and I'll sign off on it?"

"Four o'clock tomorrow?" She clamped her mouth shut in frustration. A seller who kept stalling on price after all their discussions worried her. Was he all talk? It wouldn't be the first time.

Chapter Five

About seven-twenty, Helen and the rest of the Port Anne Yacht Club Board of Governors came tumbling into the bar, desperate to lighten their moods. The Burgee Lounge bustled on this cold Friday night with local members seeking a warm harbor. Candles glowed on the tables, and the smell of fish and steak burst from the kitchen each time a server walked out with a filled tray. Joe gave her a wave from a table for two near a window to the water.

"How was your meeting?" Joe asked.

"Miserable," Helen said between gritted teeth. "Oscar accused Vince Caffrey, the friend of Georgia and Todd, of skimming money from the maintenance budget. Oscar told him his contractor's charges for the new heating system were padded. It's not the first time he's accused Vince. Building maintenance and repairs are a sore subject with the board members, so Oscar knew darn well he was hitting a nerve tonight. I thought Vince was going to slug him."

Helen took a satisfied sip of her sidecar, its edge lightly trimmed with sugar, and gazed through plate glass windows toward the dark bay and the few twinkly lights on the opposite shore. The club's marina was desolate. Abandoned. Four ice breakers hummed along the docks to protect a handful of boats enduring the winter in the water instead of in dry dock like her *Persuasion*. Certainly not the cheerful, warm setting of summer activities.

Joe raised his eyebrows. "Are you sure you want to deal with this guy? Maybe you should forget this property."

"If I only worked with nice, easy people, I'd be penniless. Oscar owns prime waterfront and he's been picking my brain for six months while he made up his mind what lots to sell and which real estate agency he hired. He's got a huge network of winery people I want to meet. Do you know there's over eighty wineries in Maryland?" She reached for her glass. "I'm never quite sure what to do at a wine-tasting. Do you?"

Detective Joe McAlister gave a sly look. "Taste wine?"

"Very funny," Helen smirked. "It's groups of strangers standing around, staring into wine glasses and making odd mouth-scrunching movements. Do you really think they have any idea what they're tasting? Can they discern the difference between a pinot and a malbec? I certainly can't."

"You might have to figure it out if you're the Realtor representing Oscar Banyon's vineyard," Joe muttered into her ear.

"I'd call on my Detection Club chums, but they won't be much help. There's never a discussion of wines in any of the cases they've solved. Jane Marple's a teetotaler, other than sherry. Agatha Raisin tosses down gin and tonics, and Nora Charles is all about her dirty martinis."

Joe chuckled. "Shall we order?"

"Absolutely. You know I'm always starving." She smiled up at their server.

"That's Oscar at the bar," she mumbled, tilting her head in his direction. A man in a black European-cut jacket and pointed leather ankle boots picked up a stemmed glass and studied the liquid, his tanned face set in total disdain.

Oscar glared at Vince, a big man with broad shoulders and a receding hairline. He wore a brown corduroy sport jacket and sat at the opposite end of the bar. Oscar groused into another member's ear while he fingered his glass. This time, his reedy voice rose a couple of octaves, deliberately carrying across the room. Vince raised his head and returned the glare.

She raised her head. "Uh oh. I can hear our commodore from here."

"Banyon certainly plays the part, doesn't he?" Joe remarked.

Helen lowered her chin to hide a snicker. "You think the wool cap and goatee is a little too flamboyant? He capitalizes on his French heritage and can pour on the charm if he wants. His image doesn't fit our Chesapeake casual, but who am I to say? He's been in the area a lot of years." She took in the curious faces of members eating their meals. "I'm afraid he's not making any friends tonight. This group doesn't enjoy confrontation. They're here for a good meal and a chance to exaggerate their boating stories with friends."

Joe raised his eyes. "Vince is the insurance agent."

Helen nodded. "Vince is our small-town hero. A local legend. He went to high school here in Port Anne. He played short stop with the Baltimore Orioles for three years until he destroyed his rotator cuff and got sent back down to the minors. Never climbed back up. Played minors for six years and finally called it quits."

"How's he doing?"

"He works for an agency on Water Street, a few buildings down from Safe Harbor. I've recommended him to some of my clients. They seem to like him. He gets his jollies repeating baseball heroics in the bar. He's the star player for the county senior baseball league and bathes in the attention. Has a thirty-minute radio show for the local station analyzing baseball Saturday mornings. Pretty mundane life compared to being on national television and kids clamoring for his autograph."

Vince rose to his feet and walked toward Oscar's end of the bar. He stuck out his chin. Diners around the small room started taking notice, stopping their own tableside chatter to listen in. Carrying trays, the wait staff began skirting around the two men. The altercation grew a bit louder.

"Oscar, you're put out because I objected to the restaurant ordering your overpriced, fake French Kool-Aid. I'm sick and tired of defending myself," Vince declared, his usual friendly face flushed and angry. "If you were willing to give the yacht club some major price breaks, we might reconsider. But you're too greedy."

The vineyard owner's eyes glowered. He pointed to his glass of house wine. "Zut. What is this? Paint thinner?"

"Don't curse in your fancy French."

"I'll do better than that." Oscar stared down into his glass, drew back, and tossed the red liquid at Vince's jacket. "Does that say enough?"

The ex-ball player grabbed Oscar's lapels. "I can't believe you! I'll take you up with the board. I'll get you removed!"

Helen slid from her seat and approached the bar. Another chair scraped back. Joe was on his feet.

"Oscar, Vince, why don't you discuss this privately?" Helen suggested under her breath, her hands on each man's arm.

The two men sputtered.

Joe stepped between Oscar and Vince, pressing his two hands against their chests. Helen stepped back.

"Let's end this debate before it gets out of hand," he said quietly. "You need to bring this shouting match down a notch. This isn't a pool hall, and you aren't twenty-five anymore. Cool off, or I'll walk you to the door."

The men reared back to glare at Joe. "Who the hell are you to get involved?" declared Oscar, crossing his arms. "Are you a member here?"

"Detective McAlister, Kent County. Come on, gentlemen, this isn't the place."

"I'm leaving." Oscar slammed his glass down. "Put this on his tab." He spun around and stalked out.

"I'll send you my cleaning bill," shouted Vince after him. Helen patted Vince on the back, and she and Joe returned to finish their dinner.

"Oscar was way out of line tonight. You never accuse another member in public of wrongdoing. It's bad form. Oscar's lucky the board doesn't toss him out of his commodore position or at least issue a written warning." She sat back. "These last few days have been a killer. He was definitely surprised you and I were together. Maybe I'll be fired before I'm officially hired if he realizes we're a couple ."

"Maybe he'd be doing you a favor," Joe offered.

Chapter Six

The sun was barely visible early Saturday morning as Helen studied the pale shades of blue and gray icy waves from her living room sliders. The wind whipped across eight miles of water from her cliff to the opposite shore, with the weather station on her kitchen wall recording nineteen-mile-an-hour winds. Her blue-eyed Siamese, Trixie, and brown and white milk-faced Dr. Watson sat at her feet. All three were grateful to be on this side of the glass. A text from Joe popped up on her cell as she poured her second cup of coffee.

Coroner rules Elison's death definitely homicide. Blunt force trauma. Metal trim pieces show pry marks from a small tool. Likely a kitchen knife.

Helen reread the text. Why am I not surprised, she thought. 'Always listen to your gut,' instructed Jessica Fletcher.

Helen texted back to Joe.

What's your next step?

Interviewing family today. Maybe someone didn't love dear old dad. Unless he knew something a client wanted kept quiet.

Yup. What are you up to?

Stopping at Five and Dime in town. Appointment later with Oscar. Let's hope he's in a better mood today.

Good luck with that.

Funny.

* * *

Helen Morrisey slammed shut the original beveled glass double doors of Five and Dime Antiques. Originally the Port Anne Hotel in the 1920s, it had advertised clean beds, basic bar food, and a welcome respite for road-weary travelers stopping midway between Baltimore and Philadelphia. A weather-worn sign named after a town founder read 'Cecil Hotel' in green letters and hung by two long chains from the ceiling near the entry. The structure had two full floors with original wood planks and a staircase running up the center. Second-floor windows stared down on Water Street. They'd been watching horse and buggies for over a century. Now they took in SUVs, hybrids, and monster trucks pulling fancy speed boats on trailers. She stepped inside the crowded shop of odd bits of local history from faded buoys and compasses to record collections spilling out into the narrow aisles. Victorian dolls, their eyes glassy and unemotional, stared down at her. A stuffed raccoon's claws stretched toward her, brushing her hair. He always gave her the creeps.

She leaned on the original hotel's reception desk and peered into a glass cabinet displaying penny candies and homemade fudge. She wondered if the candy was as old as the desk. The red gummy fish were faded, the Mary Janes dusty. When she was a kid, she never noticed. On an upper shelf, she studied a collection of antique mallets from the size of an index finger to eighteen inches long. Their hand-rubbed wooden handles gleamed. She tapped a brass hotel bell on the counter. It clanged. That's loud enough to wake up the dead, she considered.

"Rupert? It's Helen Morrisey," she called out. "I know I'm early, but your door was open." She wiggled her hands out of black leather gloves and stuck them into the pockets of her jacket. "Rupert?"

Brass fixtures hung from the fifteen-foot tin ceiling. "I'm coming," a creaky voice called out. A short, round man in a baggy brown wool cardigan and dark corduroy pants poked from around a ceiling-high stack of books and offered her a delighted, fully dentured smile. "I was getting ready to open. I'm guessing you got my voicemail?"

Bits of snow melted on her dark hair. Laughing, Helen brushed off the flakes. "You bet I did. I'm dying to see what you found me."

Easily in his eighties, the shopkeeper chuckled. "You told me you're searching for early additions for your mystery collections. I can't wait to show you." Rupert reached under the counter. Gently, he picked up two parcels wrapped in yellowed newspaper. He folded back the paper and set two faded Nancy Drew books in front of her.

Helen's eyes lit up. "Are those 1930 editions? I can't believe it," she breathed.

Rupert opened the books and laid them on the counter in front of Helen. "Patience, patience." He beamed at her surprise. "*The Message in the Hollow Oak* is 1935 with the original plain blue cover and interior end papers."

Reverently, Helen stroked the title pages as if they were the Gutenberg Bible. "*The Clue in the Old Album* is a first edition dated 1947. It has the back fly leaf advertising the *Judy Bolton Mystery Series*. Wow. How in the world did you find them?"

"The Avon estate. They had their auction last Saturday. I bid on a bookcase, and it included four cartons of books. I wasn't anxious to take them. Most old books don't sell well nowadays. When I got around to opening the boxes yesterday, I spotted the Nancy Drews."

"Thank you so much for calling me first." She ran her index finger down the copyright pages.

He beamed. "I owed you a favor for helping me hire a roofer after our December ice storm. I could have lost all my stock on the second floor."

Helen grinned. "I can find contractors. Finding old Nancy Drews is another thing."

"They'll cost you a pretty penny, I'm afraid. These are in excellent condition."

"I'll take them over jewelry any day, and I love pretty jewelry. Besides, I trust you to know their value." She paused. "I hear you found a new assistant for the store."

"I did." Rupert called out, "Tag, I have someone I want you to meet."

Average build and an inch or two taller than Helen's five foot six, a young man of about thirty in baggy jeans slipped out from behind a china cabinet. Long sandy hair topped a broad forehead and full lips. A light brown beard grazed his square chin. "Oh," he said with a shy smile. "We work together."

"Tag and I met at Safe Harbor. He joined our office in November," she explained. "I didn't realize you're working here too."

"I thought I'd help Rupert while I get my business up and running. Spending my spare time in an antique store is never work."

"I completely agree. Besides, real estate is a tough business. It's harder when you're new to the area and you're building your client base."

Tag spotted the two books in Rupert's hand. "Are those from here?"

"Aren't they fantastic? Rupert knows I collect classic mysteries, especially the older editions. These are gems."

"Helen is our local amateur detective. She's helped our Sheriff's Office solve four or five murders over the past couple of years." He patted Helen's shoulder. "If I ever get in trouble, I'm coming to you."

"A few of the Safe Harbor agents told me," Tag said. "Interesting hobby. You've got some kind of a detection club? Anyone I'd know?"

"Ignore the stories. I'm a mystery fanatic. My club is a small group of fictional women sleuths." She ticked them off. "Nancy Drew, of course. She's athletic and bold. Nora Charles from *The Thin Man* series is my throwback to the '30s. She's clever and quick. I love her personal style."

Tag shook his head. "Anyone else?"

"Jessica Fletcher from *Murder She Wrote*. She'd make a great Realtor. Doesn't miss a trick. Agatha Raisin is my British rule-breaker. She's made a career out of being where she shouldn't. Last is my brilliant elder, Jane Marple. No one observes human nature better than Jane." Helen grinned at Tag's confusion. "I figure doctors and lawyers have their favorite consultants. I've got mine. They help me through all kinds of life decisions, not only crime. Someday I'll show you my bookcases. Not a spare inch."

"That's crazy," Tag shook his head.

"I'll let you think so." Helen smiled.

Rupert wrapped up the two tomes and slipped them into a brown paper bag. "Enjoy them."

She gave the shop owner a peck on his rough cheek. "I will."

Rupert caught her arm. "I forgot. I have another treat for you."

"Oh?"

"I have a collection of unsolved crime magazines." He reached under the counter and handed her a couple. "It used to come out four times a year. They went out of business about ten years ago."

"*Unsolved Crimes We Don't Forget.* I used to subscribe years ago." Helen flipped through the stack. "They can be addictive."

Tag picked one up. "I've already read most of these. I tackle them whenever I'm home at night and I don't have a date."

"I'm sure that's not a problem, although Port Anne isn't exactly a mecca for young people. Thanks, Rupert. Now I'll never get to sleep. What do I owe you?"

The old man gave her a wave. "Return them when you're done. Bill Elison dropped them off to me a couple weeks ago. He collected them for years. I thought you'd enjoy them." He motioned to Tag. "Give Helen those couple in your arms. I've got boxes more if you're interested."

"These are more than enough for now."

"I can't believe Bill's gone," the sweet man said. "He called me Wednesday about three-thirty and offered to drop off more."

Helen's head jerked. "Are you sure about the time?"

Rupert grunted. "It was a slow day. I decided to close the store early."

"I'll tell Detective McAlister." Helen's cell buzzed. "Whoops, I've got to run. Thanks again, Rupert. Tag, catch you in the office. Don't hesitate to ask if I can help you."

Outside, she darted under an overhang, out of the wind. She texted Joe.

Talked to Rupert at Five and Dime. Bill called him late Wednesday afternoon. About four.

Great info, I'll call him now. Thanks.

Helen headed down the sidewalk toward Safe Harbor with her treasures tightly tucked under one arm. 'Good job, Nancy. We're narrowing down times.'

* * *

The streets of Port Anne were quiet this afternoon except for a few early diners. She could see the bobbing heads of a couple customers seated along the bar through The Blue Crab's windows. Safe Harbor had only two cars in the lot, one of which was Tammi's. The Captain's Bell clanged as she stepped inside.

"Hi, I didn't expect you to work on a Saturday. Why are you here?"

"I'm dropping my car off at Hogers Auto Body later. Did I tell you someone keyed my driver's side in Food Mart's lot last week? I'm ticked off." Tammi tilted her head, snowmen earrings glittering with sparkles, and studied Helen's flushed cheeks. "Got good news, or just wind chill? I'm hoping you finally nailed down your Italy trip with Joe?"

"Nooo. We're a little too busy for trip planning." Her cell rang and she held up a finger. "Darlene, thanks for calling me back. Are we still meeting at your house Monday morning? Knowing your taste, I'm excited to see it."

Her client's voice wobbled. She cleared her throat. "Helen, we've decided to hire another agent. I keep hearing about this vandal that's graffitiing your listings. It makes me too nervous. I don't want to be his next target."

Helen hesitated, trying to control her disappointment. Tammi raised her eyebrows at the news. "I'm sorry to hear you're worried. The police think he's just a bored local teenager looking for something to do. Like joy riding." The two chatted. Helen wished her well.

She leaned over Tammi's desk, piled with legal folders in perfect order. "Darlene says she can't take a chance with two children in the house." Helen sighed. "I can't really blame her."

"She's the fifth cancellation in the last two weeks. This creep is killing your business. Why can't Joe catch him?"

"He's got extra patrols out on the streets, but it's nearly impossible to predict which house this vandal will hit next." She took a deep breath. "On a much happier subject, you will not believe what I bought at Five and Dime." She unclasped her bag and handed Tammi the brown packet. "Rupert found first editions of Nancy Drews."

"That's exciting. For *you*," objected Tammi. "Are you sure you have any room on your bookshelves? I would think you'd have to add a couple support beams in your basement."

"Whatever it takes. I always have room for great detective stories. You of all people know that." She stowed them into her tote. "Any chance you want to read an unsolved crime magazine?"

Tammi waved them away. "Ugh, too creepy. I'm too busy reading Amelia Bedelia stories to Kayla."

Helen took off her jacket. "I bumped into Tag Stoltz there. He's helping Rupert." She glanced around. "Quiet in here."

"This storm's keeping everyone home. Thought I'd get some work in while Kayla has a dance lesson down the street. Aren't you expected at Oscar Banyon's today?" Tammi squinted at their calendar on her computer screen.

"At four. We have to finish the paperwork for the lots he wants to sell. Might be a tense meeting since Joe and I broke up his argument with Vince Caffrey at the club last night. I'm trying to write it off to French temperament."

"I'm surprised he's willing to subdivide."

"He wants to expand his facilities to attract larger wedding events. I think it's a smart move." Helen spotted the round antique oak clock on the wall above Tammi. "I better run."

"Be careful driving. Your Mini isn't exactly ice-worthy. When are you going to sell it and buy a practical car?"

Helen buttoned up her coat. "Practical? Since when do I want to drive practical? So boring. Nancy would hate the idea."

Chapter Seven

Blue Heron Vineyard's barns were quiet. Not a car around. The main house lights were on. Two cars sat in the courtyard, a large white Mercedes and a bright blue BMW convertible sporting a custom tag with the words 'IMMAGC.' Wouldn't I love to drive that little number. Who are you kidding, Helen? You wouldn't want to spend the money. She climbed out of her coupe and traipsed across the slippery drive to the barn's main entrance. The lanterns usually cast bright beams on both sides of the wide doors. Tonight they were off.

She stood in the winter quiet and listened to the distant swash of water ebbing along the bay shoreline in the distance. The sky was steel grey, and a sense of approaching snow hung in the air. She stepped inside out of the wind. The tasting room was dark and chill, all the warmth of wood, candles, and scent of polished bar wood absent.

"Oscar? It's Helen. Are you here?" Helen walked down to the far end, her rubber heels of her boots squeaking over the tile.

Helen dug out her cell from her pocket and dialed Oscar's. No answer. She tried two more times. She dialed his main house. No answer. Slowly, deliberately, she surveyed the empty room. She eyed a steel door to the wine processing equipment before dialing the main house number again. This time, a woman picked up.

"Hello?"

"Hello. This is Helen Morrisey from Safe Harbor. Is this Mrs. Banyon? We've never met. I'm in the tasting room. Oscar and I have an appointment to meet here at four. Do you happen to know where he is?"

"Perhaps you could tell me. Oscar came home last night, but I haven't seen him since. I thought he might have gone into Port Anne."

"When did you last speak to him?" Helen asked.

"I told you. Last night, about nine." Mrs. Banyon's voice was clipped. "I don't keep track of him."

Helen paused. "I'm not trying to intrude, but should we be concerned?"

"I'm not. Why don't I have him call you when he turns up?"

"Would Michele have his schedule?"

"Michele left this morning for the weekend. Told me she had a wine tasting in Baltimore."

Helen was struck by her cavalier attitude. "I'd call Michele, but I don't have her number."

Mrs. Banyon sighed. "I'll call her. If she knows anything, I'll call you back."

"Thanks for your help, Mrs. Banyon. I'm leaving now. Have a good evening."

Helen jumped into her car and its buffer from the cold. She dialed Tammi.

"Hi!" Tammi practically shouted, a noisy chatter of young girls' voices in the background. "What's up?"

"Any chance Oscar called and left a message today canceling our appointment?"

"No, not a word."

"He must have forgotten we were meeting, and his wife isn't the least bit concerned. From her reaction, the weather isn't the only thing that's chilly." She cursed under her breath.

"Sorry?"

"Ignore me. I'm a little annoyed. Second night in a row he's dragged me out in the cold. Go back to your weekend." Helen hung up and stared across the empty fields and back at the darkened barn. She reached for the ignition. "Chums," she declared. "Let's head for home."

She set the car in reverse, spun around, and started back down the gravel drive.

'I thought we were detectives,' Agatha growled in her ear.

'Let's check this out one more time. This place doesn't feel right,' Jessica urged.

She parked again and got out of her car. Her cell rang as she crossed the barn's threshold. It was her daughter. She flipped on a light switch. "Hi, Lizzie."

"Hi. Where are you? You sound like you're in a cave."

"You're not far off. I'm out at Blue Heron Vineyard, and without people, it's a little spooky. Right up Nancy's alley. I was supposed to meet Oscar Banyon at four, but he's nowhere to be found. He must have forgotten. What's up?"

"My annoying twin brother called me. My date canceled, and Shawn's girlfriend has the flu. He's trying to avoid his house for a few days. Has an important court case Monday and can't afford to get sick. Want company tonight?"

"Love to, as long as you don't mind Joe. He's bringing me pizza and wings at seven."

"The question is, will he mind *us*? We don't want to horn in on your cozy Saturday night plans."

"No worries. He loves seeing you." Helen stomped her feet. "I'm freezing. Let me do one more walk-around here, and I'll meet you at home."

"Sounds good. I'll text Shawn."

She wove around the round high-top tables, following the quiet hum of equipment, and in between rows and rows of oak barrels and casks from waist high to well over her head, feeling for light switches as she walked. Four stainless steel fermentation bins lined a third row. The faint scent of wine infused the air in the chilled room. She swore the tall egg-shaped vessels, ghostly images in concrete, served as sentries along one wall.

She tapped her phone and listened. A ring echoed in the distance. She raised her volume and tried again. A muffled, slightly louder echo of 'Derniere danse' floated from around the containers. Helen jerked to a halt, recognizing the music. Her heart racing, she spun slowly around, straining to hear the ring again. "That has to be Oscar's ring tone," she muttered. She followed its unusual notes. Squeezing behind two casks, she ran her hands along their sides, their tall hulks blocking the room's overhead industrial lamps.

She spotted the phone's distant flash as it pulsed with each eerie note.

She knelt in the dark and stretched forward with her right hand, only about six inches away. She stripped off her jacket, lay down on her stomach, and army crawled between the casks. Wiggling her fingertips, she grasped the tip of the device, pulling it toward her. Her missed calls to Oscar glowed across the screen. She tucked his phone into her jacket pocket and powered on her cell light.

"Damn," she winced, pulling back her hand. A jagged shard of green glass protruded from her palm. A sheen of wine puddled inches away, its smell oddly sweet yet metallic. Not the rich bouquet she'd inhaled with the proud vineyard owner the evening before. Her light washed across the concrete and picked up the reflection of a pale motionless hand with a distinctive signature ring and a Louis Vuitton insignia on the shirt cuff.

She knew she'd found Oscar, his blood mingling with his prize red. She closed her eyes for a moment and gagged, a taste of bile rising up her throat. Her heart raced. She wiggled closer, seizing his wrist. No pulse. She pulled back and hit Joe's cell number. He didn't pick up. Her hands shook. She rang again.

"Hi, I'm running late."

Helen stopped him mid-sentence. "Joe, I'm at Blue Heron Vineyard. I'm with Oscar Banyon. I found him in his main building, behind the tasting room, among the fermentation casks. He's dead."

Joe's voice dropped. "Are you sure?"

"I can't feel a pulse. Yes."

"Are you safe? Are you alone?"

"I haven't seen anyone in the building. His wife is in their house on the far side of the lane."

"We'll notify her we're coming. Stay exactly where you are. I don't want you wandering through the building."

"I'm lying in the dark. The lights over these casks are out. They should be working. Someone may have knocked them out. There's glass everywhere."

"I'm on my way." His cell clicked off. Helen drew herself up with her back against a cask, her palms on the rough concrete. She pulled her knees to her chest and shivered in the deadly quiet.

Chapter Eight

Two deaths in three days. Are they related or a coincidence? Jane Marple had taught Helen that good sleuths don't believe in coincidences. The digital time on her phone clicked off the minutes. She held her breath while she picked at the shard of glass protruding from her palm until it slid out. Beads of sweat broke across her forehead. Her stomach roiled. Twelve minutes later, she heard sirens cut through the night and travel along the water's edge.

A screech of brakes was followed by a car door being slammed. "Helen! Where are you?" Joe's deep, worried voice reverberated through the building.

"I'm here! The far side, at the end of the row." Helen stood up and flashed her cell above her and across the stainless-steel vats.

Joe flashed his Mag-Lite along the walls. Two uniformed deputies were right behind.

"Are you hurt? You've got blood on your hands."

Helen made an uneasy laugh. "I sliced my hand on a piece of glass. It's nothing."

Joe held his flashlight over her open cut. "Ask the EMT to clean it. You've got some grit under the skin."

The officers moved past her and spotted Oscar sprawled in between the vats. An EMT dropped to his knees and checked for vitals. He shook his head at the detectives.

"He's cold. He's been gone for a while."

"Ease back," Joe cautioned. "This may be a crime scene."

Helen followed them to the tasting room.

Joe signaled to another detective. "Go notify Mrs. Banyon." He glanced at his phone. "Coroner is a few minutes away. Is there anyone else at home?"

"I'm not sure. Michele Mancuso, their winemaker, is gone for the weekend. Oscar has a stepdaughter, but I didn't ask if she's home."

Joe nodded and pointed to an EMT. "Can you check Mrs. Morrisey's hand? Make her comfortable. I'll be right back." He signaled two deputies. "We need to search the area for signs of an attacker or anything they may have left behind." He studied her pale, damp face.

"Why were you here?"

Helen inhaled. "We had a meeting scheduled at four. I was a little concerned he'd taken offense when you and I broke up his argument with Vince. When I couldn't find him, I called the main house and asked Mrs. Banyon if she knew where he was." She paused. "She was very defensive, very annoyed. She told me she saw him last night before she went to bed. Her reaction was odd. If I hadn't seen or heard from my husband after almost twenty-four hours, I'd be frantic. Maybe that's their lifestyle."

Joe pulled out a wire-bound mini-pad from his jacket pocket. "Public records tell me her first name is Paula, age fifty-seven. Ever meet the daughter?"

"No. Oscar mentioned her. She's his stepdaughter and uses the name Billie." Joe jotted down her name.

The main door opened, and Ed Tarlone blew in, stomping his feet.

"Ed," Joe greeted, pointing toward the rear. "The victim is beyond those casks. You'll have a tough time reaching him."

"Who found him?"

Helen meekly raised a hand.

"Of course you did." Ed picked up his bag and signaled his crime tech team to follow.

Joe glared at her.

"What? Why are you annoyed?"

He cleared his throat. "Back to the stepdaughter. Did Oscar get along with her?"

"Got the idea she was a bit of a princess. To be fair, she wouldn't be the first stepdaughter with a strained relationship with their stepfather."

"Who else works here?"

"I'm not sure. It's a fairly large crew, but smaller in the winter, which makes sense. I only met their winemaker, Michele Mancuso, for the first time Friday night, before the club meeting. She was friendly, personable. My guess, early thirties. She's the granddaughter of Petro Mancuso, the owner of Mancuso Wines. They're a huge operation in Napa, California. If you've bought wine, you've bought Mancuso."

"Why doesn't she work for her family?"

"I asked her. She said she wanted a chance to prove herself, build her own reputation. I'm sure Oscar was attracted to her connections. It's quite a lineage of winemakers."

"Any personal relationship there?"

"Are you asking if they had an affair behind Paula's back?" Helen asked. "Anything's possible. She's quite the looker, although he was awfully old for her."

"Money and influence override a lot of flaws."

"You sound like Jane Marple."

"Let's save that discussion for another day." He raised a heavy eyebrow. "How did you get into the building?"

"All the doors in this barn have digital locks instead of keys. Oscar gave me the passcode. I didn't use it because the main door was open."

"Sounds like a lot of people had easy access. I wonder why the killer didn't lock the door on the way out."

"Maybe they didn't have the passcode."

They both looked up as Paula Banyon strode into the wine tasting room. She was obsessively thin with shoulder-length, streaked brown hair cut in a sharp wedge from back to chin. A young woman in a black Canada Goose parka and thick-soled leather boots followed behind, her eyes darting around at all the police activity.

"Mrs. Banyon, I'm Detective Joe McAlister, and I'll be in charge of this investigation. This is Helen Morrisey, the Realtor who found your husband."

Paula eyed them with cool indifference. "Your deputy tells me there's been an accident."

"Yes, Mrs. Banyon, I'm sorry to inform you that your husband is gone. We have the coroner examining him now. We're unsure if this was an accident or if someone deliberately assaulted him."

Paula wrapped a grey cashmere sweater tightly across her chest, her rings flashing in the bar light. Billie blinked at the two men and shifted her feet.

"Mrs. Banyon, would you prefer we return to the house to talk? Would you be more comfortable there?"

"I'd prefer we talk here." Her eyes were cold as she assessed the detective and Helen.

"Your preference. Please, take a seat." Joe set two more chairs around a table. Paula crossed her legs. Her daughter slouched back.

"Any idea why your husband would go between the fermentation containers? Does he have a need to check them?"

"Oscar was always poking around the equipment. He annoyed Michele and her operators. It's not like he knew how it worked."

"When did you last speak to him?"

"He walked in last night about nine o'clock. He was furious. Apparently, he had an argument with a yacht club board member. He'd been stewing over the fact that the club wouldn't carry our wines. I kept telling him they couldn't afford them." She sniffed.

"Did he say anything specific?"

"He told me a police officer interrupted them, and he was asked to leave. He was insulted. I got the idea she was involved, too." She scowled at Helen. "I really didn't pay much attention. He enjoyed having silly tiffs with people. He came into the living room, poured himself a scotch, and threw himself on the couch to sulk."

"And you never saw him later?"

"No. He parked his car in our garage, so I never noticed if it was gone this morning."

"And you had no need to check on him."

She responded with disdain. "No need."

"Did you have any sign he had breakfast, took a shower, dressed for the day, anything?"

"It's a mammoth house, Detective," she faked a small self-deprecating smile. It never reached her eyes. For a woman nearing sixty, her laugh lines were practically nonexistent.

"Mrs. Banyon, it's possible someone broke into this barn. We found a broken window at the rear. Helen says the front entrance was unlocked when she arrived. Is that typical?"

"If Oscar was there alone, it is."

"We understand your winemaker, Michele Mancuso, was out of town for the weekend."

"Yes. I told Helen when she asked for Michele tonight."

"Is it possible she wasn't really out of town?"

Paula examined her rings before answering. "She drives a red Jeep. It was gone late Friday."

"Is it possible she didn't leave the property?"

Paula pursed her plumped lips. "I suppose. I don't keep track of Michele's comings and goings." She hesitated. "She did call Oscar Friday night soon after he came in the door."

"Did he tell you?"

Paula scoffed. "I overheard them talking. He always picked up her calls." A touch of annoyance crept into her voice. "She was leaving for Baltimore to taste a new wine. He told her to bring back a bottle."

"Was it typical for her to call him at such a late hour?"

"They'd go back and forth about our competition all the time, especially with our new red weeks away from release."

"Does Michele live nearby?" he asked.

Paula gestured toward the south. "She stays in our carriage house. Oscar wanted his winemaker to live here on the property. Makes after-hours meetings convenient if you get what I mean."

"And you saw her leave Friday late afternoon." Joe's eyes narrowed.

"I told you, Detective. I saw her Jeep pull out about six-thirty before Oscar came in from his club meeting."

"Is it possible Michele returned?"

47

"Officer, we have people pulling up and down our drive all the time. Delivery people, staff, tourists. I don't keep close tabs on our winemaker. Michele comes in and out."

"Excuse me, it's Detective. Do you like Michele?"

Paula made an indifferent shrug. "I thought she was inexperienced, but he was enamored with her family name. Thought she'd help draw business. She's certainly a lot prettier than the last one. Oscar admired her Bohemian style."

"Mrs. Banyon, you're taking your husband's death rather calmly," said Joe.

"I'm in shock." Paula made a weak sob, touching her forehead.

Helen strained to keep her mouth shut. Jane Marple, the best silent observer in the sleuthing business, had trained her. Helen still wasn't good at it. Clearly, Paula didn't allow a smile or an ugly cry to mar her face. Paula stayed in control.

Joe ignored Paula's theatrical expression and studied her daughter.

Billie tucked a strand of dull black hair behind an ear and gave him an insolent stare. She glanced down to study a purple Apple watch, the screen flashing on and off. An oversized cropped pink sweatshirt with a lululemon logo across the chest was paired with baggy washed jeans, shredded at the knees, and wet with salt along the cuffs.

"Billie, to clarify, please state your age."

"I was twenty-two in November."

"Thank you. When did you last see your stepfather?" Joe asked.

"I'm sorry. I missed the question."

Joe's mouth was a tight straight line. "I suggest you remove the earpiece while we talk."

Avoiding his eyes, Billie slowly reached up, pulled out the white earpiece, and fingered it.

"When did you last see your stepfather?"

"Um. Last night, about five o'clock? I was going out with friends and asked him for money for dinner."

"How much did he give you?

"Why is this relevant?" her mother interjected.

"Mrs. Banyon, we're never sure what's relevant at this stage." He eyed the young woman and waited for her response.

"Not much," Billie muttered, twisting a streak of hair. "I asked for a hundred bucks. He gave me fifty. He was cheap. If I wanted fifty dollars, I'd ask for a hundred, so I'd end up with what I wanted." She made a self-satisfied smirk.

"Did he usually carry cash?"

"He did, but I never got any of it." She made a 'poor me' face.

"You never saw him or spoke with him afterwards," Joe clarified.

"Nope. I came in about midnight. Slept until eleven this morning."

"Any lights on anywhere?"

"I didn't notice."

"Do you work for the vineyard?" Joe asked.

Dry-eyed, Billie scoffed. "He offered me a job, but I turned him down flat."

"Any particular reason?"

"He wanted me to do inventory. So boring."

If this were my daughter, Helen thought, I'd throttle her. 'Hold your tongue,' Jessica warned in her ear. Helen gritted her teeth.

"Really, Detective," protested Paula. "These questions are not necessary."

A shuffle across the room caught everyone's attention.

The detective stood. "Excuse me." He joined Ed at the rear, then returned.

"Mrs. Banyon, Billie. The coroner has confirmed Oscar's death is a homicide. We'll escort you back to your house. If you think of any dispute that could help us determine who might want him dead, we'd appreciate hearing from you as quickly as possible. We're committed to finding your husband's killer."

For the first time, Paula's face blanched as she rose to her feet.

"One last question, for now. Billie, were you outside your house anytime this afternoon?" Joe asked. "Your pants are wet."

Billie looked down. "Nope. I've been in my room all afternoon."

He nodded.

A deputy took Paula's arm and led her out of the building, her strong French scent and her daughter following behind her.

Joe turned to his coroner. "Ed, any time of death?"

Ed unzipped his bunny suit and peeled off his gloves and shoe covers. He grabbed the fleece jacket he'd tossed on a table. "Freaking freezing back there. His body temperature is especially low. The room temperature and the stainless equipment surrounding him make it more difficult to narrow down his time of death. I'd say between six this morning and noon."

"How did he die?"

"He has a deep cut to the jugular. We've collected broken green glass. I can confirm more by tomorrow." He snapped shut his examination bag and checked the time. "Sorry, but it's after seven and I'm not missing my grandson's birthday party tonight."

"Thanks for not sending your assistant. Enjoy your family. I'll have my deputies stay with the crime tech team until they're finished and seal off the scene."

Helen spotted a missed call as she climbed into her car. "I forgot all about Lizzie and Shawn. They're probably at my house right now. Are you coming? I can get food delivered."

Joe rubbed a day-old beard. "Haven't eaten since breakfast. I'll be right behind you." He tapped the hood of her car.

Chapter Nine

Helen's cliff house was alight, and the fireplace was blazing. Her hair was damp from a quick hot shower, and she wore a heavy cotton sweater, navy sweats, and bulky socks. Lizzie greeted Joe with a Guinness in a tall Pilsner glass and a hug and handed her mother a glass of wine.

"I hear you could use this. Shawn's upstairs changing. Hope we didn't crash your evening," Lizzie said as Shawn trundled down the stairs to shake his hand.

Joe kicked off his boots and tossed off his suit jacket. He set his Glock and a brown leather holster on the mantel. It was a cop's routine, out of reach but exactly where he could grab it. "I'm happy to take a break. Two bodies, three days. Even for your mother, it's a record." He sank into Helen's deep, dark blue couch next to her. "Do I smell food?"

Lizzie laughed. "Relax. I'll bring it out." She bustled around the kitchen and returned with a large round wooden board covered with Philly hoagie rolls stuffed with sausage and peppers, along with slices of Margarita pizza.

Joe downed a bite as his cell buzzed with a text. "Now what?"

"Problem?" asked Lizzie.

"No, all good. My neighbor. He checked on Rocky and gave him dinner." Joe inhaled another bite. "He'll take him for a run before bed."

"You two didn't waste any time getting to the food." Helen tucked herself on the other end of the sofa and faced the fire. Watson and Trixie nestled next to her. She stared at the glass for a moment. "Can't believe after today I can be interested in red wine."

"How's your hand?" Joe asked.

Lizzie sat up. "What's happened with your hand?"

Helen touched the bandage and waved her away. "Just a cut. EMT wants me to have my GP check it again Monday. Let's talk about today. Any ideas?"

Joe took a swig from his glass and stood up. "I'll be right back." A minute later, he walked back inside, dropping a zippered leather satchel onto the floor. "I need to wash all the tech dust off me."

"Use my shower. There's clean towels on the rack," Helen offered.

"Don't take too long," warned Shawn. "We'll eat all the pizza."

About ten minutes later, dressed in worn jeans and a pullover, he reclaimed the couch. Helen sniffed. "You smell much better."

"I couldn't stand myself."

"Mom, tell me what happened. How did you find Oscar?" Lizzie asked.

"I hung up with you and decided to check out the barn one more time. I kept wandering around the casks and vats and redialing him on my cell. I could hear the song on Oscar's phone. It plays 'Dernier danse.'"

"It's a famous French song. The video has over a billion views," Lizzie said.

"Billion? Wow. I never knew."

Shawn chuckled. "My mother isn't exactly an expert on hot hits."

"It's an interesting choice, especially from someone who was murdered. Do you realize what Dernier danse means in English?"

"What?" Helen asked.

"It means 'last dance,'" Lizzie explained.

"My sister is good at languages," Shawn commented.

Helen spoke up. "Talk about a self-fulfilling prophecy. Spooky."

"How did he die?" Lizzie asked, her face intent on Joe.

Shawn raised a hand in protest. "Give the guy a chance to breathe."

"These two Morrisey women are cut from the same cloth," Joe commented around chews. "Why don't you hire them for your Baltimore DA's office? Get them out of my jurisdiction?"

Shawn groaned. "I've got enough political nepotism to deal with from one day to the next. I don't need my mother and my sister complicating it."

"To answer your question," Joe said. "Our coroner says he was impaled with a broken bottle and definitely not self-inflicted."

Lizzie gulped.

"The same bottle cut my hand," Helen pointed.

"Let's hope the killer made our lives simpler and left DNA behind."

"The attack didn't appear planned," Helen added, "but we've been fooled before. I'm wondering who visited him and picked an argument?"

"You tell me," Joe commented around bites. "You're the one who might know about his social connections. Oscar certainly didn't get along with Vince Caffrey. Paula Banyon and her charming daughter, Billie, said they didn't notice anyone coming or going."

"Or so they claim," Shawn added.

"To be fair to Oscar, he enjoyed playing the commodore part and he had a lot of friends. People admired him. He was a bit of an egotist, but I never thought he was hated." Helen asked her daughter, "Ever meet Billie around Port Anne?"

Lizzie shook her head. "No, never. Spotted her a few times with her mother, but she's got to be eight or ten years younger than we are."

"My guess, Port Anne is too small a town for her. Not enough action. If you and Shawn showed the same lack of respect toward law enforcement as she did, I'd disown you."

Joe eyed Helen. "The wheels are turning."

Shawn rose to his feet and stretched. "How about joining me for either a scotch or bourbon. Pick your poison."

Joe chuckled. "Got any Irish Whiskey? I hear it warms your bones." He got up and added two more logs to the fire, poking at the ashes.

"By the way, none of you have seen my newest treasures." Helen left the room and came back with a package. She removed the brown paper and newspaper wrappings and handed one book to Shawn and one to Lizzie. "Aren't they fabulous?"

"Mom, these are amazing," her daughter exclaimed as she examined them. "I'm so jealous. *The Message in the Hollow Oak*. One of my all-time favorites."

Shawn unveiled *The Clue in the Old Album*. "Pretty awesome. Do I want to know what you paid for them?"

Helen snorted. "You do not want to know. Don't worry, I'll put them in my will."

"Nice to hear, but we can wait." He sipped on his drink.

Helen took the two tomes and stood in front of her bookcase that stretched from wall to wall. Gently, she shifted a couple Agatha Raisin cases and squeezed in her new acquisitions among her Nancy Drew collection. She stood back and admired. "Perfect. Oh, I should set them on my nightstand and admire them in the middle of the night."

"I'm surprised she's not tucking them under her pillow," Joe smiled.

Helen wiggled her empty wine glass at her son. "I'm drawing a total blank. Why would someone want to kill Oscar?" She shuddered.

"What about your friend Bill Elison?" Lizzie asked. "Did someone plan to kill him? Set him up?"

Shawn frowned. "Maybe a visitor with a grudge took advantage of the opportunity to shove him down the stairs."

"Or," Helen suggested, "he or she met Bill at his house. They had an argument, and Bill fell to his death. His visitor panicked, jury-rigged the scene afterwards by raising the edge of the stair plate and cutting the carpet. Tossing the box down helped them stage the scene."

"Quite a grudge," Lizzie offered.

Shawn grimaced. "In my business, grudges can escalate. Sometimes perpetrators regret it after the deed is done. By then, it's too late."

"Jane Marple would say ordinary people can do the most astonishing things."

"Exactly," Shawn said.

Joe's cell buzzed with a text. "Our lab. Results came in. No unknown fingerprints in Bill's house." He raised his eyes. "State police are running DNA tests on Bill's cell phone. My guess, DNA won't help us ID someone. The killer could cover their fingers with their own clothes. Or grab anything nearby so they can touch Bill's phone without leaving a trace."

"Probably wore gloves," Helen said. "Or it was one of his children, and they knew his password."

"My bet, they used a face swipe ID," Joe explained. "His killer put the phone up to Bill's face to get access to the text app and respond to Tammi with a thumbs up. Bought him more time before anyone checked on Bill."

"Do you realize that they're both members of the yacht club? My Detection Club sleuths would consider that odd." Helen opened her desk in the far corner of the room and waved a legal pad in the air. "Since we have all these brilliant minds in one room," she declared, "this is the perfect opportunity to create a list of suspects."

Her son moaned and buried his head under a pillow. "Next, you're going to tell us getting those two Nancy Drews today was karma."

"Possibly."

Joe stood up and rubbed his eyes. "I'm begging you, put your Detection Club sleuths to bed."

"Oh! Speaking of bedtime reading." She dashed back into her bedroom and came out with a handful of black and white glossy magazines. She held them up like a newsboy on a corner. "Rupert gave these to me. They're old issues of *Unsolved Crimes We Don't Forget*. I haven't had a chance to flip through them, but they're right up your alley." She eyed Shawn and Joe. "They're articles about unsolved crimes dating as far back as the 1960s."

"I'm familiar," Shawn said. "You subscribed for years. When our friends' moms had *Better Homes and Gardens* and *Women's Day* on their coffee table, you had these."

"Let's not pile them on top of the Banyon and Elison cases, please." Joe reached for his Glock and holster and tucked them into his bag. "I'm more concerned about today."

"Aren't you staying tonight?" Lizzie asked.

He shook his head. "I have a Golden Retriever patiently waiting for attention. I also have to meet another detective near my house early in the morning. Thank you all for a great meal and a much-needed shower."

"I'll walk you to your car," Helen offered.

He kissed her. "It's too cold out."

She ignored him and slipped on a jacket from the hall. A few minutes later, she was back.

"Mom, you look beat," Shawn said.

"I am. If you don't mind, I'm going to make a cup of tea and crawl into bed." She reached for her Nancy Drew additions.

"Get into bed and I'll bring you the tea," Shawn offered.

Lizzie and Helen glanced at each other and back at Shawn.

"I'm sorry, who are you and what have you done with my brother?"

"I make tea for Lacey every night," Shawn tossed back as he walked into the kitchen. "I'm an enlightened man."

Lizzie leaned close to her mother, cupping her hand to the side of her mouth. "This must be serious," she whispered.

Chapter Ten

Shortly after seven am Sunday, Helen's cell rang. She groped around her nightstand, one eye open, and fell back against her pillows. It was Maggie Dyer, a reporter and friend of the *Kent County Whig*.

Oh Lord, the press. This has to be about Oscar. The call went to voicemail. Seconds later, a text popped up on her screen.

Sorry it's early. What can you tell me about Oscar's death? Hear it's murder.

Helen's index finger hovered over the keys. She sat up, pushing hair out of her eyes.

Not much to tell. You should check with Joe.

He's ignoring me. Promise you'll call me?

Yes. Long night.

Thanks.

She studied the sad face emoji from Maggie. Ever the journalist. She bundled into her comfy red robe and stumbled into the kitchen, following her nose. The coffee pot was full, a note beside it.

"Mom, Shawn and I went for a run to the lighthouse. Thought you'd rather sleep. Lizzie"

Perfect. Besides, I can't keep up with them. Another text sounded. This one is from Tammi.

Read today's *Kent Whig* news link.

Now what? She clicked open the link. In bold letters, the headline read *Realtor Finds Vineyard Owner Dead*. Three photos ran across the screen: Oscar, the Blue Heron Vineyard entrance sign, and Helen's professional headshot.

> *Oscar Banyon, well-known owner of Blue Heron Vineyard off Osprey Point, Port Anne, was found at approximately five o'clock Saturday evening in a rear room of his vineyard's production facilities by local Realtor Helen Morrisey of Safe Harbor Realty. Police were called by Morrisey, who claimed to have an appointment with Mr. Banyon. Detective Joseph McAlister of the Kent County Sheriff's Office confirmed a coroner's report. Mr. Banyon was assaulted in his wine fermentation area. Police ask the public to come forward with any information that might lead to an arrest. Blue Heron Vineyard produced a number of award-winning wines since its onset in 2002.*

Beneath the article, commentary from readers started to post. Helen scrolled through them, most offering condolences. She stopped and zoomed in on one anonymous commentary.

> *FYI, Realtor Helen Morrisey was called in for questioning by Kent County police on Thursday following the death of local businessman, William Elison. Morrisey is keeping the Sheriff's Department busy with a string of her clients' homes vandalized. Maybe she'll need to give each seller a Saint Joseph's statue to bury in their front lawn to generate offers and ward off being targeted.*

"Damn!" Helen exploded, tossing her cell onto the couch and starting to pace. Trixie and Watson ducked behind the couch and watched her from a safer distance.

Helen was marching back and forth across her kitchen when, minutes later, Shawn and Lizzie stomped onto her deck.

"Mom, what's going on?" Lizzie plucked her tight red cap off her bright hair. They tossed their wet sneakers to the side of the glass door.

Helen dug between the couch cushions for her cell. "Read this!" She thrust the phone in front of their faces. "What the heck am I supposed to do?

Shawn, you're the attorney. How do you suggest I respond? How dare they! What do they mean, I *claimed* to have an appointment? Why'd they connect the graffiti vandal hitting my clients to Oscar or Bill's murder? One has nothing to do with the other."

"Mom," Shawn said in his quiet voice. "Calm down. It's only a jerk sticking in his two cents to feel important. I deal with this type every day." He handed her a fresh cup of coffee.

"But you're a district attorney. You get paid to deal with personal accusations," she grumbled.

Lizzie reached for hot water and a tea bag. "It is a pretty nasty comment. I didn't know you had some houses hit."

"I've had three since January, and it makes people question my integrity," Helen declared, hands on her hips. "People get leery. It's bad luck. They hire someone else because the rumors make them uncomfortable. As of Saturday, I've had five other clients cancel on me. They don't want to be the next house on this creep's list. I certainly wouldn't if I were them."

"Mom, are you telling me that only your listings are being vandalized? No other agents?" Shawn looked doubtful. "Seems pretty strange."

"I checked with the police. Every client is working with me. Or had in the past. One by one, they're getting picked off." She plopped down at the kitchen island. "What do I do?"

"First of all, it's not a string. It's three. It'll die off." Lizzie set a half dozen eggs next to the cooktop. "People know it's only chatter. When I get snarky reviews on ShopTV after an airing, I've learned to ignore them. In no time at all, their comments get pushed toward the bottom of the news feed. Most people don't give them any attention." She whipped the eggs and dropped them into a buttered pan with a handful of grated cheddar. She popped three English muffins out of the toaster.

Shawn warmed their plates. "Ignore them. If it happens again, we'll consider posting a response. You don't want to engage in a dialogue. It feeds debate."

The two sat down across from their mother.

"I don't sit back easily," Helen declared around a mouthful of toast.

Her daughter glanced at her brother. "We had no idea."

"Clearly, you did not read *The Body in the Library*, although as my daughter, I'm ashamed to admit it." Helen tsked.

"Not recently, Mom," Lizzie countered.

Shawn lathered butter on a muffin. "I'm not seeing the correlation, but I'm sure you're going to enlighten us."

"Colonel Bantry, Jane Marple's good friend, is accused of murder because a young and beautiful woman is found dead in his library. It's an exact correlation to my problem."

Shawn winced. "We're not following you."

"Colonel Bantry is completely innocent, of course, but the entire county shuns him while he's unjustly under suspicion. Jane has to find the murderer in order to help him regain his reputation."

Shawn set down his fork. "You're always getting involved when innocent people are accused of crimes."

His mother's face turned red.

"I guess we can be thankful Oscar's body wasn't found in your living room," he said. "At least this time we only have to find your serial vandal to restore your reputation."

"Does Colonial Bantry have a connection to Banyon?" Lizzie asked. "Jeez, even their names sound alike."

"Frankly, I couldn't believe Paula Banyon's calm reaction when Joe gave her the news of Oscar's murder. Cool as a cucumber. Not a tear shed. Her daughter, Billie, didn't blink. It's a second marriage, by the way. I wonder if there was a pre-nup. Paula's a rich widow unless Oscar hid bad debts from her."

"Maybe Paula was in shock."

"Lizzie, that's what I love about you. You look for the best in people," her mother said.

"Anyone else to consider?" Shawn picked up their empty plates.

"Jessica Fletcher would suspect our club buildings chair, Vince Caffrey. He and Oscar had a nasty blow-up Friday night in front of everyone in the Burgee Lounge. Oscar accused Vince of accepting padded contractors' estimates and picking up the difference. The club's in the middle of some major renovations. Oscar literally tossed a glass of wine in Vince's face.

"Does Joe know about this?" Shawn asked.

"He was there when they argued."

"Let Joe do his job." Shawn dried off his hands. "Who's Vince anyway? His name sounds familiar."

"You remember, the baseball player for the Orioles. Retired about eight years ago. He's back home and selling insurance."

"I'd check out his home life and his financials. He wouldn't be the first ex-pro athlete who squanders his money and feels desperate." Shawn gulped the last of his coffee. "I'll hide upstairs in my bedroom and get some work done. I'm heading home later tonight in time to make dinner for Lacey. I think she's over the worst of her flu."

"I'm leaving for the studio at three. I'm on air and won't be home until after midnight. Don't wait up for me, Mom." Lizzie stretched.

"Any luck finding a house?" Shawn asked.

Lizzie rolled her blue eyes. "I might need a new real estate broker. The one I'm using keeps talking me out of anything I like."

"I want you around." Helen picked up her mug. "I think I'll take my coffee and stew with my sleuths."

She kissed her mother. "Am I forgiven for not remembering a Jane Marple mystery?"

"I'll set a copy on your nightstand for tonight. You can bone up." Helen's cell pinged. "Change of plans. Joe wants me to come into the station and make a formal statement at eleven."

"Good. Let Joe and his squad deal with this," Shawn warned. "We've told you before. You can't fix everything. Do me a favor. Make sure you lock your doors tonight."

"I can take care of myself," Helen declared.

Lizzie's eyes narrowed. "Mom, you've had more close calls than a cat with nine lives."

Helen reached for Watson and Trixie. "What's wrong with that?" The two cats blinked in agreement.

Chapter Eleven

The Sheriff's Office was buzzing when she walked in. "I'm here to meet Detective McAlister," she requested. A young officer ushered her into an interview room. Black Formica table, gray steel unpadded chairs, a television screen along one wall, she knew was actually a one-way window accessible from the hall. She shivered. This place is as cold as a mortuary. You could embalm dead bodies in here, she thought. 'I see they haven't improved their decorating,' Nora Charles commented in her ear. 'You complain every time. It's not the Ritz,' Helen reminded her.

Joe opened the door with a deputy behind him.

"Hi," he smiled. "We've already asked you these questions, but we need to do this by the book."

"Of course." She tugged on her jacket. "It's a refrigerator in here. Don't you guys believe in heat? It's twenty-eight degrees outside and forty in here."

The deputy chuckled. "Let me see what I can do." He left the room and returned a few minutes later with a paper cup of black tea and some sugar packets.

Helen dunked the bag a few times and wrapped her hands around the cup. "Thanks."

Joe ran through her identification. "What time did you arrive at the vineyard yesterday?"

"Exactly at four. The barn was dark, no lights."

"You met him Friday afternoon. Why did you return yesterday?"

"Oscar never signed the paperwork. We both had to be at Port Anne Yacht Club by six, and he hadn't decided his asking price for the lots. I offered to come back Saturday afternoon."

"Did you speak with him after the altercation he had with Vince Caffrey?" Joe asked.

She shook her head.

"Were you aware of any threats toward him? Any enemies?"

"No," Helen said. "Oscar could come off pompous, but overall, I thought he was admired. He was a smart businessman. We were planning a wine tasting at the vineyard to benefit the local library. He wanted to hold the fundraiser and announce the sale of his lots at the same time."

"What was your impression of his relationship with his wife?"

"I never met her until Saturday night. She never came to the club. I don't think she liked socializing with the locals. Oscar made cutting remarks about his stepdaughter. Said she was spoiled. He hoped she'd get involved in the vineyard, but she blew him off." Helen stopped. "You both met her. You can picture why they didn't get along."

Joe made a note. "From what we've found so far, Oscar bought the property in 2002. He and Paula married in 2021. We've got calls into his first wife. They had two children together. Did he ever mention them?"

"Once," Helen mused. "Oscar said they hadn't spoken in years. I suspect he and Paula were seeing each other before he got his first divorce."

"When you walked inside, were the lights on?"

"No. Completely dark. I flipped them on and walked around the tasting room. No sign of him. I decided to call the main house number. I thought he might be at home. Paula Banyon told me she hadn't seen him since the night before. When I asked about Michele Mancuso, she told me she thought Michele was gone for the weekend."

"Walk me through discovering Oscar."

"I got back in my car but decided to walk around one more time. I didn't picture him standing me up. I walked back into the barn and through the tasting room, redialing his cell number. When I got closer to the fermentation area, I thought I heard it ring. His cell plays a French tune, so it's easy to recognize. The ring grew louder. I followed it between the steel casks. The moment I saw him, I thought he was dead."

"Before your meetings with Oscar about the sale of his land, did you and he have any past relationship or business dealings?"

"I only knew him through the club. We worked on the board together."

Joe rubbed his chin. "Have you heard anything that led you to believe he had any illegal business dealings?"

"No, never."

"Do you think his accusations of stealing directed at Vince Caffrey are founded?"

Helen studied her hands, then the two cops. "Any club's financials are a balancing act. Until Oscar accused him, I never questioned Vince's invoices from contractors. Running a restaurant and taking care of our buildings is a challenge. Some months we're in the red, most months in the black. As a bunch of volunteers, the work is even harder to squeeze around everyone's work schedules. I wouldn't want Vince's position."

"Give me a minute," Joe said. He left the room. Ten minutes later, he handed her paperwork. "Please sign the bottom of your statement."

Helen picked up a pen and signed and dated the forms.

"Thank you," Joe took the papers and glanced at his watch. "I've got to run."

Helen picked up her coat and gloves. "Do you want to catch some dinner?"

"I can't. I'm meeting a Baltimore work friend at Prime and Claw. We're going over a cold case. Can you walk the vineyard property tomorrow morning, about ten?"

"Sure. I'll meet you there. Any more on Bill?"

"Techs are going over the house a second time."

"Would you mind if I checked on Georgia and Todd?"

"Not at all. Maybe they'll give you some background on how everyone got along." Joe picked up her wrist. "How's your hand?"

"It's fine. The bandage is annoying, but I can take it off tomorrow."

"I'm hoping we'll come across something near the casks since they're in a sanitary location."

She glanced around the station house and snuck in a quick kiss on his cheek. "See you tomorrow. Enjoy your dinner with your friend tonight.

You'll have to tell me about the cold case later."

Joe grunted.

* * *

Port Anne, about noon on a Sunday in February, was surprisingly busy. The parking lot behind the tiny town hall was full. Two young people carrying square white boxes stepped out of Tella's Pizzeria. A white flag with an oversized red teapot flapped in the wind outside of Jean's Coffee Pot. She could hear her chatting over the buzz of her coffee grinder as she stepped inside. Today, Jean wore a bright pink apron over her ample bosom, her signature collection of plastic teapots scattered across.

"Hello, there." Jean's gray eyes warmed when she spotted Helen. "I wondered when you'd come by."

"I'm hoping you may have picked up the latest gossip. You're my best source, remember?" Helen reached into a glass container to pull out a homemade blueberry scone.

Jean filled a paper cup with her favorite Jamaican Me Crazy and topped it with foamed milk and scattered pumpkin spice.

"A bunch of chit chat about the article in the *Kent Whig*." She leaned on the counter. "How did you happen to find Oscar Banyon?"

"We were scheduled to meet. I found him behind his tasting room."

Jean lowered her voice. "He was never one of my favorite people, but it's terrible news. How'd his wife take it?"

"She was an ice woman. Didn't shed a tear. Have you ever met her?"

"Paula comes in for coffee. Can't say she's friendly."

"Ever meet her daughter, Billie?"

"Oh, yes. She stops in after school. A bit of a snot if you ask me. She never tips, by the way. I expect she's more concerned about her trust fund than who killed her stepfather." Jean handed a customer their change and returned back to Helen. "No love lost between them is my guess."

"Ever hear rumors about the vineyard? Any financial trouble?"

"Not that I knew. He acted as if he were European old money. Where did he get his money, by the way?"

"No idea," Helen said. "When Oscar moved into town, waterfront property didn't cost what it does today."

Jean opened a white paper bag, and Helen dropped another pastry inside. "I'm stopping to visit Georgia, Bill Elison's daughter. I'll bring these along." She dusted the crusty sugar off her hands.

"So sad. Such a nice family."

"Keep your ears to the ground for me."

"I'm on it," Jean tossed back with a wink.

* * *

Georgia lived a few miles out of town in a newer community of mid-priced colonials. A garden flag with red hearts was planted near the front door. Helen rang the bell. A skinny teenager opened the door and shouted, "Mom! Dad! There's a lady here to see you!" Helen followed him into the kitchen.

Georgia raised weary eyes to her.

"I imagine you haven't gotten much sleep since Thursday." Helen gave her a hug. She spotted Todd leaning on the opposite side of the island counter. About forty or forty-five, he was medium height and fit, with the scruffy beard that was in style. Helen was not a fan. "Hi Todd, how are you holding up?"

"It's tough, for sure." They shook hands. "All the grandkids are devastated. Everyone is. Anyone who did business with Bayworks knew Bill." He pushed a white kitchen stool toward her and sat back down.

"Can we get you coffee?" Georgia asked.

"I've had more than my share today. Oh, I brought scones from Jean's."

"That's so thoughtful," Georgia replied. "We've been dealing with Dad's funeral arrangements. I told Todd you might be able to explain more of what happened." Georgia wiped her hands on a dish towel and sat down next to her husband. "I'm hoping you can help the police track down Dad's killer. Todd's not convinced."

Todd slouched over his coffee.

Helen wrinkled her brow. "We worked together volunteering at the club, and I hired Bayworks for my clients. He was very generous with a client of mine going through tough times. What makes you think I can help?"

"A customer of ours suggested we talk to you." Georgia dried shaky hands on a dish towel. "You've got a reputation for being quite the private detective."

Helen sat back and folded her hands. "Detective McAlister is in charge. You've lucky you've got an ex-Baltimore major crimes investigator working for you. I've gotten involved in a few cases, but the police weren't happy about it. They've put up with me."

"I think you're being modest." Georgia's eyes begged for help. "Detective McAlister showed us the coroner's report. We heard you spotted a bent metal piece on the threshold and the cut edge on the carpet."

"I did. Bill and I met Tuesday night. I knew I would have noticed the stairs needed repair. It's part of my usual prep work review of a house. I took notes. The entire house was in perfect condition. I can't say that about all the houses I sell. Joe's crime scene people confirmed the damage was recent."

"Todd says we should leave it to the professionals," Georgia said.

"He's probably right. Is there anyone who had a grudge against him?"

The couple eyed each other. Georgia spoke up. "We've had more than our share of financial issues and payment problems lately. Dad didn't handle getting stiffed well."

"I know what it's like to work hard and not get paid," Helen said. "Why would he get stiffed?'

Georgia studied her hands. Her nails were unpolished, square-tipped, and clean. "Do you remember when Untapped Restaurant had a fire about eight months ago?" She swallowed. "We were hired for smoke and damage clean-up. It was a huge job. They still owe us over thirty thousand dollars."

"Why didn't they pay you?"

Todd spoke up. "We're guessing the restaurant was underinsured. They got their reimbursement from their insurance company but kept stalling on our payment. I got fed up with calling them once a month. About two weeks ago, Dad walked into Untapped and threatened to sue them. He hired an attorney, and the owners of Untapped fired us."

His wife spoke up. "They hired another cleaning service. It's a shame. We hated losing their account. It was a good-sized monthly fee."

Helen raised her eyebrows. "I'm surprised. The owners are well-liked in the area. They have a booming business. Are you sure they didn't have any other reason for not paying?"

Georgia avoided her husband's eyes.

Todd scoffed. "The owners were miserable to work with, always giving our staff a hard time. They complained about every little detail and canceled us before Christmas. I was glad to be rid of them."

"Dad wasn't," Georgia shot back.

Todd grunted. "Maybe they killed Bill to avoid paying him."

Helen looked doubtful. "Killing someone for thirty thousand dollars is over the top. We're not talking millions, and their debt doesn't go away. Untapped owes Bayworks Cleaning Company, not Bill. Do you want me to contact them?"

"I'd rather you not speak to them. Our attorney is handling it," Todd objected.

Helen hesitated, studying the stubborn set of his jaw as she picked up her tote. "Can you give me a copy of your client list? I want to review the names and give it to Detective McAlister unless you object."

"I'll ask our bookkeeper to drop off a copy tomorrow morning," Georgia said.

"Thanks. I suggest you keep our discussions to yourself. I'd be careful about mentioning any of this to relatives or friends. Is that okay with you?"

"Sure." Georgia tried to smile. "I appreciate your help."

Todd pressed his lips together.

"Don't get too excited. I may not be any help, but I'm willing to try. Your dad was a kind man. He deserved better."

Chapter Twelve

Howard Travel's owner, Sarah, popped over the divider from a rear booth in Prime and Claw as Helen stepped inside the restaurant on Sunday evening. On a cold night, the strong fishy scent of fresh crab cakes grilled in butter floated over the warm, noisy crowd and offered a friendly Cheers bar-like vibe. A tray of New York strips sizzled by her on a waiter's arm. Glasses were lined along the bar with bits of cherries and orange slices lining the bottom of their bowls, ready for Old Fashioneds. Two bartenders with pony tails, one male, one female, bustled back and forth.

Helen slid into the booth and unwrapped her scarf. "I'm so glad you called me. I was about to get in my car to go home. Dinner with an old friend is a lot more fun."

"No hot date with the handsome detective?" Sarah teased, pushing her salt and pepper hair off her forehead.

"The detective has a more interesting dinner planned. He's meeting an old cop friend from Baltimore days to discuss a new development on a cold case."

"I'm surprised you didn't wheedle your way into the meeting so you can put in your two cents." They gave their server their orders for Cabernet and prime rib burgers.

"I was tempted but decided he'd already seen too much of me." Helen glanced around. "Lord, I'm hungry. Did you hear about Bill Elison and Oscar Banyon?"

Sarah sipped her wine. "I did. What do you plan to do about it?"

"Do?"

"Don't give me that surprised, innocent face. It will be only a matter of time before your Detective Club gets involved. Any chance you heard from Georgia Myers and her husband?"

"We met today. How did you know?" Helen gave her a suspicious stare.

"Bill and I went back years. I told Georgia how you saved my family from disaster last year."

Helen held up her hands in protest. "The Myers don't know me like you do. Old friends stick up for each other. Besides, Georgia may want me involved, but Todd was less than enthused. I get the idea he tried to talk her out of it, but she didn't listen."

"Ignore him. He's all talk, no action. Georgia needs you. If the police think Bill was murdered, could Georgia or Todd be suspects?"

"Anything's possible. We'd have to figure out their motive." Helen picked up her wine, her eyes wandering around the restaurant. She studied her friend. "You're the travel agent who deals with everyone in town. Let's talk about Oscar Banyon. What can you tell me about his wife, Paula? Ever plan vacations for them?"

Sarah hesitated. "They liked to travel, although Paula and her daughter hit the islands without Oscar. He never traveled far from home. Never wanted to leave. Kind of odd for a man of the world, don't you think?"

"Ever arrange any trips to France to visit his family?"

"Interesting question. I never did. Funny thing, I've traveled through Europe's wineries often over the years. I never once heard the Banyon name mentioned by French locals."

"No mention of a Blue Heron Vineyard?"

"Never. On the other hand, vineyards change names over the years. Like designer shoe styles. I'd guess Oscar chose a different name here in the states."

Helen chewed on a steak fry. "Do you think you could put out some feelers with your European vineyard contacts? I'd like to hear what they know about Oscar's family vineyard."

Sarah chuckled. "And off you go, Jessica Fletcher!"

"You're the one who suggested I put my sleuths to work." Her phone rang and she frowned. "Sorry. I'll make this call quick. It's a client of mine. She has her house in Grace Harbor on the market. It's odd she'd call me on a Sunday night."

One finger in her left ear, phone on the right, she answered. "Hi, Maureen. I'm out for dinner. Do you need me?" Her eyes widened as her client rattled on. "I'm so sorry. Was anyone home at the time?"

"No. I was visiting a friend overnight." Maureen's voice shook.

"We'll stop all showings for a day or two until we get the house back to normal. Can you stay with someone again tonight?"

"I'll call my sister."

"Good. I rather you not be alone. I'll stop over tomorrow about ten and check on you. I'm glad you called. Try not to worry."

Sarah raised her eyebrows. "That doesn't sound good."

"Maureen Nagley is so lovely," Helen said, disgusted. "Someone broke into her house this afternoon. Took some jewelry and spray painted her family room walls."

"That's terrible. Why in the world would someone single her out?"

"I'm texting Joe. It's the fourth break-in since January involving one of my clients. The stories are killing my business." Helen tapped in a message and hit send.

"Dessert solves all problems. Want anything?"

"Nothing better than chocolate to help relieve stress. I'll order the brownie. And a hot tea."

Sarah picked up her bag. "Order the cheesecake for me. I'll run to the restroom." About five minutes later, she sat back down.

"How's the brownie?" she asked.

"Delicious," Helen mumbled around a bite. "What's going on? Have you seen a ghost?"

"Not quite. Joe's seated in the main dining room with a woman."

"He's having dinner with an old cop friend," Helen shrugged. "Why?"

"She may be a cop and a friend, but she's not old, and she is a stunner." Sarah tilted her head. "They're practically nose to nose."

71

"Excuse me." Helen rose to her feet. "I've got to take a look."

Her friend grabbed her wrist. "Sit down. He'll see you."

"This is a covert operation. Nora Charles would never let him leave without scoping this woman out." Helen's green eyes flashed. "Be right back." She picked up her bag and meandered over to the bar and back. A blonde, her hair streaked in light brown and grazing her shoulder, sat across from Joe. Dramatic silver earrings glistened in the bar lights. Their heads close together, she issued a sexy laugh at one of his comments.

Helen plopped back into her seat. "Well, this is awkward. More than awkward."

"It doesn't help she's drop-dead gorgeous."

"Shhh," Helen put a finger to her lips. "Don't rub it in."

Sarah set her fork down. "Uh, oh. Guess who's walking toward the bar with him?"

The tall brunette, dressed in black jeans, knee-high leather boots, and a short-cropped grey designer jacket, ordered another drink.

Helen tossed her hair and straightened her sweater over her hips. She stood up. "Agatha won't forgive me if I don't say hello."

Sarah raised her eyebrows. "You're braver than I am."

"Damn. He sees us. I wanted to be on offense."

Joe reached their table. "Hello," he said, clearing his throat, his face flushed. "Helen. Sarah. This is Special Agent Emma Harris. Emma, this is Helen Morrisey and Sarah Howard."

Emma offered a strong, slender hand. "Helen, I've heard so much about you. Sounds like you should be on the force here in Kent County." Her voice came out in a soft southern drawl.

Helen returned a firm hand while eyeing Joe. "I'll take it as a compliment. Joe tells me you have new details on an old case. Did you work together while Joe was in Baltimore?"

Emma stroked his arm. "We go way back. I've been in the FBI Baltimore office at least eight years." The agent eyed Joe and made a coy smile. "We were engaged at one point. It didn't work out, but we've remained close friends."

CHAPTER TWELVE

Helen's head snapped. Joe avoided Helen's eyes, his hands deep in his pockets. Helen decided she wanted to make him sweat. She didn't blink. "Would you care to join us for a drink?"

Joe tugged at his shirt collar. "Thanks, but it's been a long day. I have to drop Emma off at the Hilton. I saw your text about your client's burglary. I'll give you a call tomorrow as soon as I hear the details."

"Thanks for checking." Helen, reaching for her glass, gave them a cool smile. "Emma, it's a pleasure to meet an old friend of Joe's. Good luck with the case."

Her eyes drilled Joe's back as she watched them make their way out the door.

Sarah sat back after the door closed behind them. "Well!"

"That's an understatement." Helen's pen cut through her bill as she signed her check. "I didn't know FBI agents were such trendy dressers. Those pants couldn't have been tighter. No hidden Glock on those hips. Her shoulder bag must cost more than one of my commissions." She tossed down the pen. "I didn't realize FBI agents earned that much. Public servants and all that. And how does she look so put together on a Sunday night in freaking cold February?"

"When you're single, no kids in college, you get to splurge on yourself," Sarah declared. "Joe wanted to sink through the floorboards."

Helen laughed. "She was delighted to fill us in on their personal history. Where's a voodoo doll when you want one?"

"Who would you curse?"

"I'm not sure. Weighing my options."

"What are you going to say to Joe?"

Helen grabbed her coat and shoved her wallet back into her bag. "I'd say it's his move. He dug this ditch; he'll have to dig himself out." She stood up. "Assuming he wants to."

Sarah studied her friend. "Maybe he was afraid to tell you."

"He's an ex-Marine. He ran a Baltimore homicide unit. What could he possibly be afraid of?"

Her friend snickered as she tugged on her gloves. "Have you met Helen

Morrisey? She can be one intimidating woman."

"Don't be silly. You know what Jane Marple would say."

Sarah raised her eyebrows. "No, but I think you're going to tell me."

"Never make assumptions. My bad. I should listen to Jane more often."

Chapter Thirteen

"Maureen, this is awful," Helen exclaimed when she walked into her client's living room Monday morning. She put her hands on her head and spun around the room, appalled at the graffitied walls in red and black and the words *'Your agent is a crook!'* She put her arms around the older woman. "I can't believe this!"

The older woman trembled. "I didn't sleep all night."

"What did the police say?"

"They took photos of the room and the broken kitchen door. They didn't sound hopeful about tracking down the vandal."

"Who would do this? It makes no sense. And why in the world would they accuse me of being a crook? It's bizarre."

"I've no idea. Come, I found this."

Helen followed Maureen into the kitchen. She picked up Helen's business card off the counter. "It was torn in half and tossed on the floor." Maureen clutched her arm. "I'm frightened. Can you stay a few minutes? I made fresh coffee."

Helen took a mug. "This is creepy," she agreed. "But we're going to figure this out. I promise you."

Her client offered a tenuous smile. "Glad my Realtor is my own personal sleuth."

Helen's cell rang. "It's Detective McAlister." She picked up the phone. "Detective, I'm with my client, Maureen Nagley, in Grace Harbor. Any news for us?" Her voice was cool, all business.

"I assigned officers to canvas her neighborhood for anyone who heard or saw the break-in."

"Did your deputies tell you our vandal is now leaving behind threats?"

"Say that again," Joe said. "What kind of threat?"

"They smeared the message *'your agent is a crook'* across her living room. Joe, this is getting more and more vindictive. Maureen is afraid to stay in her own house."

"I'll look at the file's photos right now. Try not to worry. We'll get this guy." Joe growled.

"It's getting harder and harder. Call me when you learn anything. Thanks."

She hung up and turned to Maureen. "I hate to leave you, but I need to get to the office. I'll ask Tammi to arrange a handyman to fix your door and repaint your walls. I don't want you to live with this for long. Do you have friends you can visit for a few days?"

"My sister lives in Far Hill." Maureen exhaled. "I'll stay with her."

Helen hugged her. "I'll finish my coffee. You go pack a bag and we'll lock up the house together. Tammi will check in with you later today."

* * *

She wove through Grace Harbor and headed to Port Anne and Safe Harbor. Her phone screen buzzed with a series of texts from Daniel Haggert, another client. She pulled into a driveway and scrolled down.

Yard trashed while at the store. Back porch graffitied. Should we cancel showings for the week? Thanks, Daniel

How awful! Did you call the police?

Yes. Here now.

I'm on my way.

Thanks.

She left a voicemail for Tammi. "Hi. I'm leaving Maureen Nagley's house, which was vandalized yesterday afternoon. Can you track down a handyman and coordinate with her? I don't want her in the house until it's back to normal. We need someone available right away. Also got a text from Daniel Haggert. Someone graffitied his porch. I'll stop there on my way to the office. Thanks."

* * *

Two police cars were parked in front of the Haggert house when she pulled into their driveway. The Haggert family lived in a brand-new house within a planned community, and easily twice the price of Maureen's. She passed the community pool and two pickleball courts. A Sheriff's Department deputy was talking with Daniel on the rear deck while more officers checked the house.

The two men gave her a wave. "Helen, thanks for coming." Daniel ran his hands through his short, light hair, his usually friendly face strained.

Helen smiled at the deputy. "I think we've met before. I'm glad you're here. What do you think happened?"

"Too early to say, although it appears more like a couple of bored teenagers than anyone out for cash or drugs." He led them around to the rear porch.

Helen stared at the marred wall. *'Your agent is a crook!'*

"I was with another client in Grace Harbor today. Someone broke into her house and painted the exact same words across her living room walls."

Daniel stepped back and stared, first at the porch and then at Helen.

"Did they get inside?" Helen asked.

"No, but I found this stuck in the screen of our kitchen door." He handed one of Helen's business cards to the deputy. It was torn in half.

He fingered the pieces. "Who would have it in for you?"

"If someone does, I don't have any idea who or why."

Daniel's lips clamped down into a tight straight line. "I think we should take the house off the market until we can get this porch repainted. Do you agree?"

"I do. We'll find a contractor who can work fast. I feel so badly, Daniel, and I can't imagine what this is about." She kicked a few pieces of broken glass aside with a leather boot.

"Not your fault," Daniel said. "A couple of days won't matter. I'm more upset about my kids seeing this when they get off the bus from school this afternoon."

"Give your insurance company a call. Take lots of pictures. You may have coverage. Tammi and I will start making calls to contractors."

"Our squad will check with your neighbors."

Helen stepped back and stared at the graffitied warning again. A chill ran up her arms. What is going on here?

"I need to call my wife." Daniel shook their hands.

"Officer, can we talk for a minute?" Helen asked, her voice low. "This is the fifth house targeted. My clients' homes are being damaged, and their safety threatened. What if any of them were at home? How do you plan to put a stop to it? We've been lucky these creeps have only attacked empty property."

The officer nodded. "I know that."

"Are there any security cameras on the house?"

"There is, but the system doesn't trigger help until someone breaks in. Only Maureen Nagley's system went off when they entered her kitchen. The security company called the station."

"Thank goodness for that." She pulled back her shoulders. "Call me if you learn anything. Anything at all."

* * *

Monday afternoon at Safe Harbor was usually busy, no matter what the weather. Helen waved hello to the receptionist. Tag Stoltz was chatting in the hall with Stella. Tammi was on the phone. Helen flipped on the lights in her office and was scrolling through emails when Tag tapped on the doorframe. He was dressed in wool slacks and a tan and navy sweater.

"Can you give me a few minutes?"

"Take a seat. I'm guessing you're not working at Rupert's store today?"

He glanced at his slacks. "Tomorrow. It's a balancing act. I keep jeans and sneakers in my car."

"I remember those days when I was just getting started," Helen smiled. "What's on your mind?"

Tag sat forward, his hands clasped. "I'm kind of curious if you've heard anything more about Oscar Banyon's murder."

Helen studied the young agent's face. "Not really. It happened Saturday. The police are probably swamped. Why do you ask?"

Tag shuffled his feet. "I've never been this close to an agent whose client was murdered. It's kind of weird, although I admit, it's kind of exciting. A couple of our agents told me. Does it worry you?"

Helen set her elbows on her desk, her face in her palms, puzzled. "I'm not sure what you're asking."

"I had a listing appointment this morning. The seller asked if I knew about you."

"About me?"

"Yeah, I may have only been here a few months, but it doesn't take much to realize you do a lot of business in Kent County. You're a recognized name." Tag studied the carpet for a moment. "The seller made a weird comment. She said you've run into crimes involving your clients before. She asked about Oscar and the man who owns the cleaning company."

"You mean Bill Elison. He owned Bayworks Cleaning."

"That's the name. I never heard of him before I read the news."

"What was this seller suggesting?" Helen frowned. "Did she know Bill?"

"She hinted he wasn't the first person you've found murdered. She thought you might be bad luck. She also mentioned you date a detective and get involved in his cases."

Helen was poker-faced. "I wouldn't give much credence to local gossip. Thanks for telling me. I appreciate it." She shifted her laptop. He took the hint and reached for the door.

"How's your business going? I realize you only joined us in November." Helen asked.

"It's slow, which I expected. It's tough competing with names like yours." He hesitated. "Actually, it's really why I wanted to see you. I wonder if you would consider being my mentor."

Helen sat back, surprised. "I'd honestly have to think about the idea, and right now, it's a bit chaotic. I'll let you know in a few days. In the meantime, don't get discouraged. It took years to build my business." She smiled. "Be patient with yourself. Working at Five and Dime might turn into a good way to meet people. One thing I've learned is that you can never predict what can lead to new business."

Tag's face brightened up. "Thanks, and thanks for the pep talk. I hope I didn't upset you about that woman's comments." He closed the door.

Helen stared after him, the conversation running through her mind. More rumors. She reached into her desk drawer for Twizzlers and started to chew. What a day. Could it get any worse?

* * *

About four o'clock, Tammi tapped on her door. Today, she wore blue and white snowflakes around her neck. "Got a couple minutes? I need to talk to you."

"Of course. Let's catch up. You sound worried."

Tammi sat down and fingered a notepad. "I'm not sure how to tell you this, with Bill and Oscar gone and now more clients vandalized."

"This sounds serious." Helen pushed aside her laptop and set her leather chair next to Tammi's. "We're best friends. We have each other's backs."

Tammi bit her lower lip. "I can't imagine how I could have gotten through the past three years with Marcus in Germany. I couldn't have managed without you and my mom. You're family to Kayla."

"I love that I'm Kayla's godmother. She gives me the chance to have another little girl in my life." Helen grabbed Tammi's hand. "What's this about? I'd be surprised if it's about one of our clients. You're tougher than they are. Do you need another raise? Are you sick? Tell me." She gave an encouraging smile.

Tammi inhaled, held her breath, and let it out in a long, quiet sigh. "I'm resigning."

Helen's face went white. "Excuse me? Why? Whatever is wrong, we can fix it."

"I've been dreading this conversation for weeks. Marcus's deployment is over."

"That's wonderful news. I'm so happy for you!" Helen stopped. "Why are you upset? Are you worried about his return and your relationship? It'll be an adjustment, but you two will sort through it."

"I know. It's not easy for military families to piece ourselves back together. But that's not the issue. He's being assigned to a base in Fort Hood, Texas. We'll be moving in less than a month."

Helen sat back. "I thought he was putting in a request for an assignment at the local proving grounds right here."

"He did. But it's the Army. You give them a list of preferences and, if you're lucky, you get your first choice. He didn't."

Helen put her head in her hands. "I can't believe this. It's not about losing you here at Safe Harbor. That's bad enough. You're what makes this office my second home." Slowly, she lifted her head. "More than anything, I can't imagine not having you in my life every day."

Tammi wiped a tear. "I can't either. I'll miss you so much."

Helen's eyes teared. "Not as much as I will." She stroked Tammi's hand. "But I'm happy for you and Kayla. Nothing is more important than having Marcus back home out of harm's way and all of you together. Family has to come first. Is your mother going with you?"

"I wish she could, but she can't leave my grandfather. He's almost ninety, not well, and depends on my mother. My mom is moving in with a friend so she can check on him."

"Kayla will miss her grandmother terribly."

"So much. I hate leaving my mother behind. She has her own share of health problems. Here I could help both of them." She stood up. "We'll need to hire my replacement."

The two women hugged each other. "Whoever that is, God help them. Replacing you isn't possible." She glanced at the time. "It's late. You need to go home and tell Kayla. Pick up a cake to celebrate. Are you writing up the job description?" Helen asked.

"I'm working on it now."

"Don't forget. My assistant needs to keep me out of murder investigations."

"I've never had success with that."

"But you've helped keep me alive." Helen blew her a kiss.

Chapter Fourteen

A few minutes after five, Helen packed up her laptop and started for home. Too windy to light a fire, she thought. Her front porch lights were on, and her front door unlocked. Lizzie was already home. She could smell dinner cooking.

"Hi, Mom." Lizzie was bustling around the kitchen. "I'm making lemon chicken."

Helen kissed her on the cheek. "How did you guess I need a home-cooked meal? I was mentally resigned to a can of chicken soup. I didn't want to cook."

Lizzie snorted. "You never want to cook. Besides, you've had a couple of tough days. Thought you'd appreciate it."

"You don't know the half of it. I've been feeling sorry for myself all the way home." Helen swept up Watson, held him to her chest, and stroked his soft chin with her own. His gentle, deep yellow eyes followed her. "I'm putting on my pjs. Be right back."

A few minutes later, Helen grabbed a stool and slumped over the island countertop. Lizzie handed her a glass of Sauvignon Blanc. "Bless you," Helen declared.

Lizzie was slicing lemons into quarters. "Are you going to tell me why you're upset? It's written all over your face."

"Let's start with Joe and the killer FBI agent."

Her daughter scrunched her eyebrows into a V. "Killer as in murderer or as in gorgeous?"

"As in gorgeous, hot, and sexy. Sarah Howard spotted her with Joe while we were in Prime and Claw last night. She used the word 'stunner.'" Helen popped a slice of cheese into her mouth. "She even has a southern drawl."

"Ouch! That can't be good." Lizzie put her knife down. "Maybe she'll turn out to be nice."

"Don't kid yourself. I got the distinct sense she's no pussycat." Helen looked down at Watson and Trixie. "Sorry guys, no offense. The last twenty-four hours went downhill from there."

"What else happened?"

Her mother heaved a woeful sigh. "Tammi gave her notice. Marcus is coming back to the States. They're assigned to a base in Fort Hood, Texas."

"Oh, Mom, I'm so sorry. She's family."

"We've worked together for fourteen years. She's my best friend." Helen's lips quivered. "We're Nancy and George."

"You're sounding obsessed. When is she moving?"

"In about four weeks. Not a lot of time to hire someone and get them familiar with their job. Life will never be the same."

"Mom, for someone who dives right into people's problems, you don't handle change well."

"I don't handle family not nearby."

Lizzie leaned on the counter, her two hands on her chin. "You and Tammi can talk by phone. She's not leaving the country. You can hop on a plane when you want to visit."

Her mother swiped a tear from her cheek. "We share everything, not just the occasional story. She runs out for coffee when we can't stomach the office dreck. She's my excuse for buying pastry. I treat, and she pretends she isn't interested. When a client is nasty, she calms me down, or I calm her down. I never miss Kayla's plays and dance recitals. You don't either."

"No matter how awful and long they are."

Helen made a wistful laugh. "She was my rock when your father died. No one will replace what we share."

Lizzie came around the island and wrapped her arms around her mother. "You need a hot meal. Let's eat." Helen hugged her back.

About nine, Lizzie was tucked into bed with a book when Helen came into her room and sat down on the edge. She squinted at her mother. "Why do you have a legal pad in your hand?"

"This is a print-out of Bayworks Cleaning Company's client list."

"Sounds boring, especially at this late hour."

"It's actually interesting. Vince Caffrey's boss at Longfeld Insurance, Blue Heron Vineyard, and Untapped are all customers."

"Does it surprise you? I would expect Bayworks services a lot of local businesses."

Helen made a long face and tossed the list at her daughter. "Must you be so logical? I'm going to climb into bed and read a few of those *Unsolved Crimes* magazines Rupert gave me."

"I'd never sleep." Lizzie wrinkled her nose. "Are you going to call Joe?"

"I don't know," Helen pouted. "I'll think about it tomorrow. Tomorrow is another day."

"Okay, Scarlet O'Hara," her daughter quipped.

"Humph. Give me back my list!" She stomped back down the stairs.

* * *

Tuesday whipped by. Tammi constructed an advertisement for her position, and Helen tracked down contractors for Maureen and Daniel.

"I hope you don't mind. I posted a notice on the office bulletin board."

"Everyone has to be told sooner or later," Helen grumbled. "What did Stella say?"

"She was surprised but happy for me. She wants to plan a sendoff before I go."

"Great idea," Helen smiled.

"We have someone to suggest to you. Tag Stotz."

Helen raised her eyebrows. " Really? What makes you think he might be interested?"

"Since he's working for Rupert a few hours a week, he's obviously trying to supplement his income. I think someone who's already licensed would be easier for me to train. Tag knows most of the language and basic systems.

It could give us a jumpstart."

"Did he tell you he asked if I'd be his mentor?" asked Helen.

"He did. Maybe working with you is a good way to learn the business. At least he could buy you some time to find a full-time person."

"What does Stella think?" Helen asked.

"She says his business is picking up, but he's got a long way to go. He doesn't say much, but she likes his attitude. He's curious about what happens here in the office."

Helen tapped a pen on her desk. "Do me a favor. Check out his former real estate company. Maybe you can get more background. I'd like to know why he left that agency. But you're right. He could be our interim person."

"You're too suspicious about everyone. He's got an Elvis smile, very cute."

Helen smirked. "He needs to lose the long hair. Any more ideas on hires? We need to be prepared for replacing Tag down the line. "

Tammi slid her ad across Helen's desk and shook a colorful nail. "Stop ignoring this. You have to decide on our ad. Is it missing anything?"

Helen glared at Tammi's write-up. "I have three issues with it. Number one, this list of requirements could choke a horse. How do you think we'll ever get any candidates? Number two, the ad is too long, it'll blow our entire advertising budget for the month of February."

"You told me you had three issues."

"You need to add the words 'crime lead follow-up, Twizzler consumption controller, romance counselor.'"

"You really are irritable today," her friend declared.

"I'm not irritable." Helen crossed her arms across her chest and pouted. "I'm feeling sorry for myself. I'm being selfish, but I don't care. I hate discussing this."

A soft tap on the door. Their office receptionist walked in, her arms overflowing with a huge bouquet of perfect white roses, orange lilies, and tall stalks of deep blue delphiniums. Helen dropped her yellow highlighter.

"Wow! Someone knew they needed to save my day," Tammi exclaimed. "Did Joe send them?"

She watched while Helen opened a florist's note. *"I miss my favorite sleuth, and I'm not talking Nancy Drew. Love, Joe."*

Tammi's earrings took a wild swing side to side. "Care to fill me in? It's too early for Valentine's Day. Unless he's hoping to avoid the florist's upcharge."

"Ha, ha. That's the kind of sarcastic comment about men Agatha Raisin would make." Helen's cheeks flushed. "Is it hot in here?" She fanned her face.

"Ah, no. It's February, and the heating system is barely working. Either you two had a fight, or you're engaged. Which is it? Come on, I want details." Tammi's endless green striped nails wiggled.

"If I give you details, will you cancel your move?" Helen asked. "Sorry. Unfair request. We're definitely not engaged. Don't even go there."

"Did you ignore Howard Travel's deadline for your May trip to Italy? If you're not careful, Joe will decide to go by himself in hopes of meeting a beautiful señorita."

"That's Spanish. I think you mean signorina."

"I'm surprised you know the difference," Tammi commented.

"Given last night, he doesn't have to go to Italy to find a willing travel partner. Remember when I told you Joe was meeting an old cop friend for dinner Sunday night? Sarah and I ran into them at Prime and Claw. His old cop friend is not only a special agent with the FBI, but she's drop-dead gorgeous and about ten years younger than I am. She informed us they'd been engaged about six years ago. With much pleasure, I must add."

"A detail he never told you." Tammi eyed the flowers. "I'd say Joe's trying to get off the hot seat."

Helen narrowed her eyes. "Although his ex-fiancée is definitely trying to reignite the flame."

"Don't be ridiculous. He's crazy about you. I feel sorry for him. And her, if she's interested in getting him back."

"Trust me, she's interested. Is this the valuable love advice I'll miss when you're gone?"

"I promise, I'll put it in the ad," Tammi chuckled.

"Come on, let's finish this dreadful project." Helen put a rose up to her nose and inhaled. "They do smell delicious."

Chapter Fifteen

Wednesday morning, Joe called her as she drove into town.

"Hi there," he said with exaggerated cheer.

"Good morning," Helen replied, her tone frosty.

"I was wondering if you received my flowers." He sounded tense.

"As a matter of fact, I did. Late yesterday. Thank you, they're beautiful. I love the colors."

"I thought you might like them."

"How's your ex-fiancée?"

"Emma's fine." Joe stumbled. "Any chance I can cook dinner for you tonight?"

"Aren't you tied up with Emma and her cold case? I get the sense things are heating up and I'm not talking about business."

He grunted. "Snide doesn't sound good on you. She's on her way to the agency's Philadelphia office. Won't be back until late tomorrow."

"I'm glad you can fit me in, Detective." She tapped on her steering wheel. "Here's the deal. I want to get your reaction to some information I picked up concerning Bill Elison. What time do you suggest?" Helen asked.

"How's six o'clock?"

"Works for me."

"See you at six." Joe sounded relieved.

She couldn't help but chuckle to herself. Her cell rang again.

"Dottie Taylor. Good to hear from you. It's usually me who's calling you for construction advice," Helen said.

"I thought if you're in Port Anne today, you could stop by. It's about Bill

Elison," Dottie's rough voice responded.

"I'm coming through town now. On my way to my office. I can be there in a few minutes."

She spun around and wove down a narrow dead-end street to Taylor's Lumber, a thorn in the side of every big box store lining the edges of Port Anne town center. The corporate bigshots probably predicted they'd shut it down long before this. They'd underestimated the local loyalists committed to spending their money at a privately owned business handed down through generations. Now Dottie Taylor, in her sixties, supervised the yard with two daughters.

The Taylor family knew their customers by first name. Helen gave a son-in-law a friendly wave and stepped inside the century-old wooden building housing hardware, paints, sample windows, and carpet. If the Taylors didn't have what you needed in stock, they'd order it. Helen and Andy restored their Victorian while raising their twins. They traipsed in and out nearly every day. Helen called Taylor's their second mortgage. After Andy died, she moved out to the cliff on Osprey Point to try to start a new chapter for her, Shawn, and Lizzie.

Rachel Taylor, the younger of the two girls, pushed her dark hair back with a denim scrunchy and smiled. "Hi, Helen. Haven't seen you in a while."

"My budget's still in recovery from the new decking material you talked me into last summer." Helen gazed across the store, its worn original oak floors and deep wooden bins crowded with all shapes and sizes of merchandise. She inhaled the smell of sawdust and fresh varnish. "Where's your grey Tabby? Why isn't he supervising the register?"

Rachel's smile dropped. "He passed away a couple months ago. He was seventeen years old."

"Oh, I'm so sorry. You must miss him so much."

"We do. He was special." Rachel leaned down and scooped up a yellow Tabby and set her on the counter. "Meet Molly. I found this sweet girl chasing mice in our lumberyard, and she's now taking charge. We couldn't function without a cat greeting customers. We're fattening her up." She gave the round kitten a squeeze, and Helen reached out to stroke her chin. "Need anything in particular?"

"I'm looking for you, Mom."

"I figured." Rachel cocked her head. "She's in the back stocking shelves. Go say hello."

"I will." Helen wove between the rows and rows of floor samples and found Dottie jotting down SKU numbers. Her face brightened when she spotted Helen.

"How's the real estate business?" Dottie shoved a pad into the pocket of a green canvas apron. Faded jeans were draped over ankle-high scuffed work boots. A rubber bracelet of keys hung on her left wrist. "I guess business is dead. Rumor has it your clients are dropping like flies." She chuckled.

"Don't joke about it." Helen leaned her back against a rack of paint cans. "If I walk into one more graffitied house, I may have a heart attack. I'm afraid to go to my next listing appointment, and I'm never afraid of listing appointments."

"I'm torn up about Bill Elison. We grew up together, building our businesses. We both had strong backs. Georgia is my goddaughter. Oscar Banyon, he's another story. Good for bringing in tourists, but not easy to get along with, in my opinion." She tsked, tsked.

"Georgia asked me to check around town. She wants me to help find her dad's killer. I'm not sure where to begin. I'm buried under complaints from upset clients who've been vandalized. Five houses in the last six weeks. I'm telling you, it's killing my business."

"Todd stopped by to pick up cleaning supplies and mentioned it. I can't say he sounded happy about Georgia talking to you."

"Why does it bother him?"

"He thinks you're an amateur and will muck up the police investigation. In my opinion, he doesn't want anyone poking into their business."

"Sounds like a man with something to hide."

"Did my daughter tell you someone broke into our yard Monday night?" Dottie asked, her voice low and distraught.

"No," Helen said. "Tell me." She pulled out a box of paint and sat down among the shelves.

"They painted threats across one of the storage sheds facing our entrance."
Helen gritted her teeth. "Did you call the police?"

"McAlister checked it out early today. I've got my yard crew painting over
it now. Come. There's something else bothering me. I want to show you
my bulletin board." Helen followed her.

"People from all over three counties pin up their business cards, hoping
to pick up business. Your card has been hanging here for years."

Helen smiled. "Every so often, I check to see if you need another one. I
don't see it."

Dottie crooked her finger, and Helen followed the lumberyard owner
behind her register. Dottie opened a desk drawer and handed Helen her
card. "It was torn in half and pinned back on the board. I showed McAlister."

Helen flipped the two pieces back and forth. Her eyes darkened. "I'm
being targeted. There's no doubt."

"Along with anyone who works with you."

"Your break-in and graffiti were because of me." Helen patted Dottie's
shoulder. "I'm so sorry."

"I'm not intimidated. When that famous chef of yours was killed, you
managed to save my business. But I agree with you. With your clients' houses
being raided, I'm worried these vandals aren't just bored local hoodlums.
This is nasty."

"Sure appears that way. Can't thank you enough for backing me up.
Between Joe and I, we'll figure this out. Will you tip me off if you hear
anything?"

Dottie smiled. "I will. Lots of scuttlebutt floats around a lumberyard."

Helen opened her bag. "Do you mind if I stick another card on your board?
Or are you afraid you'd be asking for more trouble?"

Dottie took the new one and jammed it onto the center of the board with
a red pushpin. "Old one was kind of faded anyway." They grinned at each
other. Helen headed back to the register.

"Hey, Helen," Dottie called out.

Helen spun around.

"Be careful. We don't want to lose you, too."

* * *

Tag Stotz, dressed in neat slacks and sweater, raised his eyes from a computer in Safe Harbor's resource room when Helen walked in.

"Hi. Dressed for clients?"

"Hope they show up. Do you have a couple minutes?"

"I'm running behind. Anything in particular?" asked Helen.

"I'd like to discuss Tammi's position and if I can be considered."

"I assumed you want part-time work."

Tag followed her. "I have a lot of experience. I'm pretty sure I can handle her work in fewer hours."

"I rather doubt it." Helen studied him. "Tammi's in charge of initial interviews. Go ahead and set one up with her. She'll need a current resume. If she considers you a strong candidate, the next step is a background check and recommendations." She set down her tote. "I'm curious, why did you decide to move to Port Anne? Do you have relatives here? It's a long way from Seattle, Washington."

"My mom and dad owned a farm in Washington state, and I worked for them. We visited relatives on the East Coast a few times. After my parents died, I got my real estate license. I decided to move east and remembered Port Anne. It's a lot more affordable, and I wanted to be near the water."

"Port Anne is going through a lot of growing pains with new people moving in and taking over the waterfront. If you want help with property values, ask me. I'll run through your numbers for you."

"Thanks, I will." Tag fingered her bouquet. "These flowers are gorgeous. Someone wanted to impress."

"Thanks. They are a treat in the middle of winter." Helen reached for her phone.

Tag made a just between us grin. "Who sent them? Secret admirer?"

Helen struggled to ignore her annoyance. "No secret. They're from Joe McAlister."

"I've heard of him, the police detective."

"Yup," Helen lifted her chin. "Tag, I really need to make some calls."

"Oh, sorry," Tag backed out of the room.

* * *

Tammi caught her about one o'clock. "I'm picking up a sandwich at the Wooden Mast. Can I get you one?"

"Wish I had the time. Port Anne Yacht Club Vice Commodore called an emergency meeting for today at two. With Oscar gone, we've got some decisions to make about club operations. I guarantee you, she wants us to vote to approve an outside audit of maintenance expenses. I'll head home afterwards. I'm going to Joe's for dinner and want to change."

"Oh, ho. Are you two on the mend?"

Helen grimaced. "Jury is out, but I have questions about Oscar and Bill for him."

"By the way, Leslie Tupper called this morning and canceled her appointment for this Saturday. Says she's decided to stay put."

"That's disappointing. She was excited about the houses I found for her. Wonder what changed her mind. I'll give her a call in a few days."

Chapter Sixteen

little after six o'clock, Helen's Mini trundled up a narrow, winding gravel lane past a Victorian farmhouse and made a short climb up a hill to reach Joe's carriage house. She slowed to take in the views of a winter sky meeting acres and acres of Far Hill horse farms. The nearby five-star international competition facility brought competing equestrians from around the world.

Joe's big barn mirrored the farmhouse in architecture, with turrets and hand-cut wooden shingles. He had bought it about four years ago after he left the Baltimore Police Department's major crimes division. An eclectic combination of restored architecture, incorporating three original sliding barn doors, and a roughhewn overhang protected the entry. Inside, the central room ran east to west with restored original plank floors, a two-story fireplace, and an open kitchen. A staircase of forged iron wound its way to the upper floor with two large bedrooms and private baths.

Helen made a turn in the drive and leaned back in her seat. This is the first peaceful moment I've had in six days. Her eyes traveled across the surrounding fields, touched in snow. It was an Andrew Wyeth painting. A dog leaping across the front path broke the silence.

"Rocky! How is my darling boy? I haven't seen you in a couple weeks." She tugged on the Golden Retriever's soft ears and kissed his greying muzzle. He swished his long fan of a tail in total delight.

"Rocky, calm down. Get inside, boy," Joe shouted, reining in the dog. "Hi." He flashed a happy grin. "Give me your coat." He took her bag and hung it on a hammered iron peg. Joe set his chin on the top of her glossy, dark hair and gave her an awkward hug. "You look amazing." His eyes traveled from her V-necked wool sweater that stopped just above her knees to the black tights tucked into leather riding boots. "It's been a while since you've worn red. You smell good, too."

"Thanks. Orange and blue aren't my only wardrobe choices." Helen circled around a deep tan leather couch and put her hands to the roaring fire.

"Want a glass of cabernet?"

"Sounds perfect, especially after today. What smells so delicious?"

"Nothing fancy. Rib eyes and baked potatoes."

"You've stolen my menu. Well, other than pizza and Chinese." She accepted a heavy wine glass and sat on the edge of the stone hearth. A pendulum clock sounded from across the room. They stared at each other. Helen cast her eyes around the room. Rocky made himself comfortable at her feet.

"Any news on Bill Elison? Or Oscar Banyon?"

"Umm. Can we talk about them later?"

"Sure. What do you want to talk about? Your engagement?" Her voice was taut.

He stuck his hands into his jeans pockets and shifted from foot to foot. "I called it off at least six years ago. I told you."

Helen twisted her glass, then raised her chin. "You told me you came close to getting married. You never said you were engaged. A little detail you didn't mention. Now, she's back."

"I'm sorry." Joe gritted his teeth. "She's here for a few weeks to work on a cold case with me. That's all."

"How cold is the case, Joe? Is it a police matter or a personal one? Because the vibe I got from Emma is she'd be happy to rekindle *that* fire." Helen began to pace. "I can't blame you if you're reconsidering. She's obviously smart and beautiful. She's in law enforcement. I'd guess she's willing to plan lots of trips anywhere you'd like with no hesitation. Probably a lot more fun than a widow at least five years older. I've got family, personal hangups, and a posse of fictional sleuths who get in your way."

Joe turned his back to her and leaned on the stone kitchen island, his hands spread apart, gripping the edge. He turned again to face her, a nerve

95

in his left jaw clenching in and out. Helen knew his sign of tension. No upside-down smile tonight.

"I didn't tell you about our engagement because, in my mind, we should never have gotten engaged in the first place. I'd been searching for a long time, met a lot of women, and thought she was the one." His brown eyes were cloaked in the shadows of the dark room. " I realized we'd rushed it. Neither of us knew what we wanted. I certainly didn't. I called it off."

"Do you know what you want now?" She lifted her chin, stubbornness in her eyes.

"I want what you had with Andy."

Helen bit her lip, her voice low and soft. "Let's not bring up Andy."

"Why not? If he hadn't died, you'd be together. You wore your wedding ring on a chain until last summer."

"You're right, and it's taken me five years to reach a stage where I can picture a life without him."

"What does that mean? Have you decided there's room for someone new?"

"Have you decided if you want Emma back in the picture?"

"Until two days ago, I never gave her another thought since I left Baltimore. I haven't changed my mind. I'm not the least bit interested in Emma." Joe took her hands. "I want to be that new someone for you, and I'm willing to wait."

"No regrets about leaving the Baltimore force?"

"Sometimes. I miss their quick access to outside agencies' assistance." His anxious eyes grazed her face. He reached down to stroke her hair.

She took a deep breath, her eyes studying the detective in the firelight. She gave him a tentative smile. "You're tensing your left cheek again. Are you willing to put up with my Detection Club? They're part of the package."

"Even Agatha Raisin, as annoying as she is." His lips brushed hers. "I've told you, I have three sisters. I'm used to being around a bunch of opinionated women." He kissed her hard.

"You may have convinced me." She lifted her eyes, her shoulders relaxing.

"Why do I sense you have something to ask me?"

She stroked his cheek. "I'm curious if you ever plan to feed me. And when we can discuss your cases."

Joe laughed. "You are so predictable. Get out your notes and I'll fire up the steaks."

* * *

The two shifted a small table over in front of the hearth. She set the table while Joe brought over the steaming plates. Helen pulled out her pad and slid it under his nose. "We have a theory."

"We? Oh. Your Detection Club." Joe lopped sour cream onto a potato.

Helen pulled back her shoulders. "Actually, we've got a couple. I sketched them out on my Pro Con list."

Joe read out loud, "Motive plus Opportunity equals Murder. Why should I be surprised?"

"Don't push it. You're on thin ice, remember? This is my sleuthing process, and it's worked in the past."

He set down his fork. "I'm listening."

"These are the basics. Who wanted to kill Bill Elison? Calli at Tomes and Treasures made an important point. Bill had access to a lot of people's houses."

"Like you," Joe interrupted.

She ignored him. "Which means he had access to their personal information. Tax returns, past due bills, drug prescriptions, family disagreements. Maybe access to guns. My sleuths think it's possible one of his customers didn't like what he knew. Someone who didn't want to take a chance he'd tell someone else. Oscar could have been the customer who decided to shut him up."

"Must be an awfully big secret to need to kill him. Who do you suspect?"

"Do you remember the five-alarm fire at Untapped Restaurant about eight months ago? According to Georgia and Todd, the owners of Untapped Restaurant owed Bayworks Cleaning Company at least thirty thousand dollars for clean-up. When the restaurant received its insurance payout, it never passed it on. It put a financial strain on Bayworks. They covered the equipment and employee expenses and need their payment."

"That's good info. Could the owners of Untapped be desperate enough to kill him?"

"Todd was adamant." Helen circled Untapped Restaurant's name. "I find it difficult to believe. I doubt $30,000 is enough motivation for killing anyone unless Untapped would go out of business without it. A lot of restaurants have razor-thin cash margins."

"Sounds a stretch. An established restaurant like Untapped could go to a local bank for a loan."

"I told Georgia and Todd the same thing. It's a respected local business."

"What else do your sleuths have?" Joe cleared their dishes and topped off their wine glasses.

"Oscar accused Vince Caffrey of fiddling with repair bills. Vince is also Bayworks' insurance agent."

"Ah, yes. The ex-ball player. Oscar definitely hit a nerve. Vince may have paid him a visit, and their conversation got out of hand. Doesn't sound as if he had any issues with Bill."

"What about Bill's son-in-law Todd?"

"Why?"

"You've trained me. Family and friends are often the killers. My gut tells me Georgia did not kill her dad. But Todd? My impression is he doesn't carry his weight at Bayworks. They let it slip that Todd lost the Untapped account because Bayworks staff were accused of poor workmanship. He was the person in charge of the account. He also doesn't approve of my sleuthing. Maybe Todd and Bill argued, and Bill fell."

"Pretty short list of suspects so far."

"I've only been on this investigation clock for the past few days, Detective. And you don't pay me very well," Helen teased. "Oh, wait. You don't pay me at all."

"No budget." Joe held up empty palms.

"Do you want to hear what I found out about Oscar?"

Joe ran his hands up Helen's arms and along her neck. "As fascinated as I am, couldn't we shift this into a more personally rewarding conversation?"

"Business before pleasure." She gave him a quick kiss. "I have a list of Bill's customers. Guess who's on the list?" She handed him a folder. "Blue Heron Vineyard, including the house and the wine rooms. It was an important account for Bayworks."

Joe stood up and stretched. "That's interesting. I'll be knocking on Mrs. Banyon's door tomorrow." He reached over and started to pull Helen toward the couch. He stopped and watched Rocky's ears spike. The dog jumped to his feet, a growl deep in his throat. "Speaking of which, is someone pulling into my driveway?"

He followed Rocky to the front door as headlights flashed across the façade of the house. Rocky let out a string of wild barks, and Joe eyed his Glock tucked onto a high windowsill.

"It's Emma." Joe let out an annoyed groan and swung open his door. "Hello, what brings you out at this hour?" He did a poor job of sounding happy to see her.

Emma stepped inside, flashing white teeth and bright lipstick. "I finished my meetings early and decided to come back to Port Anne tonight." She handed Joe a bottle of wine and tugged off her gloves. She stopped short, spotting Helen on the couch in her knee-length red sweater and stockinged feet, a roaring fire reflecting in her glass of wine. "Oh, hello. This certainly feels cozy." Her voice had dropped into cool and a bit condescending.

"We were about to call it a night."

Emma's eyes shifted from Joe to Helen. "Am I too late for a nightcap?"

Joe held onto the door knob. "Be glad to, but it's been a long day. Another time?"

"Of course." Emma lifted her fur hood up over her light hair, forming a halo around her face. She gave Joe a seductive wink. "Let's plan on tomorrow."

Helen tugged on her boots and grabbed her down coat. "Why don't I walk out with you?"

"It's late. Why don't you stay?" Joe asked, his hands back in his pockets, the muscle in his jaw clinching again.

"Maybe next time. Thanks for a delicious dinner." Helen took a few steps across the drive and then twirled around. "I almost forgot." She reached up and pulled Joe's head down to hers, planting a long, deep kiss before letting him go. "Good night." She wiped a smidge of lipstick off his cheek with her finger and ran it around her wet lips.

She flashed a coy, little smile at Emma. "Nice to see you." Helen stepped around Emma and crunched across the snow to her Mini.

Chapter Seventeen

Thursday morning, Helen worked her way down Water Street. Her Mini crawled around the town street crew as they took down Christmas wreaths hanging from black arched lampposts and replaced them with 'Discover Port Anne' flags, their background T blue and the foreground yellow daffodils in anticipation of spring. 'Welcome to Port Anne, Top of the Chesapeake' flags alternated. Kind of early for spring messages, Helen mused. Her first stop, Calli's Tomes and Treasures.

"Good morning, everyone! I've got news," Helen exclaimed, waving a large yellow envelope in the air.

Calli and Val were engrossed in tagging new merchandise. Calli's face lit up. "Is this my contract?"

"It is," Helen chuckled. "Signed, sealed, and now delivered. You are officially the purchaser of one of the prettiest spots in The Harbor community." She handed the thick packet to Calli. "I never get out the champagne until settlement day, but I've brought three of Jean's scones to celebrate. You'll be in before Mother's Day."

Val clapped her hands. Calli gave Helen a hug. "Thank you so much. If it weren't for you, I would have gotten cold feet."

"I wasn't going to let you," Helen declared. She reached for the front door knob. "I'll keep you posted on next steps after I set up your inspections."

Calli touched her arm. "Have you spoken to Georgia lately?"

"No. I owe her a visit. Why?"

"She stopped in yesterday to wander around. She needed a good book to take her mind off everything that's happened."

"I'm sure she's depressed," Helen said.

"She misses her dad, of course. We sat down in my back room, and I made her a cup of tea. She started to cry. She told me running Bayworks with Todd alone isn't going well. Bill spent a lot of time calming Todd's unhappy customers. Bill didn't trust Todd, and Todd was insulted. Todd's abrasive. He ignores requests and complaints. Now, Georgia's left to handle the problems Todd creates. It's straining their marriage and affecting their income."

Helen shook her head. "I feel sorry for her. She's carrying a lot on her shoulders. I'm glad you told me." A message popped up on her cell. "I have to get to the office, but I'll stop in to check on her."

Next stop, Rupert at Five and Dime. The lights were on, and the open sign hung on the door. "Rupert? It's Helen Morrisey. I got your message." She glanced around. Behind her, the front door swung open.

"Lord, I thought Washington was cold in February." Tag stomped his feet. "Oh, hi. Sorry, I thought I was talking to Rupert. Can I help you?" He unwound his plaid wool scarf. "By the way, I submitted my resume to Tammi yesterday. We're meeting today."

"Good." Helen took out her cell and scrolled down. "I swore Rupert left me a voice mail to stop in this morning. He said he remembered more about his conversation with Bill about a local crime. Thought I'd like to know. Any idea what he's talking about?"

Tag looked confused. "He's never mentioned it to me. Rupert tends to ramble about the old days." His eyes traveled the first floor, jammed full of collections. "Isn't he here? I told him I'd be a few minutes late. Might be in the storage room." He hung up his coat on a wooden rack behind the high wooden check-out counter and gasped. "Rupert!"

Helen dashed behind the counter. The old man was collapsed face down on the bare floor boards, his head bruised, his blood pooling around him. His eyes closed. A bloodied antique mallet lay two feet away.

"Is he alive?" asked Tag as Helen kneeled down and put her fingers on the older man's neck.

"Faint pulse." Quickly, she hit 911 on her phone.

102

"Kent County Sheriff's Office. Is this an emergency?"

"I'm Helen Morrisey. I am in the Five and Dime Store on Water Street in Port Anne. We found the owner unconscious. He's bleeding and his pulse is weak. We need medical attention and the police as quickly as possible."

Tag knelt down next to her and began to shift Rupert onto his back.

"Don't move him," cried Helen, grabbing his wrists. "We're not sure what's wrong. You could hurt him even more." She stood up and hit Joe's name on her phone. "Joe," she said, her voice shaking. "I'm at Five and Dime. Rupert's been assaulted."

"Did you call for an ambulance?"

"It's on its way." She took a breath.

"Good. Don't touch anything. I'm ten minutes away." He clicked off.

"Tag, find a clean cloth and give it to me. Quick! Then stand outside on the sidewalk and flag down the ambulance," Helen ordered.

Tag stepped back, his face white, then pulled rags from a closet. Helen grabbed them and sat on the floor. She pressed Rupert's head and prayed.

* * *

One by one, Joe took them aside while the EMTs checked Rupert's vitals, applied an oxygen mask over his nose and mouth, and placed him on a stretcher. Helen began to breathe a little lighter as they threw on their sirens and headed toward the county hospital.

"You're both free to go. We'll be contacting you to review your statements."

"Should I close the store for today?" Tag asked.

Joe nodded. "Give me your key. We'll lock up after we've finished and inform you when you can reopen."

Numb, Tag picked up his jacket.

Helen waited, then turned to Joe. "Did you notice how Rupert was hit from behind on his right side? Our assailant might be right-handed."

"Like eighty-five percent of Americans."

"Detective," interrupted a deputy, handing him a clear plastic bag. "We found these items in his pockets."

Joe flipped the bag from one hand to the other. Keys, chewing gum, a pen, cough drops, and a business card torn in half.

Helen caught her breath, her eyes startled. "My business card." A chill ran across her neck. "It's the sixth or seventh one torn in half and left behind. I'm beginning to lose count. The same thing happened at Taylor's Lumber. Did Dottie show you my card posted on their bulletin board?"

"You talked to Dottie?"

"I did. Wednesday morning. Dottie called me. She told me their storage barn was graffitied." She pointed at the evidence bag. "This is the sign of a stalker."

"Absolutely."

The detective shoved the bag into his jacket pocket. "Let's walk down the street to Chessie Café. You need sugar and a shot of espresso."

* * *

At the cafe, Helen opened a six-by-eight-inch orange leather journal. "I decided it was time to upgrade my Pro Con list from a legal pad. Do you like it?" She struggled to sound positive. "I think journals are inspiring."

Joe squeezed her hands. "I would think your Detection Club is enough inspiration."

She flipped a few pages. "With this, I'll have an ongoing record of past cases."

Joe's phone started to buzz on the wooden tabletop. "It's the chief. Hi," he said. "Can you give me ten minutes? Thanks."

Helen bit the end of her cannoli. "We don't have much time. Notice these photos I took. Each time there's a break-in, the perpetrator leaves my card behind, torn in half. They're not just threatening my clients, they're sending me a message too. They're trying to break me."

A text pinged on her phone. She held the message up to Joe. "As Agatha would say, 'snakes and bastards.' It's Maggie Dyer, the newspaper reporter we worked with from *Kent County Whig* on the Barto case. She's warning me. There's a news story running in their morning edition with photos of my two sale signs in Maureen and Daniel's yard and shots of Elison and Banyon's properties."

"Pretty inflammatory."

She kept scrolling. "It gets worse. There's a public comment posted today in the *Around Town* column. Listen to this: 'Kent County Sheriff's Office is trying to get ahead of a rash of break-ins, properties defaced, and the murders of Bayworks Cleaning owner William Elison and Blue Heron Vineyard owner Oscar Banyon. There's one common thread. They are all clients of Safe Harbor real estate broker, Helen Morrisey, known for her personal crime-solving efforts. Is doing business with Morrisey getting dangerous?'"

Joe set down his mug with a thud. "Who submitted the comment?"

"Write-ins don't have to give their last name. This one is from a John E. Good luck figuring out who he is. I wonder if it's the same person who made a comment about me after Oscar's death. The one who said I *claimed* to have an appointment with him."

They picked up their coats and stepped out onto the sidewalk, the wind whipping around them. Helen shivered.

Helen's lips pressed together. Her face was ashen. She held up her hands and spread her fingers, counting each one. "Two in January, then Bill, Oscar, Maureen, Daniel, Dottie. Today it was Rupert. Seven locations. Seven clients that we know of. Our stalker doesn't steal but scares the daylights out of everyone. People are getting hurt. Two have been murdered! My business is getting destroyed. Whoever posted a comment in the *Kent Whig* and said I'm the one common thread is correct."

"We don't see any connection to Bill and Oscar's murders. Your graffiti artist didn't leave warnings."

"Thank God for small favors."

"Your vandal's an amateur. One step above a bully with a personal vendetta directed at you."

She inhaled. "But Joe, what can we do about him?"

"I've got extra patrols out in neighborhoods, but your guy is traveling all over the county. Other than his vindictive actions against you, there's no common thread to help us predict his next hit."

She glanced down at her cell, her hands trembling. "Another text. Another buyer client. They've decided to work with another agent. That's three buyers in the past two weeks. The cancellations are piling up. So are my bills."

* * *

Helen walked back to Safe Harbor to find Tammi tugging on a curly strand of hair. Gnawed off lipstick replaced her positive smile.

"By the expression on your face, I assume you've read the *Kent Whig* this morning and the neighborhood gossip posts." Helen tried to offer a brave, reassuring grin. It fell short. Tammi followed her into her office to find her rooting around her desk drawer.

"Ah," Helen said, waving three red Twizzlers at Tammi. "What do you want to tell me? I'll retract my question. What do you *have* to tell me?"

"You won't be happy." Her assistant sank into a chair with a stack of notes in her hand. "The Nelsons canceled their appointment for next Saturday. They're working with an agent from Grace Harbor. 'It's more convenient.'" Tammi made air quotes with her blue fingernails. "I deleted them from our calendars."

Helen grunted. "The blanks across my screen are becoming routine."

"Are you ready for this one?" Tammi lifted her eyes. "I noticed Leslie Tupper this morning in our parking lot."

"Why? Leslie canceled her appointment with me a few days ago. Said she's putting off moving."

"She was getting into a car with another Safe Harbor agent."

Helen gnawed on another Twizzler with a vengeance. "Traitor."

"Are you referring to Leslie or the agent?" asked Tammi.

"Both," she muttered.

"What do you plan to do about all this?"

"I don't know. Drink heavily?" Helen put her chin in her hands, her jaw set. "After we get through this nightmare, I'm going to have to put out a full-page ad across all our local news sources telling people I'm back in business. Any good news?"

"I interviewed two candidates. One might be a possibility. Tag dropped off his resume, and it's not bad. We're meeting later today."

"Since when do we hire people who aren't bad? Talk about lowering the bar. Did he tell you he thinks he can fill your position part-time?"

"He did," Tammi chuckled seditiously. "I wonder what he'll think after we go over my schedule together. Instinct tells me he'd work full-time if you required it."

Helen walked to her window and listened to the traffic chugging south in one lane on Water Street. Shop flags flopped around in the wind, trying to entice shoppers. A tough sell in this weather. "When you interview him, ask what he's heard about the gossip posts. Maybe he's overheard other agents talk about trying to pick off some of my business. Maybe he can help be our eyes and ears."

Tammi's wiry, dark head snapped up from her notes. "Another agent? I find that hard to believe. You'll get through this."

"Correction, we always do."

"You're making me feel bad again," Tammi pushed back her chair. "I'm running out. I'll bring you back a salad. You can't live on candy."

"Wanna bet?" Helen balked. "It's a lot cheaper than therapy."

Chapter Eighteen

Helen spent the entire afternoon on the phone, shoring up clients. "Knock, knock." Joe opened her door. "It's late, and you look tired."

"Hi! That obvious?" Helen patted her hair. "Putting out fires. Trying to keep my ship afloat. Hold down the fort." She stopped and laughed. "Any other cliches that might fit?"

"Glad you're retaining your sense of humor. Get that from Jessica Fletcher?"

"And Nora Charles. It's not easy. I'm trying to be Mother Teresa and the Warrior Princess tied into one. Why are you here?"

"Thought you'd want to hear about my conversation with Vince Caffrey."

"Oh? Anything worthwhile?" She set down her pen.

"Vince claims he didn't leave the club until after ten o'clock Friday night. He stayed to help close the restaurant. He was upset about Oscar and the scene he made, but he never went to the vineyard. Never saw Oscar again. He gave me the name of two neighbors who confirmed he attended his son's baseball game Saturday afternoon at the Kent Arena. His alibi is loose. He could have slipped out during a game and returned without anyone noticing."

"Maybe he was coaching."

"He wasn't. Another coach was in charge that day."

"Did Ed narrow down the time Oscar died?"

"Not by much. You found Oscar at five o'clock Saturday. The wine storage is well below normal room temperatures, closer to fifty to sixty degrees.

Oscar, lying on a cold concrete floor, makes Ed's calculations more difficult. Oscar could have been killed between midnight Friday and two pm Saturday." He stopped, glancing down at his notepad. "I interviewed your club chef after Vince, and he confirmed his story. Your new commodore gave us a copy of the last two years' invoices for improvements and maintenance. I've got a deputy checking numbers with the contractors who did the work."

Joe took her coat off the wall hook. "If Vince asked them to pad their invoices and throw him a percentage of the job, it's almost impossible to prove it. No contractor is going to admit they slid him some cash on the side. Comes back to Oscar pushing Vince's buttons until Vince strikes back."

Helen snapped her fingers. "There's the cliché I wanted! Pushing buttons. Are we going somewhere?"

"Down the street for tacos and quesadillas?"

"With all these tongues wagging, are we sure we want to face the public tonight? Our photo together will be up on social media by tomorrow morning. There'll be a separate line, 'Realtor attracts vengeful vandal,' and you'll be seen with a tainted woman."

He gave her a light kiss. "Come on. Admit you're hungry. Nora wouldn't care about the tongue wagging."

Helen wrapped her scarf around her neck. "You're right. Nor would Agatha, or any of them. Besides, I sense a margarita in my near future. I'll try to pretend I'm on a beach somewhere warm."

As they locked the front door of Safe Harbor, she peered up and down the sidewalk. "Wait. Where's your Olivia Benson? The long-legged brunette in the leather pants?"

Joe grabbed her hand and covered it in his big, warm glove. "I assigned one of my single deputies to her for the night."

"For the night?"

"Up to him. I told him he was off the clock at eleven. This way, Jane Marple, we get a few hours to ourselves."

"I thought you didn't enjoy taking elderly women out to dinner."

Joe chuckled. "I enjoy her conversation. Besides, even senior sleuths need a good meal."

* * *

Helen stumbled into her kitchen about six-thirty the next morning in socks and a robe, followed by her furry companions. Watson, the vocal one, demanded breakfast for the two of them.

"Don't you dare make me feel guilty. I'm already on overload." She measured coffee into her Cuisinart. Hands in her pockets, she stared out her glass sliders at the icy grey water. The sun was struggling to pierce the early mist sitting along the horizon. The house was quiet. Lizzie had stayed overnight at ShopTV for her two a.m. show.

Digging inside her pantry, Helen unearthed an unopened box of Bisquick. She read the expiration date. 'Over by six months,' Jessica pointed out. Helen ignored her and started measuring.

Her phone rang. Shawn.

"Good morning."

"What are you doing? Those can't be pots and pans clattering in the background. You must be in someone else's kitchen."

"As a matter of fact, Mr. District Attorney, I'm making biscuits for breakfast." Silence on the other end of the phone. "Are you there?"

"Mom, what are you talking about? You don't cook. You don't bake. What's gotten into you?"

Helen made a nervous laugh. "Grandma loved to make homemade biscuits for my brother and me. I could never get enough of them when I was a kid. I need a distraction, and I'm craving biscuits. Of course, I'm using a ready-made mix."

"Of course you are. After all, when you only make a batch every five years, you need to budget your baking time."

"They'll be slathered in butter. Delicious."

"You never fail to surprise me," Shawn chuckled. "Check your cholesterol lately?"

"I'm ignoring you. Why'd you call so early? Aren't you on the way to court?"

"I'm walking into the courthouse right now. Lizzie called me last night about the *Kent Whig* news posts. What's going on?"

"I can't begin to explain it all. We don't know who's targeting my clients or why. They leave the same nasty message. *'Your agent is a crook!'* He's up to five houses. Buyers and sellers think I've got the plague."

"Do you realize anyone associated with you over the years could be on their hit list? That's a lot of people."

"Believe me, I'm worried. Lizzie, Tammi, people in my office. I didn't get much sleep last night."

"Lizzie told me you're reading those damn crime magazines. They can't help," he snorted. "Take a break. Joe will handle this investigation."

"I'll work from home."

"Give Joe the space to do his job. Murder cases are way beyond trashing people's houses."

"Exactly. He doesn't have time to track down my vandal. I need to do it."

Her son let out a long groan. She could hear him walking through courthouse security. "Mom, are you there?"

"Yes, I'm here."

"You are so stubborn. I don't know how Joe puts up with you."

"That jury's still out," Helen declared.

* * *

By ten o'clock, she'd drunk too much coffee and stuffed herself with three buttered biscuits. She decided to track down Lizzie. Her text got a 'call you back' automatic response.

Plan B, get out her Pro Con list. These cases were different from those she'd worked on before. All the victims here are tied to her business. Nothing made sense.

"Tammi? I'm on my way into the office. I've got a project for us."

"Will I like this project?" she retorted.

"I need for you to print out a list of clients we worked with over the past twelve months."

"Easy enough, but why?"

"We need to find someone unhappy with me."

"A public campaign accusing you of being a crook requires someone who's angry. Unhappy is when they march into your office and pound on your desk, which, by the way, has never happened. Defacing your clients' houses is a whole new ball game. They're risking going to jail."

"You're right," Helen said. "We have to start digging. I've already waited too long."

* * *

After three hours of pawing through files, they gathered them into two tall piles and stacked them on the floor in a corner of her office. Tammi headed off to pick up Kayla after her ballet lesson. Helen texted Lizzie. Her response popped up a few minutes later.

Mom, what do you need? Tied up at the studio. Going on air.

What time are you finished?

About three? Why?

You and I are doing some sleuthing.

Helen watched her screen as her daughter typed out a few words and then deleted them.

Will we come home in one piece?

Not to worry. I got this.

Famous last words. Shawn would have a stroke.

Don't tell him.

Where should we meet?

Home. You need to get into costume.

Lizzie responded with an emoji of a woman with her hair on fire, brandishing a dagger.

Helen ignored her. She picked up her phone and dialed Paula Banyon.

"Paula? This is Helen Morrisey. I wanted to check on you and Billie. How are you managing?"

Paula gave her a cryptic answer and began to hang up.

"I don't want to be insensitive, but we need to discuss Oscar's plans to sell those twenty acres on the north end of your property. What you decide could have a significant impact on your financial stability."

"I'm listening."

"You have an opportunity to generate cash this spring and either invest in the vineyard events expansion or pocket for yourself."

Paula went quiet. "I can meet you at four."

"Thank you." She hung up and studied her phone. I knew she'd take the bait.

* * *

Lizzie opened Helen's front door about three-thirty. "I'm home!"

Her mother jumped to her feet. "Thank goodness, you're almost late."

Her daughter checked her watch. "Actually, I believe we call it on time."

Helen scrunched her nose. "Wasn't that a line from a famous movie?'

Her daughter chuckled. "What are you getting me into?"

"You know what Jane says, don't you?"

"I'm afraid to hear."

"A good dose of sleuthing brings color to your cheeks."

"I'm familiar with your assignments." Lizzie rolled her eyes. "I need specifics."

"This is an easy one. We're visiting Paula Banyon, Oscar's wife, so I can learn more about her financial situation now that Oscar is gone. She and Billie, her nightmare daughter, are impressed with other wealthy people. You need to get jazzed up, lots of make-up, and play the eastern shore spoiled singleton. Endear yourself to Billie."

"In other words, you need Nora Charles." Lizzie's eyes lit up.

"Nora would be perfect."

"Is there an extra dirty vodka martini in it for me?"

"If Paula doesn't offer one, I'll make one for you after we're home." Helen offered. "Extra dirty. Believe me, you'll need a stiff drink after spending time with those two."

"How much time do I have to dress?"

"Twenty minutes?"

Her daughter leaped to her feet. "Lucky for you, I'm a professional change artist."

Chapter Nineteen

At three fifty-five, the two passed the Blue Heron Vineyard entrance sign and swooped around the circular drive to the front of the Banyon mansion.

"Nice cars," Lizzie commented, ogling the white Mercedes sedan and a BMW convertible. "Do those license plates actually say '1STCLASS and IMSPECL? That's over the top obnoxious."

Helen opened the car door. "Wait 'til you meet them. Matched set. They make Oscar come across as Pope Francis. I take that back. His Tesla plate read TOPGRAPE."

Paula Banyon opened the door. They stepped in, out of the cold.

"Paula, thank you for seeing me. I hope you don't mind. My daughter Lizzie was visiting, and I invited her along."

Lizzie unwound an elegant Burberry scarf from her neck. "My mother told me about your husband and everything you're going through. I'm so sorry."

Paula took in her calf-length, caramel color wool coat, matching gloves, and leopard-patterned ankle boots, and made a mournful sniff. "Let's sit in here," she offered, leading them into an expansive living room with views of the bay. Billie glanced up from her cell, her lips an insolent straight line, her feet tucked under a couch cushion.

"Billie, do you remember Helen Morrisey? She's a Realtor and found Oscar. This is her daughter, Lizzie."

She gave Helen a cursory smirk. Her eyes hesitated over Lizzie. She set down her phone and sat up. "Have I seen you before?"

"Are you a ShopTV fan?" Lizzie deliberately settled next to her on the deep white linen couch.

Billie did a double-take. "You're Lizzie Morrisey. You're on air all the time." She edged closer.

Lizzie made a soft, self-deprecating Nora chuckle. "Not all the time, but, yes, I am Lizzie Morrisey." She leaned in. "Your stepdad's death had to be a shock. What are you doing to keep your mind off this police investigation?"

Billie made a pout. "I'm stuck inside. My friends are afraid to come to the house."

"Are you working in the vineyard?"

"Billie is trying to get into television," her mother interjected. "She was a theatre major."

"Oh," Lizzie exclaimed. "Where did you graduate?"

Paula made a cursory wave. "She didn't finish. Her classes were too basic."

"You obviously have personal style," Lizzie studied Billie. "Have you ever considered an internship at ShopTV? It's how I got started."

Billie straightened up. "How would I apply?"

Lizzie tapped her index finger along her teeth. "Why don't I send you my contact in our HR department? You can use my name. You'll need to apply and be interviewed. They get a ton of applicants. I'll warn you, interns don't have much time for partying. They work a lot of hours." She smoothed her skirt and waited for Billie. She beamed.

"An introduction would be wonderful," her mother purred.

Lizzie glanced at Helen and Paula and back to Billie. Her voice dropped. "They need to talk business. Why don't you show me the kitchen? You can make me a cup of tea and tell me more about yourself."

Billie sprinted from her chair. Helen took her cue.

"You're probably in shock and overwhelmed with decisions. Have you decided if you're keeping the vineyard open?"

"For now, Michele will stay with me as our general manager. If I sell it later, she tells me the vineyard will be worth a lot more as an ongoing operation."

"I'm not sure you're aware. The night I found Oscar, we'd planned to finalize his paperwork to sell off those acres. Do you have any interest in the sale?"

"What did he hope to gain?"

"Based on my numbers, you could net about three to four million. Of course, I can't predict how quickly we'll flush out the right buyer. The spring market is a month or so away. That will help."

Paula's eyes gleamed. "Would I need to wait until Oscar's estate is settled?"

"I'd need to discuss it with your attorney. I'm hoping a buyer is willing to wait for deeds to be revised into your name."

Paula didn't hesitate. "Here's his contact information. I want you to call him ASAP."

"Happy to do it." Helen jotted down his number. "Did Oscar have any other family who might inherit?"

"My husband had no interest in relationships with his family. He never spoke of them."

"And his first wife?"

"They haven't spoken in years."

"Lucky for you. How did you meet?"

Paula fingered a sparkling diamond stud in her left ear. "We met at a garden party. Friends of mine on the Severn River outside of Annapolis. They told him this property was for sale. Oscar fell in love with the location. There aren't many vineyards on the water."

"I can only imagine how much money he needed to bankroll this operation. To get it up and running." Helen's eyes traveled around the elegant room. "Did Oscar tell you who funded it?" She glued her lips into a sweet, even smile while Jessica Fletcher warned her to count to ten. 'Be patient,' she urged Helen.

"Oscar told me he'd made a lot of timely investments in tech and energy stocks." Paula examined her nails. "Before I put this ring on my finger, I hired a private detective to check out his finances. He gave me the go-ahead. I hired one before I married my first husband. Smartest move I made." She winked. "Now I have investment advisors. I also believe in large insurance policies. These men don't get any younger."

"A girl's got to do what a girl's got to do." Helen returned her wink with an admiring little grin and scanned her notes. "Your winemaker, Michele, should be told we're going ahead with the lot sales. Do you mind if I talk with her?"

"Go right ahead, although I'd be surprised if she isn't interviewing for another job."

"How well do you know Michele?"

Paula followed the sound of Billie and Lizzie's chatter. "The question is, how well did Oscar know *her*?"

Helen folded her hands. "She is young and beautiful. If she lived on my property, I'd probably wonder the same thing." She dripped sympathy as she stood up and reached for her coat.

"The day I hire her replacement, she's out of here," Paula hissed.

* * *

Helen studied the gray skies scuttling across the bay as she and Lizzie climbed into the Mini. She flipped on her windshield wipers and pushed aside a wet coating of snow. "Let's get home. We're getting at least three or four inches tonight." Lizzie flipped on the heat.

"You did an amazing job endearing yourself to Paula and her daughter. You're brave to introduce Billie to your HR contact."

"I decided the worst that could happen is HR tells her there's no openings. If they hire her, Billie will be working her rear end off. If she doesn't last, so be it. Maybe she'll surprise us and step up to the challenge. For her own sake, I hope she does."

"From what I've seen, she needs to be around people who will put up with her attitude. Paula is a hover-mom liability. Did you get anything from Billie about the night Oscar died? Do you think she or her mother could have killed him?"

"They are quite the pair," Lizzie declared. "I wouldn't want to be left alone on a lifeboat with either of them. They'd sooner push you out to save themselves. And they're cocky."

Helen jerked her head at Lizzie. "Cocky? I haven't heard you use that word in forever. Did Nora Charles suggest it?"

"Subconsciously. It's very *The Thin Man*. You've shamed me into bingeing on black and white movies lately."

Helen reached over and patted her leg. "Nora and your grandmother would be proud of you. Do you think Paula and Billie could have planned Oscar's murder together? They knew his schedule better than anyone, even if Paula denied it."

"They had the advantage of proximity and opportunity."

"They had a huge motivation, money. It sounds as if her marriage was hanging on by a thread."

"Billie said he was a miser. Of course, I don't think there's a teenager who doesn't want more. Could she have killed Oscar?"

Helen strained to find the two white lines defining the sides of the narrow road ahead. "It's possible. He's not her blood father. She's greedy, lazy, and completely untouched by his gruesome murder." Helen turned into her drive. "Ever hear of the classic movie *The Bad Seed*? That's Billie."

"Makes me angry. There's plenty of kids throughout this county who are grateful they don't need to share coats to get to school." Lizzie stared out the window. "Were Shawn and I so unappreciative?"

Helen chuckled. "You had your moments. I'll never forget the time your dad came home from work and Shawn hadn't cut the grass. Shawn never made that mistake again, not if he wanted to go out with his pals on weekends."

* * *

They ate dinner in their pajamas in front of a cheerful fire. The howl of the storm picked up. Lizzie announced she was getting into bed with a mystery. Helen, too keyed up, thumbed through her rows and rows of mysteries for advice, adding a few notes into her new journal. The lights in the house flickered and went off. The refrigerator's hum stopped. She tilted her head to listen. Fifteen seconds later, her backup generator kicked in. Her lights popped back on, and the refrigerator started up. She could hear the boiler thermostat click. "This is a Cotswold winter night, isn't it, Agatha?" she said out loud. Her phone rang.

"How's the storm? I hope you're home," she answered Joe.

"Got in about an hour ago. Roads are bad."

"How was your day?"

"Long and frustrating. So far, there isn't a neighbor near any of your clients who saw anyone suspicious. Both Elison and Banyon's bodies were released for burial to their families. No question, they were both assaulted, although Oscar may have survived if he'd been found earlier. He bled out."

Helen gulped. "What a horrible way to go. Any news on Rupert? I'm afraid to ask."

"He's the reason I called. He was helicoptered to Johns Hopkins Shock Trauma late yesterday. The doctors induced him into a coma, but they are not optimistic. He's seventy-eight with heart issues."

"Being beaten with an antique mallet didn't help," Helen muttered.

"No, it certainly did not. We haven't found any records of family to contact. Thought you might be able to help."

"He has a sister living in Germany. The people of Port Anne are his family. He was at my house for Thanksgiving. You visited your sisters, so you two didn't meet. I could dig around his store for her name." She sighed. "Lizzie and I visited Paula and Billie Banyon today. It's painful to be with them. So entitled. Can't say we learned much that can help you. All it did was confirm they are two perfect specimens of miserable people. Any chance you learned more about Oscar's final will?"

"Unsealed tomorrow at four. I'll be there."

"I've one idea. Do you think you can run a background check on Paula's first husband? I'd love to know if Paula benefited."

"Can do."

"Oh! A tidbit on Georgia and Todd. Bill ran interference between Todd and the customers he'd antagonize. Now, those problems are falling in Georgia's lap."

"Maybe she'll open up to you." He yawned. "Can I go to bed now?"

CHAPTER NINETEEN

Helen laughed. "Sleep tight."

Chapter Twenty

The pale light of her deck lamps facing the bay spread a blue cast on the snow layered across the rails. The slow-moving water slogged along the shoreline in icy waves. Helen closed the glass doors on the fireplace and blew out a candle on her kitchen island. She moved through the darkened house to bed, content to have Lizzie under her roof.

She stopped. A car door closed nearby. Who in the world would be out in this frightful weather? Are those footsteps? Standing at the bottom of her staircase, she could see the lights in Lizzie's bedroom were out. She flipped off her porch light and checked the lock. A faint crunch of footsteps. She halted, tugging her robe's cloth belt around her waist. Quickly, she flipped on her porch light, jerked open her front door, and thrust her head out into the dark. "Who's there?" she shouted.

The frigid roar of the wind through the trees caught her breath and traveled down her throat. The cold seeped through her socks as she stood on the wet threshold. A single township truck slowly trundled past, spreading a layer of salt, its red lights flashing caution. She shoved the door to shut out the wind.

She felt foolish. Tiptoeing into the dining room, she hid in its shadows and stared out. She pinched the bridge of her nose. I'm tired. I've lost my mind.

Every neighboring house was dark. Only her lonely lamppost at the end of her drive reflected the icy sheen. It was about to be buried in the snow.

She held her breath, straining to listen. Careful footsteps crunched over the glaze, and with it, a tiny beam from a cell phone hugged the side of her house. It traveled down the drive and disappeared into the trees. A minute later, a truck's motor roared and taillights beyond her next-door neighbor's house glowed red between the pines.

Watson and Trixie sat on the windowsill, their backs raised and their tails switching along the chilled glass. When she flicked on all the lights, they voiced their displeasure. "Come on, mates. I need a pot of hot tea, and you need a midnight snack," she declared.

About twelve-thirty, her cell phone rang. No caller ID.

"Did you get my note?" a low voice whispered. "I'm watching you." The connection went dead. She stood in the living room, gripping the phone. Her heart pounded. Her head roared. She hit her recent calls button to call back. Unknown.

She unlocked her front door and stepped gingerly onto the front porch. A plain white envelope, its edge tucked under her black doormat, fluttered. The name Helen Morrisey was sprawled across the front in a wide black marker. She unfolded the note inside. *You are a crook. Soon EVERYONE will know!"*

* * *

"You look terrible," Tammi declared the next morning as Helen stomped clumps of snow off her boots.

"Thanks. Thanks so much. I didn't fall asleep until after two."

Tammi glanced at her rhinestone watch. "You never come in before nine."

"I was up at six, had two cups of coffee, and was in the shower by seven. Here, I picked up coffee for us from Chessie Café. Yours is a caramel latte. Mine is a tall black, lots of sugar." She closed her office door behind her.

Tammi gave her fifteen minutes.

We've got business to discuss.

Good business or bad?

Not good.

Helen texted a red angry face with fire instead of hair.

Here I come.

"Let's have it," Helen whimpered, laying her head on her desk.

Her friend clapped her hands over Helen's ears. "Come on. Time to rally. Your eyes are puffy. Have you been binge drinking?"

Helen sat up and pulled back her shoulders. "I have never!"

"We came pretty close the night Marcus was deployed." Tammi laughed.

"That was for a good cause." She inhaled. "Okay, let's rip this Band-Aid off. Tell me the bad news."

"An email came in early this morning from Daniel Haggert."

"Did our contractor finish painting over the graffiti on their porch?"

"Yes. He thanked us for it."

"I'm sensing a big 'but' coming."

"Daniel wants to cancel his listing agreement with us. They plan to relist with an agency in Setting Sun."

Helen cursed under her breath. "Fill out a release, and I'll sign it. Send it over today."

"You don't have to. You could hold him to your contract."

Helen ground her teeth. "Send it out this morning. They're frightened, and I don't blame them."

"I knew you'd let them out."

"Humph. What's next?"

"The events coordinator at the library wants to discuss the tasting scheduled at Blue Heron Vineyard in two weeks."

"We'll have to cancel and reimburse people for their tickets, or we'll get every bloodthirsty goon from Pennsylvania, Maryland, and Delaware out to ogle a murder scene."

"Like the people who read true crime magazines?"

Helen grinned. "Are you referring to me?"

"If the shoe fits," Tammi retorted. "By the way, we have four more candidates for my job opening. I've met with three and they're terrible."

"Did you meet with Tag? He seems anxious to get the job. Dressing better."

"He's not your type."

"What is my type, anyway?" she asked, tapping her index finger on her chin. "Never mind. When you've gone off to Texas and I'm left here on my own, you can FaceTime me to discuss it." She sneered into the cold paper coffee cup. "Like rats leaving a sinking ship."

Tammi groaned. "Now you're wallowing in self-pity."

Helen chuckled. "A little too much?"

"Even for Nora Charles. This will make you feel better. Maureen Nagley called. She's ready to allow showings."

"Bless her. She's got a lot of Jane Marple courage in her. I'll call her this morning."

"Alex Jordan, your builder for Baywood Estates, emailed."

"Please don't tell me he's moving his twenty-two houses to another agent. I'll kill myself." She held the back of a dramatic hand to her forehead.

Tammi shook her head. "Alex wants you to give him input on the staging in his latest model."

Helen sat back. "Thank goodness. A man with integrity. Or he hasn't read the news yet. I'll call him too."

"In the meantime, I am meeting Tag at ten."

Chapter Twenty-One

Alone, she studied the plastic baggie with the warning delivered in the middle of the night. She stepped to her office window. Town snow plows cleared the streets, and shopkeepers scraped snow off their sidewalks. Port Anne was busy in spite of the storm. She picked up a photo of Andy polishing their sailboat, *Persuasion*, with the kids. They were eight years old and trying to help. She stroked her finger across their happy faces. It had been a long time since she felt this low.

An ambulance, its lights flashing, was maneuvering down Water Street and jammed to a halt in front of Tomes and Treasures. Two medics jumped out and grabbed their kits. She drew her brows together at the activity. A text pinged on her cell. Joe.

Calli found unconscious this morning.

A second text buzzed from Val.

Helen, Calli unconscious. Need you.

Her heart dropped to the floor.

Jamming on her coat and hat, she bolted out of the office and down the street. "Excuse me, excuse me," she pushed through the little crowd gathered on the sidewalk.

A deputy stepped forward. "Ma'am, you're not allowed here."

She stood on her toes and spotted Joe in the shop. "Joe!"

Turning around, he strode to the entrance. "It's okay, deputy. I've called her to the scene." He placed his right hand on her shoulder and drew her aside as the EMTs maneuvered their gurney through the narrow aisle. Calli was swathed in blankets, her colorless face covered with an oxygen mask.

"Oh, Joe!" Tears filled Helen's eyes as she spotted her. Val rushed toward Helen, and the two women threw their arms around each other. "Oh, Val, what happened?"

"We're not sure." She buried her face in a Kleenex. "She came in early today, about nine. She wanted to do inventory. I found her in the back room when I arrived."

"How would anyone know she'd be here this early? The store doesn't open until ten."

"We think the intruders broke in to deface the store and raid the cash box. She surprised them," Joe said.

"Calli signed a sales agreement with me a few days ago."

"Val told me."

"Can I take Val back to my office? Or home?"

Val spoke up, her shoulders shaking. "I'd rather go to the hospital and stay with Calli."

"I'll take Val."

Joe agreed. "Stay with her. I'll send someone from my squad to the hospital to take Val's formal statement after we've finished here at the scene."

Helen drew her arm around the smaller woman's shoulders. "Val, my car's across the street." She made an about-face and grabbed the sleeve of Joe's overcoat. "I have a message you need to see," she whispered. "I'll text you when I'm back at Safe Harbor."

Their eyes met. His eyes grazed over her tired face, and he reached down to stroke her cheek, but stepped back as an officer jostled around him. "I'll be a while."

"I'll wait for you."

"Detective," a deputy interrupted, tilting his head toward a back room, "you need to inspect this." Clenching his jaw, Joe followed.

* * *

It was easily two o'clock before Helen and Val were admitted into Calli's room. She had a concussion but was somewhat alert. She gave them a wan little grin and reached for Val's hand.

"Now I know how Nancy Drew feels when she confronts a bandit."

"Shush," Helen replied, her fingers at her lips. "I didn't expect you to take my request for sleuthing seriously." Her eyes dimmed. "I am so sorry you're caught up in this."

The older woman swallowed. "After Rupert, I guess it was my turn."

"Joe's sending a deputy here to take your statement if you're able."

"I'll do anything to get the attention of a handsome detective."

Helen smiled at Val. "She must be alright. She's still got her wicked sense of humor." Val made a little choking sound.

A nurse strode in to check her patient's vitals. "You ladies have to leave. Any conversation is too much for her at this point."

Helen squeezed Calli's hand. Val leaned over to kiss her forehead. "We'll be back." Calli gave them a weak thumbs up.

* * *

Tammi sat back to examine her friend. "You look terrible."

"Didn't you say that this morning?"

"You look even worse if that's possible. I got your text about Calli. How is she?"

"The good news, she's alive and awake. Doctors think she suffered a slight concussion. Someone hit her with a bookend off her desk. If I take a guess, the police won't find any fingerprints. I dropped Val home after we were kicked out of Calli's hospital room."

"They've been friends for years and years."

Helen made a sad smile. "It's what people say about us."

Tammi chuckled. "We're not that old."

"Speak for yourself. I'm aging by the hour." Helen pawed around in her desk drawer for Twizzlers. She bit off a chunk and studied her friend. "Sit down. We need to talk. When are you leaving Port Anne?"

Tammi scrolled through her iPad. "The official date is March first. We've got about sixteen days to hire my replacement and train them."

CHAPTER TWENTY-ONE

"Is your house on the base ready?"

"Yes. Why?"

"I want you and Kayla to leave tomorrow. As long as your clothes are packed, Lizzie and I can get the rest shipped out to you. I'll get your house on the market as soon as I prep it."

"I'm sorry, have you lost your mind? Why should we leave so early?"

Slowly, Helen pulled out her note. "This was slipped under my front doormat late last night." She held up the envelope with her name and flipped it over to show the threat inside. "I got a phone call about midnight."

Tammi stared. *"You are a crook. Soon EVERYONE will know!"* Her jaw dropped and her dark skin paled.

"In January, we had three houses graffitied. We thought it was a bunch of kids getting their jollies by making other people miserable. February first, a Tuesday. I meet with Bill at his house. Someone kills him Thursday. I meet Oscar on Friday. Someone kills him on Saturday." Helen held up her hands. "Our stalker went to Maureen Nagley's Monday. Thank God she wasn't home. Next was the Haggert house, followed by Rupert and Dottie. This morning it was Calli. I want you and Kayla to leave town. I don't want you to be next. It's almost four o'clock. Go home, pack your things, and get out of here. Every day you delay is a day too long." Helen's face was stone.

Her friend's knees gave way, and she sank back down in her chair. "Why is this happening?"

"I wish we knew. It's a hate campaign. It's destroying me." Helen's voice trembled.

Tammi swallowed. "I'm not leaving you. I'm not running."

Helen stood up and crossed her arms. Her voice was steel. "You're going. Leave me your interview notes and your passwords. I'll hire Tag, even if he's temporary. This isn't up for discussion. I want you out of my office. Let the Fort Worth base know you're arriving and arrange a car."

Tammi dropped her pen.

Helen held up her phone. "I went online and bought two tickets to Austin while we waited to visit Calli. You're leaving tomorrow on a six fifty-two p.m. flight from Philadelphia. You'll arrive in Austin about ten Texas time."

Tammi's chin wobbled. "I'm not leaving a day earlier than planned."

Helen stood up and stared her down. "Once I hear you're safe, you can work remotely with Tag. What I do here is not that important to risk you. In the meantime, if someone asks, I'll tell everyone Marcus's transfer date was moved up. You can fly back after this creep gets caught to say goodbye to everyone here." Helen smiled. "You aren't getting away without an official send-off party. Besides, it'll give you an excuse to visit your mother."

"She wasn't expecting me to leave this soon." Her friend's shoulders dropped. Her hands trembled.

"I'll help her get moved over to her friend's house. Lizzie and Shawn will give me a hand."

Slowly, Tammi rose and walked toward the door. "Are you sure about this?"

Helen came around the desk and wrapped her arms around Tammi. She could feel Tammi's heart beating under her sweater. "Absolutely." She held Tammi's hands in hers and reached for the door. "Tammi?"

"Yes?"

"Call the elementary school. Make sure they understand no one is to pick up Kayla. No one. No exceptions. No one with a note or a phone call. Does she take the bus home?"

"Yes." Tammi checked the time. It read four-eighteen. "She has gymnastics until four-thirty."

"Go. Meet her inside the school. Drive her home yourself."

Tammi's dark brown eyes filled. "Oh, Lord."

Helen heard her friend dump a few items into her bag and grab her coat and her keys. She walked to the window and watched her pull out of Safe Harbor's parking lot toward Kayla's school.

Chapter Twenty-Two

"Maureen? It's Helen." She chewed on her lip as Maureen made a cheerful response. "Tammi tells me you're ready to start showings. I'm so grateful you want to continue working with us."

The senior made a chortle. "I'm not afraid of a couple lowlifes. Now that they've been here, I doubt they're interested in coming back. Nothing to steal."

Helen paused. "Maureen, I have a favor to ask."

"Ask away."

"I want to delay your showings until the police catch this person. Between you and me, I don't think it was a burglary. If they found money or drugs, it would have only been a bonus. This is a campaign against me."

Maureen was quiet.

"I realize you're anxious to sell the house, and your new condo is waiting for you." Helen inhaled. "I do have another solution."

"What do you have in mind?"

"I have another agent here at Safe Harbor I'd highly recommend. He could come to your house, and you can meet him. I could also arrange for you to work with a Realtor from another agency. Either way, I'll terminate our agreement, and you can go ahead with your plans. What do you think?"

More silence from the other end.

Maureen made a derisive snort. "I don't like either of these choices. Let me think about it tonight, and I'll call you in the morning."

"Think about your options and let's talk tomorrow." Helen stopped. "One more thing. If you hire another agent, you can call me for second opinions if you want my advice. You know me, I'm good for second opinions."

They laughed together.

Her next call was to Daniel Haggert.

"Helen, how are you?" His voice was tense, a bit uncomfortable.

"A bit swamped. Tammi told me you want to be released from your listing agreement. I'm emailing the signed release over to you in a few minutes."

His tone warmed. "Thank you. I realize you could hold us to it."

"I wouldn't do that. You're upset about all the rumors circulating around. I understand. You need to think of your family first, and I'd never forgive myself if they were hurt."

"I hate to cancel our agreement."

"Thank you. Hopefully, the police will get this sorted out quickly. I have no idea at this point who this stalker is or, frankly, if there's more than one."

"We realize you're an innocent party. If I hear anything that might help catch these guys, I'll call you."

"Thank you. Good luck with the sale of your house. We'll work together another time." Helen hung up and dropped her head into her hands. She opened a spreadsheet on her computer screen. It outlined her predicted income and deleted the dollars next to Daniel Haggert, Maureen Nagley, Bill Elison, and two new buyers.

'Buck up,' Agatha hissed in her ear.

'What can I do the police can't?' Helen snapped back.

Agatha snorted. 'You never let it stop you before.'

* * *

The streetlights were flickering on up and down Water Street. Helen shut down her laptop and put on her coat. "Damn," she cursed out loud. "Joe's supposed to be coming by." She texted him.

I'm leaving for home. Let's talk by phone when you can.

No answer. He's swamped too.

* * *

She was on the last turn toward home and the lighthouse beyond. She drew a deep breath, watching her peninsula narrow through the trees as more water on both sides came into view. Joe called.

"Hi. I'm sorry I couldn't get to you. The good news is Calli is doing well."

"Thank God. Anything on Rupert's condition? I called the hospital, but they won't give me any update."

"Still in an induced coma. I think it will be a few days."

A squawk from his car radio interrupted them. "Sorry. I'd come out tonight, but I'm leaving for Albany, New York, early in the morning." He paused. "With Emma Riley. I'll be back either late tomorrow night or the next morning."

"No comment. What is this cold case about?"

"When we get a minute to talk about anything other than these break-ins, I'll fill you in."

"Who's taking care of Rocky while you're gone?"

"Probably the teenager who walks him during the day."

"Come for dinner and leave Rocky here while you're out of town. He'll be good company for Lizzie and me. I might actually get a good night's sleep. Even Watson and Trixie won't mind."

Joe hesitated. "Is this an invitation to stay overnight?"

"I'm sorry. Was I not clear? I was inviting Rocky overnight," she started to laugh. "Your invitation depends upon how helpful you are with my Pro Con list. A bottle of cab would be nice."

"This day is improving."

"Doesn't take much right now," Helen said. "Lizzie is cooking, but you have to like Water Street Market's crab cakes with her linguine."

"You mean real food? Even better, unless you think an overnight visitor is too much for her."

"She's a big girl. I think she can handle your stay."

"Is seven-thirty too late?"

"Perfect."

She texted Lizzie. **Joe and Rocky coming for dinner.**
Lizzie responded, **Woof.**

* * *

Helen pressed her garage door remote, closing the door behind her. She sat back and gripped the steering wheel. She needed to think alone before everyone arrived. The pain of someone being so vindictive pierced her chest like a knife. She'd dealt with competition. She knew she couldn't please everyone. Clients didn't always appreciate honest advice. She spoke up when she shouldn't, thank you, Agatha. She got involved when she wasn't wanted, thank you, Nancy, and Jessica. But her life was centered around feeling respected and trusted. Feeling welcomed. "What have I built over my lifetime? Have I fooled myself?" she asked aloud.

The house was quiet. She climbed into a hot shower, washed her hair, pulled on navy sweats and a short white sweater. She jammed her feet into heavy socks and her favorite moccasins. Definitely not Emma Riley sexy. No Nora Charles silk robe and pink feathered slippers. She added a touch of makeup and a spritz of Chanel. She only had a smidgen left. It boosted her ego and helped calm her down. She climbed into bed with Watson and Trixie snuggling in at her feet.

* * *

"Mom," Lizzie reached for a bedside light and shook her shoulder. "It's almost seven."

Helen sat up. "I was dead to the world." She made a little smirk. "Maybe that's not the best choice of words given this past week." Lizzie gave her a sympathetic little pat.

By the time Rocky bounded through the door, her candles were lit, Andrea Bocelli was singing in the background, and the whiff of crabs and butter floated from the kitchen.

Joe beamed, handing them two bottles and a white Ling's bakery box of cream puffs. "We could hear Bocelli in person if we were in Italy."

Helen kissed him. "We can hear him right here on Osprey Point."

Lizzie shot Joe a sympathetic look. "We set the dining room table."

"I realize you pick red in winter, but since we're having linguine, I added a Sauvignon Blanc."

"My favorite. Open them both." Helen handed him a corkscrew and set hot French bread on the table.

"You smell good," Joe sniffed.

"Nothing better than a hot shower and a short nap," she declared. "Or are you smelling the linguine?"

"Who's going to fill me in on this crime streak?" interrupted Lizzie. "Will I be totally stressed by the end of the evening, and rather not know?"

"We're both totally stressed. Why should you be left out?" Helen retorted.

Joe started. "Tomes and Treasures was broken into, and Calli assaulted about nine am this morning. Thank goodness Val arrived soon after it happened and called an ambulance in time. Her doctors tell us she'll be okay."

"Shawn called me this afternoon to ask about Calli," Lizzie said.

"News travels fast and as far south as Baltimore."

"A friend in the D.A.'s office picked up the county news online."

"No idea who did it?" Lizzie asked. "She's such a good person. I worked in her shop when I was a teenager."

"Her back room was graffitied with the same words we found at Maureen Nagley's and Daniel Haggart's houses. *'Your agent is a crook!'* Your mother's business card was torn in half and left behind. Eight deputies were in and out of stores asking if anyone saw anything suspicious. Nothing so far. I also got more than an earful from the Mayor and the Police Commissioner. Bill and Oscar's murders have made national news. Local businesses are nervous about customers being afraid to come into Port Anne. Now the state police are involved."

"Three of my clients canceled doing business with me in the last twelve hours," Helen added. "Not counting two killed and two more in the hospital. I've got people crossing to the other side of the street to avoid talking to me.

I've got one measly appointment for all of the next month."

"It's that bad?"

"That bad."

"Sounds like your stalker is someone who found a list of your clients," Lizzie commented.

Helen shook her head. "I wish it were that easy. My clients are public knowledge. I advertise their addresses for open houses, just listeds and just solds. Real estate is an odd business. Agents try to keep their clients' names confidential, but once they've entered the marketing mode, their clients' locations are easy to find. If you're interested in property for sale or settled, you can find the info everywhere. Thank you Google."

"Any clients sticking with you?"

"Dottie Taylor from the lumberyard is holding her ground and, oddly enough, Paula Banyon. Her eyes lit up when I told her she might get three or four million for her lots."

She passed a roll to Joe. "Did I tell you Vince Caffrey suggested the board hire his brother-in-law to complete the club's financials audit? It's the action of someone with something to hide. So sneaky." Helen stared down and made circles on the tablecloth with her knife.

"Lizzie, I've decided I want you to stay with one of your girlfriends up near ShopTV. Too much happening around here."

"I am not leaving you alone. It's ridiculous," Lizzie declared just as the front door swung open with a cold whoosh. Rocky scrambled to his feet to do guard duty. Joe, Lizzie, and Helen dropped their forks.

"What's ridiculous?" Shawn dropped his briefcase in the foyer.

Everyone let out a collective exhale and shoved back their chairs.

"Why in the world are you here in this weather?" his mother demanded. She grabbed him in a hug.

He wriggled off his winter dress coat and draped his wool scarf over the banister with a blue-striped tie tossed on top. His light brown hair stood up from the wind. "I want to hear news straight from the horse's mouth."

Lizzie started to laugh. "Does anyone use that expression anymore? How old are you?" It broke the tension.

CHAPTER TWENTY-TWO

"Lizzie, get a plate. I'm guessing your brother hasn't eaten all day."

"A granola bar at seven a.m.," Shawn grumbled as he picked up a piece of Italian bread from the table.

Joe handed him a wine glass. "Red or white?"

"Any chance there's bourbon in the house?"

"Unless the bottle I brought last time is gone," Joe said. "I'll join you. Your mother's about to get out her Pro Con list, and it's going to be a long night." He started to dig around Helen's liquor cabinet.

Shawn stripped off his suit jacket. "Have mercy. I have to change my clothes. You staying?"

"You're officially out of spare bedrooms."

Shawn raised an eyebrow and grabbed his leather duffle off the floor. "I'm sure my mother can move over." He took the stairs in his heavy footed, two steps at a time stomp. Rocky joyfully trotted up after him.

Lizzie muttered to Joe as they cleared the table. "A ballerina he is not."

"Glad he's got a good legal mind."

Chapter Twenty-Three

Shawn hauled in firewood and struck a match. Building fires was his favorite pastime since his Boy Scout days. Once he had it blazing, he sat and crossed his stockinged feet on the edge of the coffee table and scooped up a mouthful of linguine from a dish he balanced on his lap. "You make this?" he asked, pointing at his sister.

"Obviously."

He finished the last bite and sat back. "Okay, Mom, let's get this pow-wow started. Why is your career going up in flames?"

Helen rubbed her forehead. "Can't we describe it another way?"

He gave her a dubious grunt. "Let's start at the beginning. Bill Elison 'accidentally' falls down his basement stairs and dies," Shawn said with air quotes. "The coroner's evidence tells us he was assaulted. Your business card was found stuffed in his shirt pocket, intact."

Helen held up a hand. "We need to backtrack a little. It's taken me time, but today I realized Bill's 'accident' was not the first one. I missed warning signs starting back in January."

"What are you talking about?" Lizzie asked.

"Early January, a client of mine who owns a horse farm in Far Hill near the equestrian center invited me to dinner. A week later, the wife falls off a horse and breaks her wrist. She was lucky. She could have broken her neck." Helen set down her glass. "Her saddle buckle came undone. They blamed themselves for not noticing the pins on the buckle had popped out. I don't believe they were at fault. These are meticulous, experienced horse people. I think someone sabotaged them. At the time, I didn't ask if my card was

138

left behind. I called them early this morning."

"And?" Joe prodded.

"My card was in the stable, torn in half, the morning she was hurt." She reached for her wine and took a gulp. "A few days later, Tammi told me someone scratched the driver's door of her Prius and drove away. I think her car was deliberately keyed. Everyone in town knows she works for me. Fast forward to my first meeting with Oscar about selling his lots."

"Who knew about your meeting?" Lizzie asked.

"Agents in the office. A few board members at Port Anne Yacht Club. He didn't keep it a secret. Nor did I."

Shawn took over. "You scheduled your second meeting with Oscar at his vineyard for Saturday at four. Who knew about your second meeting?"

"Tammi and I discussed it in the office. Anyone could have overheard. Oscar confirmed it in front of our board members. I assumed Paula knew. I mentioned it to Michele when we first met. It was time to start spreading the word."

"Basically, the entire Port Anne world," Shawn noted. "Fast forward, you find your infamous client's neck sliced open with a broken bottle."

"And not any bottle on his racks. It was his highly anticipated red," Helen added. "There was a display on a shelf in his tasting room. Anyone could reach for it."

"Monday, you told me two more of your clients' houses were defaced. Am I missing anything?"

"Tuesday morning," Joe continued, "Rupert from Five and Dime Antiques is beaten," Joe adds. "He's in a coma. The following morning, I'm called to Taylor Lumber. Dottie's storage barn was graffitied with the words '*Your agent is a crook*'! This morning, Calli from Tomes and Treasures came early to work. Someone knocked her out. She's in the hospital, but alive."

"Calli," Helen explained, "signed an offer with me and probably told all her customers about her plans."

Shawn shook the ice in his rock glass. "Besides being your clients, is there anything else in common?"

"Your mother's business cards were torn in half and left behind," Joe said.

Shawn sat up. "Every time?"

"Except when Bill and Oscar were murdered," Joe said.

Shawn studied his mother's drawn face. "That's bizarre."

Joe stuck his hands in his pockets. "There's a message in here somewhere."

"Any connection between Oscar and Bill?" asked Shawn.

"Bill's company cleaned Blue Heron Vineyard. Oscar told me they talked the week before Bill died. Bill enjoyed stopping by and talking wine."

"We haven't traced any connection between the two men other than the yacht club and Bayworks cleaning services." Joe draped his arm around Helen. "In the meantime, my squad's been in and out of every neighborhood where Helen's clients were hit. No one saw anyone or anything out of the ordinary."

"Are they just keeping their mouths shut?" asked Shawn.

"I doubt it. People see things and don't realize they're significant."

"Todd told me Bill had a couple major arguments floating around town," Helen said.

"Who did he argue with?"

"The owner of a popular restaurant in Grace Harbor called Untapped. They had a fire eight months ago. Bayworks did the damage remediation, but Untapped refused to pay their $30,000 bill."

"Nice people." Shawn grimaced.

"According to Todd, Bill got so frustrated he stormed into their restaurant and made a huge scene right in the middle of their dinner hour. The place was packed."

"Lucky Untapped didn't countersue him for loss of income and slander."

Helen held up her hand. "It gets worse. Georgia called me yesterday.

The owners of Untapped dropped off a check, paid in full. In exchange, she released them from their one-year contract. Todd never told her the restaurant held back payment because the county health department shut them down for four days. Their kitchen, which Bayworks cleaned, failed their bi-annual inspection. The owner was mortified and furious at Todd. He denied any responsibility."

She paused, consulting her journal. "A few days before Calli was struck,

CHAPTER TWENTY-THREE

Georgia told Calli her husband is one big liability."

"Big enough to want to kill her father?" Joe asked.

"I wondered the exact same thing. Why would Todd suggest the owner of Untapped is a suspect and send me out on a witch hunt? Georgia asked me to help her find her dad's killer. Her husband didn't want me involved. I think he's got something to hide. Lucky for Todd, I'm so busy trying to put out my own fires, I haven't had ten minutes to follow up on theirs. I feel I'm letting Georgia down."

Her son stood with his back to the fire. "It always amazes me that people, basically strangers, feel comfortable enough to tell you personal bits about their lives they probably don't tell family."

Joe chuckled. "Your mother has a unique talent."

"And it seems to get her into trouble far too often." Shawn glared at his mother. "We've told you before. You can't fix everything for everyone."

Helen stuck out her chin. "I promised."

"You always do," Joe muttered.

"Joe, anything from forensics?" asked Shawn.

"No fingerprints, no hair follicles. Whoever tampered with Bill's stair treads used one of his kitchen knives. We found the broken tip on the kitchen floor and the knife tossed into the woods."

"And Oscar Banyon?"

"Our accountant is digging through his bank records. So far, everything seems healthy."

"His wife, Paula, and her daughter are two pieces of work," added Lizzie. "Mom and I stopped in to meet them a couple days ago."

"You went with Mom?" Shawn interrupted. "Now they know you, too?"

Lizzie's blue eyes met her brother's. "Were *you* going to be her Nora Charles?"

"I need coffee," he moaned. "How's Tammi handling all this?"

"She's a rock. I don't know how I'll manage without her," Helen said.

"What?" Shawn's head jerked. "She's leaving you?"

"Marcus got his new assignment. Fort Hood, Texas. Tammi is leaving tomorrow."

"You told me she had a few more weeks here," said Lizzie.

"I bought Tammi and Kayla tickets to Austin while I was walking the hospital halls, waiting for news about Calli. I sent her out early."

"Mom!"

"I had to." Helen defended. "There's this." Slowly, she took a baggie off a bookshelf and handed it to Joe. "I wanted to show it to you today, but Callie got hurt, and you were tied up. It was delivered to my front door last night about eleven o'clock. I showed it to Tammi today and told her it was time to pack her bags."

Joe held the baggie under a lamp. Shawn and Lizzie leaned over his shoulders. *You are a crook. Soon EVERYONE will know.*

Lizzie's face went white.

Joe set the bag next to his Glock on the mantel. "Walk us through it. Did you see anyone?"

"The storm last night was wicked. No one was on the roads. Lizzie had gone to bed when I heard crunching sounds on the front porch. I decided the wind was dragging branches along the roofline. I heard it again. I opened the door and shouted. Nothing. I crept up to the dining room windows in the dark. That's when I saw someone walking down my driveway and into the trees. They were using their cell light to make their way."

"Did they see you?"

"No. They were halfway down the street. A truck engine started up, and their brake lights flared. I turned on all the lights on the first floor and checked all the locks. At about twelve-thirty, my phone rang. A voice asked me if I got their message. They hung up. I didn't know what they were talking about. I went to the front door and found this envelope stuck under the mat."

"Was the person on the driveway a man or a woman?" Shawn asked.

"I couldn't tell. Average height, wrapped in a heavy coat. It was pitch dark. The snow was hitting the window glass. Everything was distorted."

"What about the caller?"

"I could barely hear them, and the call didn't last ten seconds." Helen paced in front of the windows facing the bay. "What I don't understand is why someone is doing this. If they hate me, why don't they kill me instead of haunting everyone I do business with?"

Joe glanced at Shawn. "Someone wants you to suffer. Killing you is not enough for them. They may never try to kill you. They want to take away your life. What you've built."

"I've prosecuted these people. They're twisted," Shawn responded.

"So what's the plan? Hide in a bunker? Move out of state and start over?" Helen's voice rose. Her green eyes flashed. "Not happening." She stared at the dark water. The wind had picked up. It was keening around the edges of the house.

She faced her children, her cheeks flushed. She dug her nails into her palms. "Do you know what Jane Marple would say?" Helen straightened her shoulders. "This is a fiendish business."

Lizzie spoke up. "She also said the wicked should not go unpunished. Don't worry, Mom. We'll catch him."

Shawn's eyes traveled from one person to another. "Where is everyone over the next few days?"

"I'm taking an early flight to Albany," Joe said. He turned to Helen. "We're interviewing a potential witness for Emma's case."

"I'll be here," Lizzie spoke up. "And Rocky." The dog lifted his head when he heard his name. He thumped his tail on the oak floor.

Shawn shook his head. "I think Mom's right. Stay with a friend near ShopTV. These assaults feel local. I doubt if anyone will follow you two counties away. I don't have any court time tomorrow. I'll work from Safe Harbor and stay here tomorrow night. I'll leave the next morning."

"I'll be back in town by then," Joe said, handing her a card. "This detective will be around if you need him. He'll arrange regular patrols around this neighborhood." He pointed at Helen. "You stay put. Home or office."

Helen crossed her arms. "I am not hiding behind my desk waiting for the next hit. It's time I asked more questions. Go on the offensive. Stop pussy footing around." She reached for Trixie and held her to her chest. "Sorry, Trixie." She scratched her under the chin.

"When you're on the offense, it usually means trouble," Lizzie warned.

"I'll try to stay under the radar. I want to talk to Vince Caffrey tomorrow morning. If I can, I'll meet with Michele Mancuso. I'm also calling Maggie Dyer at the *Kent Whig*. Maybe she can dig up some more personal background information."

Shawn looked over at Joe and shrugged. "We can't chain her down."

"I've never known your mother to be good at working under the radar," Joe said. "Let's all try to get some sleep. We'll need it."

Chapter Twenty-Four

Friday morning, Shawn moved into a conference room while Helen made calls. She left a message for Maggie Dyer.

A tap on the door. "Come in," she called out.

Tag stuck his head into her office. "Hi, I got your text."

"Tammi told me you had a good meeting. You're techie. I like that."

The young man beamed. "I might have some suggestions on your systems."

Helen threw him a wary look. "One day at a time. Tammi told me you're operating Rupert's while he's in the hospital. I'm glad. If he survives this, I'd like to know we've kept his business going for him."

"I reduced the hours. We're open one to five."

"Did Tammi tell you she's leaving town tonight? Her husband's schedule got moved up."

"We talked about it. Kind of sudden."

Helen ignored his probe. "You think you can handle all this?"

"Piece of cake."

"It's strictly a temporary position. Let's see how it goes."

He offered a cocky grin. "I'm not concerned."

"I'm hoping to run out to Blue Heron Vineyard today. Do you want to come along? Walk the property?"

"I saw it in December. They had a tasting, and I got to meet some people."

Helen sat back. "Good for you. Detective McAlister wants me to check Rupert's office for an address book. I'll probably stop by. Tammi will set up a remote training schedule with you in a day or two. Stay in touch with her. She's the best."

"I doubt it. Everyone in the business knows your name. From what I hear, you're also in tight with the Sheriff's Office."

Helen hesitated. "I assume you've heard some of my clients got hurt lately. Someone doesn't like me very much, and they're taking it out on innocent people. Does that make you nervous?"

"Not a bit. I'm a fast runner."

She raised an eyebrow. "Let's hope there's no reason for you to run."

* * *

Longfeld Full-Service Insurance Broker was on the second floor of a pretty brick building, originally a bank. Helen felt a pang of nostalgia. She missed the sense of stability banks brought to towns. Across the street, a local bank still operated, a throwback to George Bailey and his Bailey Brothers Building and Loan. A Dollar Mart, shabby and neglected, was overdue for a makeover.

She'd dressed in a Jessica Fletcher, *Murder She Wrote* style wool suit jacket, a collared white blouse, and Jess's signature black and tan shoulder bag.

The agency's name was stenciled in scroll across the glass on the upper half of a mahogany door. She stepped into a neatly furnished front office, and a young woman lifted her head.

"May I help you?"

"Good morning. I'm Helen Morrisey. Vince and I have worked together. I don't have an appointment, but I hoped he could see me."

"I'll ask if he's available."

A few minutes later, she was back. "He's off the phone. Third office on the left."

Vince Caffrey was sitting in front of his laptop, his dark head down, his shirtsleeves folded up to the elbows. His large form overwhelmed his small desk.

"Hi Vince. Working hard?"

Vince raised his head. He chuckled. "Or hardly working. I'm better at swinging a bat than using new software." He offered Helen a warm hand. "I wasn't expecting you this morning." He gestured for her to take a seat. "Can I offer you a cup of coffee?" He gestured toward a pot sitting on top of a mini fridge.

She motioned it away. "Thanks. I'm already on caffeine overload."

"What's our hometown mystery sleuth doing lately?"

"Not much. I was in my office and feeling restless, thought I'd stop by. I wanted to tell you how badly I felt about your dustup with Oscar last Friday night. You didn't deserve to be confronted in the middle of the Burgee Lounge."

Vince's lips twisted. "That's nice of you. I was embarrassed. He's lucky I didn't take a swing at him." He stopped and shook his head. "Regardless, when I heard you found him dead Saturday, I felt terrible. Oscar could be a pompous jerk during board meetings, but I sure didn't wish him ill." He rubbed his forehead with beefy hands. His nails were short and neat, his ring finger marked with a pale circle. "Your detective friend making any progress?"

"Bits and pieces," Helen said. "Between Bill Elison and Oscar, the Sheriff's Office is stretched. The coroner narrowed down Bill's death to sometime late Wednesday night or early Thursday."

"Bill and I went back a lot of years. Bayworks was one of my first insurance clients." Vince's face turned dark.

"Do you remember when you last saw him?"

"I ran into him in January at the club. He was at the bar having dinner."

"Anyone he didn't get along with?"

"Your guess is as good as mine."

"It's terrible. He worked all his life to build a business for his family, and now this." Her eyes roved his office. One wall was crowded with framed articles and awards from his baseball days. "I guess other county teams hate playing you. Wasn't Bill on your baseball team?"

"He was."

"Did Bill have a decent life insurance policy? I'm hoping Georgia and Todd have enough money to keep Bayworks going without him." She gave him an innocent look.

Vince hesitated. "They updated their policies the week after Thanksgiving. I encouraged them. Bayworks had grown, and their coverage was too low. I'm relieved they took my advice."

"Thank goodness they did. Are you sure you didn't meet him since January? Ever need to stop at his house?" Helen waited for his reaction.

He took his time to think, then shook his head. "Nope. I stopped by his house to have him sign his new policy in December."

Helen touched a round holder chock-full of silver pens. "I'd better get out of your hair. Mind if I take one of these? I'm always losing pens."

"Help yourself. Take a couple and pass them along. They're the new ones. Longfeld updated our slogan and the barrel to silver." He opened a desk drawer and came out with a handful of red pens. "Want a bunch of the old ones? Might as well use them up." He hesitated. "If you have an excuse, I'd sure appreciate some referrals. The calls into our front desk get funneled right to Longfeld."

"Sounds kind of greedy. Our front desk circulates any leads coming in." She studied his face. "I have an idea. I send a newsletter to my past clients once a month with helpful market updates. Could you write a few paragraphs about the importance of increasing homeowners' insurance when market values climb, or owners make improvements?"

He brightened. "I'd appreciate the exposure."

She tapped her temple. "One more question. A couple of clients I share with you had their houses raided lately. Have you heard any rumors around town? Seems like someone is out to hurt my business by hurting them."

Vince walked her to the door. "I heard you were having problems. A couple of our clients called me about their coverage. The damages are so minor, I advised them to pay for them out of pocket. I can't imagine who'd be so vengeful."

"Thanks. If you hear anything odd, call me." Helen gave him a friendly wave.

Helen passed an open office on the way out and spotted the owner of Longfeld Insurance. He was on the phone, his back toward the door, in an office easily three times the size of Vince's. An average-sized man, he faced two large monitors flanking a glossy mahogany desk. A print of the Chesapeake stretched across the far wall. A sideboard held a handful of files in brass holders.

The receptionist lifted her head as Helen passed her.

She stopped and reached for a silver pen. "Excuse me. Any chance you know the company that makes your pens? I need to place a new order myself."

"I do." The young woman opened a file drawer. "I'll make you a copy of our invoice. Help yourself to these. They just arrived a week or two ago."

"Thanks. This is so helpful." Helen headed down the stairs and out onto the street.

* * *

Two doors down, she walked into Jean's Coffee Pot. Not a table was open.

"Hi! How's my favorite sleuth?" Jean greeted.

Helen wrinkled her nose. "I've been better, a lot better."

"Buzz around here is someone's trying to discourage people from working with you."

"Their scare tactics are working. I feel like the teenager with no invitation to the prom." Helen snapped a lid over her cup.

"Wish I could help."

"Any idea how Vince Caffrey is doing? I stopped in at Longfeld Insurance. Longfeld's private office is the size of a bowling alley plus two assistants. Vince is working out of a broom closet. Can't help but wonder how he handles being treated like a second banana. Tough to swallow after a pro-ball career, don't you think?"

"I don't think he's happy with how life has turned out. He and his wife are separated. I feel badly for him," Jean replied. "What's happening at the vineyard?"

"Paula Banyon's running the show with the help of Michele Mancuso, her winemaker."

"Is she a cute girl with fluffy dark hair? I've seen her around town."

"Most likely. Ever hear of Mancuso Wines from Napa? That's her family."

Jean made a low whistle. "I never made the connection. I spotted her at The Blue Crab a few nights ago with a young man."

Helen raised her eyebrows. "Did you recognize him?"

"Not sure. Medium height, thin, wears his hair kind of long." Jean tugged at her earlobe. "Has an earring."

Helen dropped her wallet back in her bag. "Might be Tag Stolz. He's a new agent with my office. Moved here in November. I hired him to fill Tammi's job. Not sure if we're a match, but he seems to be trying."

"From what I saw, the young lady thought he was her match."

"He met Michele at one of Oscar's wine tastings. Can't blame him for asking her out. Let's face it, Port Anne isn't exactly the dating capital of the bay." Helen stopped. "I've got an idea. Give me another cup of coffee. Tag's working at Rupert's part-time. Maybe he'll tell me more about Michele if I butter him up."

* * *

The Maryland state flag hung from the store's upper floor. An 'open' sign in red and white hung next to the double door. Helen stepped inside.

"Tag? You here?"

Sneakers slapped down the wooden main stairs. "Hi!" Tag pushed his hair back behind his ears. "I'm moving some cartons upstairs. Trying to neaten this place up."

"Brought you a cup of coffee and a scone from Jean's. I'll try to find his address book."

His eyes lit up. "Thanks. Rupert's coffee pot was invented during the Prohibition." He took a healthy gulp. They stared at Rupert's rolltop desk piled with scraps of paper. "I'm upstairs if you need me. I'm sorting his stacks of *Unsolved Crime* magazines into chronological order. There's dozens. If you ask me, it's time to torch some."

"Rupert's a pack rat." She tossed her coat on a counter. "I'll shout if someone comes in." She inhaled.

150

She rolled up her sleeves. About an hour later, her hands smelled of dust and old newspapers. She sat back on her hindquarters and eyed the crevices inside the rolltop desk.

'Nancy, this is right up your alley.' She took up a letter opener and slid it into the gaps between drawers. A decorative panel a half inch by three inches sprung open. "I'll be damned," Helen said out loud. Gingerly, she fingered a tiny cloth-backed address book in brown. Inside, most of the pages were blank except for the first ten or so. Helen recognized Rupert's meticulous cursive in pencil. Are kids today taught cursive? A woman's name under 'w' with a birthdate was circled. Beatrice Weber. Has to be Rupert Weber's sister. 'Well done,' Jane commented. 'Let's hope she's still alive.'

* * *

As Helen walked into Safe Harbor, her cell pinged. The ID read Maggie Dyer.

At Chessie Cafe. Got a few minutes between interviews.

On my way!

Helen slid into a chair in the corner of the cafe. "Hi, thanks for suggesting we meet."

Maggie's short, dusty, grey-blonde hair was stuck under a woolen cap. Her bookbag hung off her chair. "I got your message and, given how rumors are flyin', I thought you could use a little help." Her smile was lopsided, her face a bit windburned.

"A little is an understatement," Helen rubbed at her temples. "I need to figure out who's torpedoing me. My business is sinking without bubbles."

"What can I do?"

"What do you know about the comments popping up on the online neighborhood chats? Anything that might help me know who they are?"

Maggie pushed her pencil over her ear. "Nothing worthwhile. There's a couple people who seem to have opinions on everything. Be glad you're not running for office."

"Can you sniff around? You're a bloodhound." Helen sipped her coffee. "I could also use some background on two people. One is Tag Stolz, and the other is Michele Mancuso. Tag transferred his real estate license from Washington State. He's getting cozy with Michele Mancuso, the official winemaker at Blue Heron Vineyard. They planned to release a new wine this month. There's no love lost between Paula and Michele. Sounds like Michele might have been fiddling around with Oscar. Not sure if it's true. Her family is the famous Mancuso wine producers from Napa. I do wonder why she gave up her family legacy to work here."

Maggie scratched down a few notes in a dog-eared pad. "Why are you checking on Tag Stolz?"

"I'm being cautious. He's taking over Tammi's position."

"You can't be serious. Tammi left you?"

"Her husband's deployment is over. They're being assigned to Fort Worth."

"Bummer."

"More than I can say. I already miss her, and she hasn't even left. We were thick as thieves." She stopped. "Bad choice of words given my circumstances."

Maggie tucked her pad back into her backpack. "I'll keep you posted." She hustled out of the shop.

* * *

Last stop, Tomes and Treasures. "Hi, Val. How are you managing?"

Val's face lit up. "Taking it day by day. Calli's being released from the hospital tomorrow morning."

"I heard. Do you have help here?"

"I do. Of course, Calli is calling me three times a day. She wants to be back to work, and I told her she'll have to wait." She chuckled. "She can come into the shop, but I'll have her glued to her chair."

Helen's cell rang. It was Shawn. "Ready to head home?" she asked.

"Checking on you."

She winked at Val. "Checking on Calli. Meet you in the parking lot. I'm glad you're with me tonight." She clicked off. "Gotta scoot. Shawn thinks he's babysitting his mother today."

"Wish him luck."

Helen called back. "Children always think they can supervise their parents. We know better."

A text from Tammi popped up.

Boarding now. A photo of an excited six-year-old was attached.

Kayla says see you soon, Aunt Helen.

Helen squeezed her eyes shut. Her heart hurt.

Chapter Twenty-Five

Shawn strode down the walk from her office, swinging his briefcase. He folded his legs under the dashboard of her coupe. "When are you going to buy a bigger car?" He complained, adjusting the seat.

"I'm already driving a Mini four-seater. Can you picture Nancy Drew driving around town in a Suburban? I don't think so." His mother tossed her head. "Can you at least move your knee. I can't shift out of first."

They started to laugh.

"Mom. There's a reason this car is called a Mini."

"On another topic, how can I find out how much life insurance was taken out by Bill Elison?"

"Where's this coming from?"

"A comment Vince Caffrey made this afternoon. He told me Bill, Georgia, and Todd all updated their life insurance policies a few months ago. Kind of convenient, don't you think?"

Shawn watched the narrowing road out of town and gripped his ceiling handle hanging over the passenger door. "It could have been good financial planning."

"You didn't answer my question."

"The National Insurance Crime Bureau is a resource. I have a contact I could use if you want me to check."

Helen smiled at Shawn. "Any chance you're willing to come with me to Blue Heron Vineyard? I'm hoping I catch Michele Mancuso."

"Their winemaker?" Shawn eyed her mother with suspicion. "Do I have a choice?"

"Not really. It's just a friendly drop by."

"Liar."

His mother grinned as she picked up her cell.

"Michele? It's Helen Morrisey from Safe Harbor Realty. We met a week ago in the tasting room. Oscar introduced us. I wonder how you're doing.

"I'm in limbo, not sure how we should move ahead with business. My crew is worried about their jobs."

"It's horrible," Helen agreed. "Paula asked that I review the lot plans she wants to sell with you. Do you mind if I stop by now?" She hung up and lifted an eyebrow at her son. "We're good to go."

"Does Michele need the details on the lots?"

"Let's say it's a good excuse to pick her brain about Oscar's death. Your sister plays a great Nora Charles. I need you to infuse some Nick Charles charm in your personality when you meet Michele."

Shawn moaned and gripped his ceiling handle tighter. "I thought my high school revival days were over. Besides, I've got plenty of charm. I don't need to learn from Nick and Nora Charles."

"Don't kid yourself. You haven't seen them in *The Thin Man* series in a long time. Men can learn a lot from Nick Charles. Maybe we should watch one tonight."

* * *

A few miles outside of town, she turned off Osprey Point Road and down the vineyard's lane. They bumped along, the low car's undercarriage scraping over an ice mound. She eased between the iron gates.

"Wait 'til you see this location. It's spectacular." A minute or so later, they wound up past the main house to the barns. Helen tucked the hood of her coat up around her ears, and Shawn followed her. Their boots crunched as she led Shawn around the barn and onto the open field facing the Chesapeake Bay.

"Wow. You weren't exaggerating. This is an amazing view. How much do the Banyons own?"

Helen swept her arm north to south along the waterway. "We're putting twenty acres at its farthest point north on the market. It won't have any impact on the views from the vineyard and only claims about two thousand feet of waterfront. We have county approvals for the lots."

Helen led to the front entrance. The lantern lights made the crusty snow sparkle. Shawn swung the grand door open. Michele had lit most of the mellow electric lanterns on the round tops, along with the string of white lights running down the bar.

"Hi. Michele, this is my son, Shawn. He's up from Baltimore for the day," Helen explained.

Shawn shook her hand. "Hope you don't mind my coming along." He took in the length of the barn and made a low whistle. "This is a serious operation."

"One of the largest vineyards from here to southern Virginia," Michele spoke up. "It's one of the reasons I wanted to work with Oscar." Her dark eyes took in the tall young man. "Are you interested in wineries?"

He laughed, the dimple in his chin flashing. "I enjoy drinking wine if that's what you mean. I'm sure it would take an expert like you ten seconds to recognize I'm more of a local beer connoisseur."

"Baltimore is famous for its IPAs." Michele offered. "Where do you work?"

Shawn hesitated. Helen knew he tried to keep his role as a district attorney to himself. "I'm an attorney." He walked toward the rows of casks. "Any chance you're willing to give me a tour?" He encouraged her with a smile.

"Happy to. I'll try to convert you from beer to wine. Why don't we start with one of our cabernets? I'm guessing you're not a Rosé guy."

Shawn flashed the dimple on his chin. "You got me."

Michele reached for a bottle on the bar and deftly pulled out the cork. She lifted three glasses off a rack above her head and poured the deep red liquid. She twirled the wine in the first glass and handed it to Shawn, with another to Helen. She held her wine glass to her nose and inhaled. "A toast to good reds." She tapped Shawn's glass than Helen's. "And to Oscar."

Helen broke the silence. "This is delicious. I don't think this is the same red Oscar served me the Friday I met him here. It was the same afternoon I met you."

"You're starting to recognize your wines. With Oscar gone, Paula and I are trying to decide when we should go ahead with our next event.

Helen took another sip. "Did you decide if you're staying?"

The winemaker set down her glass. "Two vineyard owners want to meet me, and I'm weighing my options. I told Paula I wouldn't leave her in the lurch. We can't afford to delay our reopening."

"Do you think you can work with her? She strikes me as a strong personality."

"You're being polite. She may think she's a businesswoman, but frankly, she understands zero about running a vineyard."

"I was surprised at her reaction when the police told her Oscar was dead. She's tough. Didn't blink an eye."

Michele topped off their glasses. "She and Oscar had more than their share of knockdown fights. She wanted to travel, and he wasn't interested. She wanted to send Billie to a fancy private theatre program in L.A. He refused. After a while, I ignored their arguments."

"Billie definitely isn't easy. Oscar told me he tried to get Billie to learn the business. She wasn't interested."

"She has this ridiculous idea she can make it big in Hollywood. Thinks it's all fancy clothes and makeup, no work. With Oscar gone, I guess Paula can spend his money any way she wants," Michele said with disgust. "Billie doesn't appreciate what's right in front of her."

"Tough spot for you." Shawn's voice was sympathetic. "Who informed you Oscar was dead? Had to be a shock."

Michele studied her glass. "One of the detectives called. At first, I didn't believe him. I spoke with Oscar Friday about ten. I was on my way home Sunday morning when I got their call."

"Who do you think would kill Oscar?" Helen leaned closer.

"I can't tell you. We got along fine, but he was definitely a rare bird. He could tick off people. He had an edge to him."

"I'd agree with you," Helen said. "Anyone in particular?"

"He was furious with some guy from your yacht club."

"You must mean Vince Caffrey," Helen said. "They definitely didn't get along. Oscar was always baiting him."

She tilted her head at Helen's roll of drawings. "Do I need to review these?"

"It'll only take a couple minutes. I wanted you to be aware of the lot plans in case someone asked." She ran her fingers along the roll.

Michele pushed the sleeves of her thick sweater back and studied the drawings. "I was excited Oscar wanted to sell these lots. We both wanted to expand the wedding venue side of the business." She directed doe eyes on Shawn.

Helen's gaze traveled up Michele's left arm. "Wow. What did you do to your arm?"

Quickly, Michele tugged the sleeves back down over her wrists. "It's not the first time. I scrape my hands and arms on our steel casks all the time. The stainless edges are sharp." She made a little toss of her head. "Part of the job."

"I hope you treated it," Shawn said. " I grazed my arm on a boat cleat, and it got infected."

"I can't help but notice, these rooms are immaculate," Helen admired. "How long has Bayworks been your cleaning service?"

Michele followed Helen's gaze. "It's been a few years. They clean all the public areas once a week. More often during the summer months. My staff goes over the fermentation section again after the cleaners leave. Everything has to be sterile. Oscar and Bill enjoyed talking about wines together." She hesitated. "Except for the last couple visits. They'd stop talking whenever I walked in. Odd vibes."

Shawn pointed at framed photos of rolling hills, stone walls, and rustic buildings. "Where is this?"

"Oscar's family vineyard in France."

"Do you ever have time to visit your own family?" Helen asked.

"Around the holidays. Getting time off with this job isn't easy, especially during growing season. If I miss anything at home, it's the Southern California beaches." Michele's cell buzzed. "I hate to leave you, but I have a client on the West Coast expecting my call. You're welcome to stay."

"I need to get in a couple calls myself," Shawn said. "Thanks for the wine. It was outstanding."

"By the way," Helen turned to Michele, "someone mentioned you know my new assistant, Tag Stolz? How'd you two meet?"

"He came to a tasting here a few months ago. We catch dinner every so often. He's a nice guy."

Shawn opened the door. A blast of cold air hit them.

"I'm hoping he works out. Thanks again for your time," Helen said.

The young woman studied Helen. "Tag told me you've solved a few murders around here."

"People exaggerate. Call me if you hear anything that might help the Sheriff's Office with their investigation."

"You can count on it." The winemaker gave a flip of her dark hair.

* * *

Helen and Shawn climbed into the coupe, and she cranked up the heat. Shawn was quiet.

She glanced at her son's profile. "What do you think of her?"

"My instinct, don't count on her help to solve Oscar's murder. Maybe she doesn't want to get involved. Not the first person."

"What do you think about the cut on her arm?"

"Nasty. I wouldn't think a stainless-steel cask would be so rough. She could have hit Oscar with a bottle and nicked herself. She wasn't happy when you spotted that bandage. I'd dig more into why she's here."

"As a matter of fact, Nick Charles, I have Maggie Dyer, my reporter friend, working on it."

He laughed. "Should have guessed." He dropped his seat back, trying to stretch his legs. "Could this car be any smaller?"

"Stop complaining and leave my car and me alone. We're kindred spirits."

"Remind me to never take a road trip with you."

"If you don't behave, I'll pull over and leave you on the side of the road."

"Wouldn't be the first time." He smirked. He leaned his head back and folded his arms across his chest.

"You and your sister were about ten. You wouldn't stop squabbling in the back seat. Your dad stopped and told you both to get out. The shock on your faces as we drove away was priceless. I'll never forget."

He scowled at his mother. "You're lucky we didn't suffer from permanent mental anguish."

"Oh, please. We stopped two houses down the street and waited for you."

Shawn put his head back and closed his eyes. "Cruel and unusual punishment," he muttered. Helen chuckled.

* * *

Joe called about nine that night. "Checking in. Everyone okay?"

"Of course. Rocky's at Shawn's feet, and Trixie and Watson are patrolling the woods from my windows. How'd your day go? Solve your case yet?"

"I'll only say it was an interesting day." He yawned. "That's code for not much progress."

"How's the FBI's answer to Wonder Woman. She and her boots ready to go home yet?"

"Very funny. You're showing your age."

"Don't dare go there in the same sentence as your ex-fiancée."

"My mistake."

"I've got a few bits of info on Bill and Oscar. Are you too tired to talk?"

"Go for it. If I don't respond, you can assume I fell asleep with the phone in my hand."

She laughed. "I stopped at Vince Caffrey's office. He encouraged Bill and his kids to increased their insurance policies a few months ago. He wouldn't tell me any details."

"Never met an insurance agent who'd try to talk you *out* of a policy increase," he said dryly.

"Shawn says you should be able to find their coverage through the NICB. He's got a good contact there if you need one."

"Ahead of you. A deputy worked on their policies this afternoon."

"Shawn came with me this afternoon to meet with Michele Mancuso. I convinced him I needed a Nick Charles." She could hear Joe moan. "According to her, Paula wanted to travel, and Oscar refused. He was an internationally respected wine expert but refused to travel. Don't you think that's weird? Why wouldn't he enjoy experiencing other countries, especially their wine regions?"

"Good question. On the other hand, I'm acquainted with a highly respected real estate broker I thought might want to see the world. I can't get her to leave the state of Maryland."

"Ha, ha. Very funny."

"Anything more?"

"Apparently, Paula wanted to send Billie to a fancy, overpriced theater school, and Oscar refused. I guess she can do anything she wants now that he's out of the picture."

"Like a lot of rich wives after their husbands are gone."

"Let it be a lesson for you. Find yourself a rich wife."

"It's a little late for that." He cleared his throat.

"Michele had a long bandage above her left wrist. When I asked about it, she was quick to cover the bandage. Said she scratched herself along the stainless-steel storage tanks. Claimed it came with the job."

"You just woke me up."

"I thought it might," she chuckled. "What do you think?"

"I think we need to stop by and have another chat with Ms. Mancuso before her cut heals. Our crime tech team detected another blood type at the scene surrounding Oscar's body."

Helen inhaled. "Oh, ho! That is news."

"Unfortunately, we don't have a match with any criminal records yet. Emma requested more blood samples through Quantico's lab, but they may take days to respond."

"You're the one who tells me my Detection Club needs to be patient."

"Your sleuths are the bane of my existence."

"Do you understand the definition of 'bane'? It means a source of harm or ruin."

"It also means a source of unhappiness," Joe countered.

Chapter Twenty-Six

Early Monday morning, Helen was at her desk in Safe Harbor, ignoring sympathetic glances from her coworkers. Tag was officially on Helen's payroll. Given how her business was tanking, Helen wondered how long she could afford him, even part-time.

She'd be inputting her own reports if these raids on clients continued much longer, she thought. She was sucking on another cup of office swill and a day-old donut from their kitchen when Tammi called.

"Hi, I'm so glad to hear your voice," Helen exclaimed. "I thought after your flight, you might be sleeping in."

"I'm calling before Kayla wakes up. By the time we walked into the apartment on the base, she was comatose."

"I sure miss you. I'm drinking the office God-awful burnt coffee instead of your delivery from Jean's."

"Stop. Many a time you'd bring it in for us." Tammi ignored her whining. "How is it going with Tag? Can't he pick up morning coffee?"

"He's trying. He's upped his dress code, thank goodness."

"He's scheduled for training with me this afternoon. I sent him the Zoom link. Any progress on our stalker?" Tammi stopped. "What are you eating? I can hear you chewing."

"What I always eat, Twizzlers, although these are kind of stiff and stale."

"It's nine o'clock in the morning there," Tammi chastised.

"It's your fault. You left me for your husband," Helen puffed.

Tammi ignored her. "Getting back to my question, any progress?"

"Nope. Zero. Nada."

"I've been thinking."

"I'm all ears."

"You have a reputation around town for tracking down criminals connected to your clients."

"Or family.".

"I've begun calling it the friends and family plan," Tammi chimed back.

"You're so clever."

"Is there a chance this vandalism has nothing to do with a grudge against you? Neither of us can unearth a single client of yours who could possibly be this upset."

"Then who is making me and my clients miserable? I have one appointment next week because they're from out of town and haven't heard the rumors. Give them a few days in Port Anne and I'll be fired."

"Stop feeling sorry for yourself. I wonder if you're putting your Detection Club brain power to enough use. Your Jessica Fletcher is a detail person. Jane Marple would be studying your stalker's actions from every direction. Is there a chance your stalker is Oscar and Bill's killer? Could they have launched this campaign to distract you from solving these murders?"

Helen stopped chewing. "You're saying the killer wanted to get rid of Bill and Oscar. Knowing my sleuthing habits, they decide to keep me so swamped with client problems, I can't focus on these murders."

"Exactly. The stalking also keeps the Sheriff's Office on overload."

Helen went silent. "My God. Maybe you're Jessica Fletcher incarnate."

Tammi laughed. "Not likely. Besides I'm a much better typist."

"This is why I desperately need you."

"Stop." The line went quiet. "Hello? Did I lose you?"

"I'm thinking over your idea. It's brilliant."

"Who said killers try to divert our attention from the truth?"

"Jane Marple," Helen replied. "When are you coming back?"

"Not anytime soon. You and I can work on Tag together. In today's world, I can handle a lot online. Ms. Sexy Special Agent leave town yet?"

"Not yet."

"She will."

"About Tag, can you email his former broker's name to me? I keep putting it off."

"Will do. Got to go. Kayla's up and begging for breakfast."

A tap at the door. "Tag, do you need me?"

"Sorry. You had a call from a Maureen Nagley. Said she's a client of yours. Wants you to call her back."

"Good. I'll call her now."

He handed her an envelope. "A guy named Alex Jordan called. Needs to hear from you. Said you had his number."

"Should have called him back four days ago."

"I'm surprised you have time for business with all these houses getting graffitied."

"Tell me about it." She reached for her phone.

"Alex? Helen Morrisey. I'm sorry I didn't return your call sooner. It's been a bit crazy here. My new assistant is getting his sea legs. Did you want to meet? I could stop by tomorrow about eleven o'clock. Gives me an excuse to see your progress."

Helen flagged Tag.

"I think we should go over my current client list. It's getting shorter as we speak. Alex Jordan is a well-known builder, and I've been working with him for three years. It's important for you to recognize names."

The young man wrinkled his brow.

She paused. "Do you mind if I ask you a question?"

He looked wary.

"I heard you're friends with Michele Mancuso at Blue Heron Vineyard. Do you know much about her? It strikes me odd she isn't working for Mancuso Wines."

Tag made a sheepish little grin. "I met her at the vineyard in late December. We've gone out a few times. She told me she didn't get along with her dad."

"What a shame."

"If I had a name as famous as hers, I wouldn't pass it up. Michele's hoping she'll take over Oscar's business now that he's gone. She described him as tough to work with."

"I'll bet he was. Even more reason she might be happy he's out of the picture." She watched his reaction. "Any idea where she was Friday night, and the Saturday before Oscar was murdered?"

Tag shifted his feet. "Not sure about Friday. We drove down to a wine tasting south of Baltimore Saturday. We came back Sunday after she got the call from the police about Oscar."

"Where'd you stay?"

He shrugged. "I didn't pay any attention to the name. Some place on a back street of Baltimore's Little Italy."

"Did the police ask you to confirm she was with you?"

"An officer met with me Sunday afternoon." He fingered his phone. "I have a few pictures." He opened it up and held it in front of Helen. "Michelle took selfies."

Helen studied the photo. "Gave her a good alibi. What time were you back in Port Anne?"

"The police called her about eight o'clock in the morning. We stopped in the breakfast place here in town. She dropped me off home and drove to the vineyard."

"Was it The Wooden Mast. Canvas awnings? Across from Kent Bank."

He nodded.

"Okay, let's run through my list."

* * *

About twelve-thirty a text popped up on her phone from her favorite reporter.

Want to grab a sandwich? Got more on Michele Mancuso.

You bet. Wooden Mast?

See you there at 1.

* * *

Walking into the Wooden Mast was a sweet throwback to *Happy Days*. Red leatherette seats on chrome stools lined a long, speckled Formica countertop. A steady stream of contractors rotated in and out. One chewed their last handful of hand-cut fries dipped in ketchup. Another claimed an open seat. Helen spied Maggie at a square table in the far corner. She stepped around a group of teenagers and grabbed a wooden chair.

"Sounds like you've been busy. Contrary to me," Helen greeted.

Maggie shifted her gray canvas satchel aside. "I'm sure you're sleuthing around town for Oscar and Bill's killer."

"You're assuming they're the same person. Besides, I'm a little distracted. Got another call from my new assistant on the way here. A seller canceled my appointment with them for tomorrow. It was a nice house, and I was excited about marketing it. This scare campaign is winning."

A server stopped by and took their orders. Maggie stuck a straw into her Coke. "Maybe my info will help. Had a reporter pal in San Fran poke into the personal lives of the influential Mancuso family."

Helen unwrapped a thin paper napkin and laid out her set of utensils. "Tell me."

"Michele didn't exactly leave the family business voluntarily."

"I knew it," Helen declared, her eyes gleaming.

"She had a history of getting into skirmishes. She disappeared from her private high school and took a flight to Malibu with a couple boys. They got tossed into jail for a few hours because of underage drinking. Another time, she went joyriding and plowed into two bikers. No one was seriously hurt, but it cost her father some bucks to keep her from being charged. The final straw happened about eighteen months ago. She stole eight bottles of a rare port wine from her uncle's private collection and sold them for twenty thousand dollars. He was furious."

"The uncle has expensive taste."

"My reporter friend said collecting specialty wines is part of the Mancuso world. The uncle, who's equal partners with her father, wanted to turn her in to local police. He was fed up. Her father convinced him not to file a complaint. Michele is banished from the family compound until she cleans up her act. That's the real reason she's working for a stranger here in

Maryland."

"Stiff punishment, although I don't blame her father. Tough love."

"My friend says Mr. Mancuso is definitely old school. Strict."

"Do you think she's capable of killing Oscar?"

"It's possible, but what does she get out of his death? If Michele's deal with Oscar didn't work out, she could crawl back to Daddy. Eventually, he'd take her back inside the family fold."

Helen pushed her plate aside. "I need to give this a little thought."

Maggie flipped her wire notebook back a couple pages. "You mentioned Georgia and Todd Myers."

"What about them?" Helen zipped up her coat.

"Bayworks comes across squeaky clean. Georgia takes after her father."

"Anything on Todd?"

"Nothing much. Has friends. Buddies around with Vince Caffrey reliving their high school days. More often since Vince's wife kicked him out."

"Jean at the Coffee Pot told me they separated. He isn't wearing a wedding ring."

"He's got an expensive house over on Cliffview. He couldn't make the mortgage payments, and his wife was fed up."

"I kind of feel bad for him. An injury killed his career when he was at the top of his game. Talk about a bad break," Helen mused.

"True. You know about Todd's boat, don't you?"

Helen stopped fussing with her gloves.

Maggie's lips twitched. "You remember. His powerboat caught fire near the town docks last summer. It went up in smoke."

"I forgot that boat belonged to Todd."

"He tried to sell it for top dollar but couldn't. Needed at least thirty thousand in repairs. Talk around town was the fire solved all his problems and put a lot of money in his pocket. Vince handled his insurance claim."

"Any chance *Kent Whig* covered the story?"

"I'll email it over to you."

Helen grabbed their check. "Thanks, Maggie. I owe you lunch."

* * *

Helen called Joe as she cranked up the heat in her Mini. "Have some interesting tidbits. Maggie Dyer dug up some info on Michele Mancuso."

"Let's hear it."

Helen rattled off the highlights.

"Explains why she landed in Port Anne," Joe said.

"This morning, Tag Stolz and I met in my office to review my client list. I asked him if he'd been interviewed by the police.

"So far, he doesn't seem to have any connection to the Banyon case. He and Michele match stories. They could be covering for each other. A little early to tell."

"I agree. He showed me a couple selfies of their weekend. They had breakfast Sunday morning at Wooden Mast as they came back into town. The photos of Michele in Baltimore showed the bandage she's wearing."

Joe lowered the volume on his office dispatch. "She could have killed Oscar late Friday night or Saturday morning before she left town with Tag. We'll check all the area urgent care offices. Find out when she got that cut treated."

"It's possible taking Tag to Baltimore gave her an excuse to get out of town while Oscar's dead body was discovered. Maybe Michele thought she'd take over the vineyard if Oscar were gone. Run the show with Paula Banyon as her partner." Helen hesitated. "But how could she be certain Paula wouldn't sell the business, take the profits, and go find her next rich man? Leave her in the dust. I think Paula would be thrilled to leave this town behind and head south. It's definitely her M.O."

"On the other hand," Joe said, "if Paula used Michele and later dumped her, she's taking a big chance. Sounds like it's time for Michele's second interview in our station." He paused. "Speaking of MO, we had another strike off Dove Lane early this morning. They didn't get inside the house, but one side of the garage is a mess. A deputy's there now."

Helen gulped. "Who's the homeowner?"

"A Dr. Gavin Kahn. His partner, William, called it in. Name sounds familiar. Isn't he the doctor you helped last summer?"

"How could you forget? We took a float plane down to a lighthouse south of Annapolis to deliver his offer."

"How that Coast Guard pilot managed to land us on the water in twenty-mile-an-hour chop was a miracle."

"Gave me nightmares for a week. I'm afraid to ask. Did Gavin find one of my business cards?"

"Yup. We think the garage was hit late last night or early this morning. Gavin discovered it as he backed out his car for his hospital shift. Your card was torn in half and stuck under his windshield wiper."

"Let me guess. No security system."

"A good one, but it wasn't directed at the garage. Where is this person getting all your cards?"

"That's easy. They're all over town. In shops, restaurants, bulletin boards. No one needs to come into Safe Harbor to pick up a stack."

"We'll figure this out yet. Sooner or later, this guy will give himself away," Joe said.

"I hope so. My bank account is draining as we speak. Any news on Bill Elison's case?"

"We're working our way through his customer list. Had an interesting interview with Vince. Let's say he was very careful with his responses. Polite but careful. We're meeting Georgia and Todd again today."

"Why would they ask me to help them find their dad's killer if they did it? They'd be better off if this case goes cold."

"Good question."

"Maggie reminded me of a story about Todd. His boat caught on fire last summer. It was a one hundred percent loss, completely gutted. Worth about a hundred thousand dollars."

"Nice boat. Are you suggesting he set it on fire to collect the insurance money? Why wouldn't he sell it for the hundred thousand?"

"I don't have the answer, but as soon as we hang up, I'm calling an insurance agent I trust."

"Fill me in on what she says. Your imagination might be running away with itself."

"Not my first time. Could you email me your forensics photos of Bill's house? I'd like to study them. Walking through the day he died was a blur."

"I'll send them now. Got to go." Joe's radio squawked.

Chapter Twenty-Seven

An unknown number rang her cell as she walked into the office.

"Mrs. Morrisey, this is Beatrice Weber, Rupert's sister, returning your call."

"It is, but please call me Helen. I'm so relieved you called me. It took some digging through Rupert's records to find your name and number."

"Is Rupert all right? He calls me once a week. When I didn't hear from him, I got worried and left him a couple messages."

Helen inhaled. "Rupert was hit in the head by someone who came into his store eight days ago. We found him soon after it happened. I'm sorry to tell you the doctors induced a coma to give him time to recover. I spoke to his floor nurse early this morning. He's stronger, and they plan to bring him out of his coma tomorrow morning."

The elderly woman's voice caught. "My poor brother! I'm in Germany. If I make plans today, I'll arrive in five or six days. I'm afraid I don't travel well, but he's all I have."

"I'm sure he'd love to have you here."

Beatrice blew her nose. "My brother mentions you often. I think he had Thanksgiving with you."

"He did. Try not to worry too much. He's in very good hands. Johns Hopkins Medical Center is one of the best in the country."

"Thank the Lord. I'll start checking flight schedules."

"Do you receive texts?"

"I do. I like them. Exciting to hear from people." Beatrice made a soft chuckle.

"Feel free to text me anytime. I'll pick you up at the airport. Good night, Beatrice."

Her voice quaked a bit. "Good night. I'll say my prayers."

"We both will." Helen set down her phone. You think you've got problems, she berated herself. 'Helps keep your perspective,' Jessica Fletcher admonished.

Her next call was to Lane Morgan Insurance in Grace Harbor. Lane picked up.

"Helen, what in God's name are you up to? Every time I turn around, someone tells me one of your clients' properties was hit." She issued a hearty laugh. "I'm glad I'm not their insurer."

"Easy for you to laugh. I can't sleep."

Lane cleared her throat. "I can imagine. Can I help?"

"I need your professional advice. If someone wanted to get insurance money out of their boat and can't afford to sell it, how would they go about it?"

Lane paused. "They'd put in a claim for damages for repairs. Of course, to re-insure it going forward, the owner needs proof of its latest value."

"Be devious for me. Let's say the boat owner has a hundred-thousand-dollar policy, but the boat has a fifty-thousand-dollar repair problem."

"The owner could torch the boat," Lane explained, "but claim the fire's accidental. The insurance company doesn't know about its true value and pays the entire hundred thousand."

"Is that possible?"

"Absolutely. Insurance companies are awash in fraudulent claims. Sorry for the pun. In boat world, it's called barratry." Lane hesitated. "Any chance you're talking about a boat fire last summer near the Port Anne town dock?"

"Should I be?"

"There was talk about that fire. The owner had a large policy and collected on it. Claimed diesel leaked onto some hot electrical wires and set off an explosion. Between you and me, I wondered if there was a problem with that boat, and the owner couldn't sell it. It sat in the harbor for months without moving. If the owner set fire to his boat and collected the full hundred thousand, the insurance company got swindled. The owner could pay off their bank loan and pocket the rest."

* * *

The sky signaled more snow as Helen started for home. "Lord, I'm ready for spring." The two lanes of Osprey Point Road through the park were coated, and the shoulders of the road blurred. A four-by-four in front of her kept tapping on its brakes. She followed its taillights all the way into her neighborhood, before swinging into her driveway. The house was ablaze in lights, top to bottom.

"What in the world?" she swore out loud. "Don't tell me it's my turn to get raided."

She reached into her glove compartment for her ten-inch stainless-steel flashlight and switched on its high beam. It was a much better defense device than her cell phone light. It was Nancy Drew approved.

She crunched up the walkway and peeked into a window. Lizzie! Helen rang the brass bell hanging at her front door while digging for her keys.

"Hi!" Lizzie greeted. "Did I surprise you?"

"I thought my house was being raided. Weren't you staying with your girlfriend?"

Lizzie laughed. "I overstayed my welcome. Her boyfriend arrived. Besides, hiding away from home is for cowards."

"You're as stubborn as I am."

She picked up her mother's bag. "Hungry? Chicken in pesto sauce is waiting in the oven. Here." She thrust a glass of white into her mother's hand.

Helen collapsed on the couch. "Bless you. It's been another exciting day in the life of real estate agent Helen Morrisey and charming Port Anne. Do you remember Dr. Kahn? I sold him a lighthouse south of St. Michael's last summer. His house on the point was graffitied in the middle of the night."

"Why can't the Sheriff's Office catch these people?"

"Too much happening and not enough investigators. Joe's tearing his hair out."

"I'll bet. You want to eat in the living room with your feet up?"

"Sounds perfect. Give me a minute to change." She was back in a flash. Lizzie handed her a filled plate, and Helen inhaled. "Heaven." She sat back. "You haven't told me what's happening with Billie and her attempt to enter the real world."

Lizzie settled in next to Watson and tucked a teal-colored Afghan around him. Trixie leaped up to steal some of the attention. "ShopTV put her into their training program."

Helen gulped. "I can't believe it."

"No more than I can. The studio is so short-staffed, they're willing to give her a shot." Her daughter smirked. "I wonder how long she lasts. They don't have much patience with young prima donnas. It'll be a real culture shock."

"You're being polite. She's got the maturity level of an eight-year-old. Maybe I need to stop by and chat with Paula while I'm on her good side. If Billie gets fired or quits, I won't have ShopTV as leverage."

"A friend in HR told me a bit of interesting background on her mother."

"Oh?"

"Apparently, it's standard protocol to check the applicant's social media posts. It led to information on Billie's mother. Paula's a former CPA."

Helen sat up. "Seriously? Which means she's a lot more aware of Oscar's financials than she lets on. She played the innocent wife uninvolved with his business when we met."

"Which made me curious, too. So I googled her."

"I'm all ears, Nancy Drew."

"Are you aware Oscar is her third husband?"

"Third? She told me Oscar was number two."

"Maybe the CPA forgot how to count. Would you like to hear how they died?"

"Can't wait to hear."

Lizzie preened. "I got curious. Her first husband was only thirty-eight when he died of heart failure while scuba diving. She sold his tech business. Number two was Billie's father. He died on vacation. They were taking photos of the Grand Canyon, and he fell. The police declared it an accident. Paula left her husband behind but brought home a fat insurance settlement."

Helen started to laugh.

"What's so funny?" asked Lizzie.

"Sorry." Helen tried to control herself. "Maybe Oscar was afraid to travel with Paula. Let's face it, Paula's got a bizarre track record when it comes to husbands on vacations."

"Mom, you're losing it."

"You've got to admit, it's pretty bizarre." Helen wiped a few tears from her cheeks and started digging through her *Murder, She Wrote* mysteries.

"What are you doing?"

"I'm trying to remember. Jessica Fletcher solved a case involving two women partners in crime. What if Paula wanted to get rid of her husband and dump the vineyard life? She knew the young and beautiful Michele was hitting on Oscar. Paula decided to be proactive and kill Oscar. Or she convinced Michele that Oscar wasn't worth chasing. Too tight-fisted. Paula says she'll share Oscar's estate if they plot his murder together." She ran her fingers along the book spines.

"Do you think Billie could be in on it?"

"Billie's nasty enough, but I doubt it. Paula probably wouldn't want to drag her daughter into her plans. Billie might break down if she's interviewed by the police."

"I thought Michele was gone the weekend Oscar died."

"She was, or at least she claims. Tag Stolz, my new assistant, went with Michele to Baltimore Saturday for the weekend."

"Maybe they made up the story of their trip," Lizzie offered.

"It would mean Tag covered for her."

"He could have provided her an alibi and never realized he was being used."

"That's true."

"How is he working out?"

"He's not Tammi."

"Mom, no one is Tammi."

CHAPTER TWENTY-SEVEN

"Are you sure you don't want the job?"

"Never. Tammi had the patience of Job." Lizzie got to her feet and stretched. "Time for bed." She gave Rocky a few strokes under his belly. "I'm surprised Joe hasn't reclaimed him."

"He thinks he's providing me a guard dog."

Rocky gave her a plaintive whine and hid his kind eyes under two clumsy front paws.

* * *

Early the next morning, Lizzie took a run down the park trail to the lighthouse with Rocky. Joe had sent the photos from Bill's house the day he was found. One by one, Helen opened them and zoomed in. The kitchen showed the dirty dishes in the sink and a notepad on the table next to the pens. She scrolled to the next. The hallway opened to the dining room. More shots of his home office. They all felt foreboding.

She squinted at the screen as she zoomed in on the kitchen table shot. Bill's coffee mug, my Safe Harbor pen, and another from Longfeld Insurance. She zoomed in on the tile floor with a decorative black mat set inside the back door. What is that on the floor? She hesitated, scrolled backwards, and enlarged the photo. Bits of dirt, maybe grains of sand, were scattered across it. She opened a photo of the flooring near the entrance to the basement stairs. Helen sat back. It was dirt, maybe rough grains of sand similar to the grit on the mat. Where did it come from? Bill's house was cleaned Tuesday. Who tracked it in on their shoes?

She reverted to the kitchen table photo. Two pens. One she gave to Bill on the Tuesday they met. Why was a Longfeld Insurance pen on the table? Bill's new policy was issued in November, before the holidays, and Vince claimed he only saw Bill at the club once in early January. Helen played the possibilities in her mind.

"Joe? Can you call me?"

About twenty minutes later, he rang. "I'm about to sit down with Michele in the station. What's up?'

177

"I'm staring at the photos of Bill's house. A couple things bother me."

"Shoot."

"I think Vince Caffrey was in Bill's house after he and I met and before the cleaner found Bill."

"Why are you singling out Vince?"

"I gave Bill a Safe Harbor pen when we met. He put it on the table. Vince had a pen on the table the day we found Bill. He told me the new pens arrived two days before Bill died. I have a copy of the invoice. If Vince hadn't seen Bill since early January, why was Vince's new pen found at Bill's house?"

"Helen, people keep free pens around their house for years. I've got pens from people I don't remember ever meeting. Vince was his insurance agent. If I accuse Vince of murder based on a pen, I'd have to accuse you, too."

"Very funny. Don't forget, I admitted I was in the house. Vince denied it."

She was quiet.

"Helen?"

"I'm thinking," she explained. "We both believe Bill knew his killer. His house was cleaned Tuesday morning. I arrived Tuesday afternoon at four. When I zoom in on the photos of the floor, there's a trail of light tan and dark grit across the tile. Why would that be? Did the killer track it in from Bill's driveway? I never noticed it when I was there."

"Maybe Bill tracked it in?"

"He may have. Should we check his shoes? What if he didn't?"

"Maybe it's a salt and sand mix for defrosting sidewalks. It's everywhere."

"Hmm. Could be," Helen admitted. "I was hoping we found a way to identify our killer."

"I'll send someone from my squad to Bill's house for a sample."

She ran her fingers over her right palm. "We might need two samples. Remember when you asked an EMT at Oscar's to clean the grit out of my cut? Any chance forensics found the same grit at the vineyard?"

"You're suggesting the same person who killed Bill murdered Oscar?"

"Let's face it. We don't have a motive for either killing, but I'm convinced they're connected. There's no way Jane Marple or any of my sleuths would consider two murders in three days as unrelated. We need forensics to tell us if the grit on the floor near Oscar's body is the same as I saw in Bill's kitchen photos."

"I'll ask forensics to run a comparison."

"Shoes too?"

"Shoes too."

"Can I stop by Bill's house and take a close-up photo of those pens? I promise I won't step anywhere near grit."

He was silent.

"I know I'm annoying," she prodded.

"Nothing new there."

"Are you giving me a yes?"

"Absolutely not. I'll take care of it. How's Rocky?"

"Spoiled."

"Want to eat in Port Anne about six?"

"Only if I get to keep Rocky. We're in love. We might run away together."

"He's making better progress than I am."

* * *

A text popped up as she drove into Port Anne. Calli.

Hi! Good news! Checked with hospital. Rupert is awake!!

Helen dialed Calli.

"Calli, it's Helen. So excited! Best news I've heard in weeks. Can we visit?"

"Yes, ten until three."

Helen glanced at her dashboard clock. "Would you like to come with me?"

"I was hoping you'd suggest it. I'm not allowed to drive yet."

"I'm heading to an appointment. I'll pick you up at the store about one o'clock."

"You're the best," Calli declared.

Helen laughed. "Haven't heard those words in a while."

Chapter Twenty-Eight

"Helen?" It was Tag.

"Hi. How was your training with Tammi yesterday? Did it help?" She was on her way through the park, her coupe's blower fogging the windows.

"Easy. I think I taught her a few things."

Helen held back a retort. Please, God, give me patience. "Anything I need to know?"

Tag hesitated. "Did you see this morning's post in the *Kent Whig*? I'm worried about you."

"What are you talking about? Read it to me."

"It's in the *About Town* section again. *Looks like Realtor Helen Morrisey's unknown graffiti artist is getting even more creative as he continues to work his way down her client list. A homeowner on Dove Lane is at least number nine over the past four weeks. Now he's leaving a message – 'Your agent is a crook!'"*

"This is a nightmare." Helen gritted her teeth.

"Any chance this guy might attack you next?"

"Don't worry. This someone gets their jollies out of defacing people's properties and destroying my name. We'll get him."

"I want you to know, I appreciate this job."

"Thanks. I'm stopping at Dr. Kahn's house and later the vineyard. I won't be in the office until late. If anyone calls about these posts, pass them on to me."

"I'm at Rupert's store later."

"The hospital told me he's awake and alert."

"Really? I thought he wasn't going to make it."

"You don't sound very pleased. Worried about losing your job at the store when he gets back?"

"Not likely. Besides, my business is picking up."

"I'd expect you to be bored working in a dusty old shop like Rupert's."

"I like it. Gives me something else to do when I'm not in the office."

Maybe Tag would work out after all, Helen considered. Wish he didn't sound like such a twit sometimes.

Her cell buzzed. Tammi left a text.

Checked your online calendar. Don't forget your appointment with Alex Jordan. 11 am.

On my way. What would I do without you? Oh, wait! I am without you. Helen followed it with a red heart symbol and drove toward Ferry Point.

* * *

Baywood Estates at Ferry Point offered twenty-two spacious colonials on a beautiful, wooded piece of land. It rolled down to the Chesapeake facing Osprey Point peninsula and her house. The builder, Alex Jordan, had taken Helen's advice and reworked his site plan to save the trees. It set the development apart from so many built on farmland and increased his sale prices.

"Hi," Alex greeted. She offered a hand, and Alex hugged her back.

"How's my favorite builder?" Helen asked, turning to admire. "This model is gorgeous!"

"It may be my favorite."

"Be careful. We have to sell all the models, not only your favorite."

"Come see the upstairs floor plan. You're the one who talked me into the connecting bedrooms for kids."

"This upstairs layout is a parent's dream. So much space," Helen exclaimed. "Andy and I wallpapered the smallest bedroom for our first baby. We found out four days before my due date that we were expecting twins. Andy insisted we keep them in the same room." She rolled her eyes. "What a debacle. Two cribs side by side. Our first parenting decision and definitely not our best."

She leaned on a windowsill and gazed out. "This water view is spectacular."

Alex leaned next to her. "Winter or summer."

"What did you want to work on today?"

"I'll show you in the kitchen." They headed downstairs. Alex opened a file on the island. "I can't hold this back from you."

Her face went white as he placed three color photos on the counter in front of her. She stared at the new walls smeared in red paint with the words *'Your agent is a crook!'* "Oh no! Not here!" Her voice broke. "I'm so sorry, Alex. When did this happen?"

He sat down on a stool. "The morning I first called you."

She swallowed. "Which house?"

"Two houses. One of my crews was painting fresh drywall in the garages. The houses were locked, thank goodness, but the garages were open. We repainted the walls later that day."

She studied them. "Why didn't I hear about this from the Sheriff's Office?"

"I never called them. You don't need the publicity, and neither do I."

"Thank you. You're so kind." Helen's eyes welled. "This is the twelfth client whose house has been graffitied since January, and I'll be damned if I know why. We also have two people dead, Oscar Banyon and Bill Elison. The police don't think they're connected to my vandal, but I'm not sure anymore."

Alex studied Helen. "I've only heard their names, no details."

"The police are treating deaths as unrelated. The vandal acts too much like a teenage smash-and-grab personality. All the hits on my clients are so arbitrary. It makes it almost impossible to come up with a motive." She glanced around, then back to Alex. "I can't thank you enough for your loyalty. If you think it's best for you to have this project reassigned to another Safe Harbor agent, you need to tell me."

Alex picked up the photos and handed them to her. "Take these." He squeezed her shoulder. "You've worked on this job for three years. Every step of the way. We're fine."

Helen gave him a grateful hug. "Thank you. I was afraid you were going to take me up on my offer."

Approaching Port Anne village to pick up Calli, a thought came to Helen. She hit speaker. "Alex, was my business card left in either of those garages?"

"A card was in each of them. Weird thing, they were torn in half."

"Thanks, Alex. Talk soon."

* * *

"Knock, knock. Rupert?" Helen and Calli tiptoed up to Rupert's hospital bed. The old man slowly opened his eyes. He made a weak smile and reached out a thin hand.

"Ladies, I'm so happy to see you."

Taking each side of the bed, they leaned over and kissed him on his cheeks.

"No more than we are," Calli declared.

Helen stroked his hand. "How are you feeling?"

"The doctors say I'm doing well for an old dog. I feel ready to run around the block." He chuckled.

"That I'd love to see," Calli said, studying his face. "You couldn't run around the block *before* you were hurt." She shifted her chair.

Rupert studied his old friend. "I hear you had a close call, too. How are you feeling?"

Calli straightened up. "Nothing compared to yours."

Rupert studied Helen's pale face. "I hear I'm part of Kent County's own crime wave. Fill me in."

Helen protested. "Must you call it a crime wave? I feel responsible."

"Don't be silly," he retorted. "How's my store?"

"Tag is running it most days from one until five. He works for me in the mornings. Last time I stopped in, he was sorting through your magazine collections. I'm not the only true crime follower."

"Glad he's around. Let's hope he doesn't rearrange everything while I'm gone. Can you hand me some water?"

Helen held up a plastic cup and a straw to his lips. "I tracked down your sister, Gretchen. She's booked a flight to Philadelphia."

"I read her text this morning. I wish she hadn't gone to the trouble." His voice quivered.

"She's your sister. She wants to know you're okay with her own eyes." Helen looked at Calli and back to Rupert. "The nurse says you're allowed thirty-minute visits at a time. Do you mind if we talk about your attack?"

"Give me a boost," Rupert said, struggling to sit upright. He grinned at Calli. "If anyone is going to catch this bastard, it's our Helen."

"Do you have any idea who attacked you?"

Rupert rubbed his chin. "I don't. His face was covered with a scarf, and he wore thick gloves."

"Like the rest of the world in this weather," Calli commented.

"You say 'he'. Do you think the attacker was male?"

"Not sure, could have been either. He moved fast."

"Did he say anything?"

"Keep quiet, old man." Rupert's voice quivered.

Helen squeezed his hand and looked up at Calli. "You had to be terrified."

"It happened so quickly, I didn't have time."

"'Keep quiet'. What could you possibly know that your attacker wanted to keep quiet? Could it have to do with your shop?"

Rupert leaned back and closed his eyes. "I've been reliving the attack. Nothing makes sense."

"It's okay. We'll figure it out." Helen lightened her tone. "Remember those Nancy Drews you gave me? Love them."

His eyes warmed. "They are beauties."

"Shawn and Lizzie will be fighting over them someday," she laughed.

"If you like those crime magazines I gave you, I've got more. Ask Tag. He's probably flipping through them instead of watching the store." He chuckled at his own joke. "Tell him he's welcome to keep some. He's been a big help." He rubbed his beard.

Helen stood up and started to pace. "Rupert, you told me that the last time you spoke to Bill, he said he may have discovered an old local crime. Is there any chance he came across a crime in those magazines? Could they remind him of something that happened in Kent County?"

"I can't tell you. He sounded excited."

A tap on the room door. "Ladies, Mr. Weber needs to rest. Times up," the nurse declared.

"Of course." Calli leaned over her friend and gave him a gentle hug. "We'll be back."

Helen squeezed his wrist and pointed to the nurse. "Make sure you follow this woman's instructions." She blew him a kiss as they walked out.

Chapter Twenty-Nine

It was after four o'clock when Helen dropped Calli off at Tomes and Treasures and headed south out of Port Anne. Seeing Rupert on the mend lightened her heart. One piece of good news, thank goodness. Her phone rang. Joe.

"How's Rupert?"

"Weak, but much better. Looking more like himself."

"Good, good. We're working down the interviews of Bayworks employees. A woman who works in their accounting department swears Bill and Todd had a nasty argument in January about increasing his life insurance. Georgia was in the room."

"I don't understand. We all know about their new policies. Vince Caffrey wrote them."

"They weren't arguing about Bill's million-dollar policy he signed in November. Todd wanted Bill to get a second one. He kept pushing it, and Bill kept refusing. Georgia backed her father."

"So what happened?" Helen asked.

"Bill stormed out of the office. It's the real reason he was working from home."

"Why was Todd forcing this policy on Bill?"

"For some guys, it's never enough. Maybe Todd and Vince went to Bill's house to try to convince him. They argued. Bill was killed." Joe's radio squawked. "Where are you now? Home?"

"Soon. I'd really like to examine those pens left behind."

"You can't enter a crime scene without me. I'll meet you there in fifteen minutes."

* * *

Two porch lights marked Bill's front door, but his kind face wasn't there to greet her. A lump formed in her throat.

Silently, they ducked under the yellow crime tape running across the yard. Joe handed her blue latex gloves and shoe covers.

"I'm wearing shoe covers for crime scenes more than house showings," Helen muttered under her breath as they stepped inside. His kitchen had all the signs of being searched. Deputies and the Sheriff's Office forensics techs had opened every drawer, every cabinet, and photographed every room from front to back. The dirty dishes had been taken from the sink to be tested. The silt of white fingerprint powder covered the floors, counters, doors, and windows. Forensics had been there a second time to remove the sample sand and grit from the floor near the basement door.

Helen's heart thumped. She'd met Bill in a cheerful, warm kitchen with his grandchildren's drawings in crayon hanging on his refrigerator. This afternoon, the house felt cold and abandoned.

Two pens sat in the center of the table. Helen opened her phone to its camera and took three pictures from different angles with Joe in the background. Then she started a video as he removed two plastic baggies from his jacket and picked up her Safe Harbor pen. He dropped it into the bag and held up the clear bag to the camera. He picked up Vince's Longfeld Insurance pen from the table and set it into the second bag. He held the bag up to the light, and Helen videoed the pen's print along the barrel. The insurance agency's new slogan was clearly imprinted on a silver background.

She continued to video her own movements as she reached inside her orange tote. Out came the handful of pens Vince had given her two days before. She held one close to the camera, showing the old slogan on the side. The barrel was red.

Their eyes met. "Vince was here after I met with Bill. We can prove it." Helen handed him a folded piece of paper. "This is the invoice for the new

187

silver pens ordered by Longfeld Insurance. It's stamped 'received'. The pens arrived three days before Bill died. Vince lied to us. I believe he showed up at Bill's house to get him to sign the second policy."

"I'd need to prove he lost his temper and shoved Bill down the stairs. I'll take these back with me to the station." Joe twisted his watch. "Ready to go? I'm late for an interview."

"Sure. I'm going home."

At the end of road, Joe waved. Helen peeled off the latex gloves and turned toward her peninsula.

"Darn it! My gloves." She dug into her pockets and her bag. Nothing. She made a three-sixty back to Bill's.

Helen pulled out the latex gloves and shoe covers. She locked herself inside and searched the kitchen, then headed straight for the office, flipping on switches along the hall. More dust on Bill's desk and across his bookcase. His wines were displayed on one shelf. The police had taken his signed purchase agreement from his copier. She spotted her black gloves on Bill's black desk pad.

'Do I dare one more look around?' she asked her sleuths. 'Absolutely,' Agatha declared. Helen opened the drawers in his desk. Check books, bank statements, information on cruises, photographs. Back in the kitchen, a shiver traveled up her arms as she approached the basement door with dread. She touched the light switch and softly took the stairs. She tiptoed around Bill's blood stains, scarring the concrete, her stomach roiling. The cardboard box had been removed. Helen turned on her cell light. On hands and knees, she crept in a tight circle, peeping under the nearby washer and dryer and a folding table. Turning, she held her light along the floor, flashing it beneath the oil burner and hot water heater. She sat back on her knees. Suitcases were tucked beneath the open stairs. Carefully, she lifted them and ran the light underneath. She shifted a box of Christmas decorations. Nothing. She'd been here too long. Time to get out of here.

Back in the kitchen, she approached the back door and froze. She watched the knob slowly turn before her. Todd stepped in.

"Todd! You scared the life out of me!" Helen struggled to smile and keep a guilty quiver out of her voice.

Todd jumped. "Helen, why the hell are you here?" His eyes blazed. "Who let you in?"

"I, I have a key. Bill gave it to me," she stuttered, backing up against the kitchen table. "I came in with Detective McCallister, but I forgot my gloves on Bill's desk, so I came back." She held them up. Todd stared at them, then her face. His eyes traveled around the room.

"I wasn't trying to intrude." She trailed off, trying to sound helpless. "Would you rather I return the key to you?" She gambled her offer would mollify him. She reached inside her bag, pulled out the key, and held it out.

Todd stomped past her, casting his eyes down the darkened hall.

He swooped a hand forward and grabbed the key. "Helen, we don't want you here. Understood?"

"Completely."

Thirty seconds later, she was safe inside her Mini. Reaching Osprey Point Road, she hesitated, her turning signal pointing south toward home. She needed to reach Georgia before Todd. He'll make her sound like a brazen busybody. Well, was she? She chastised herself.

Her finger over the phone, she sat back, bone weary. The deep snow-covered pines surrounded her. Helen wanted home, her cats, and a bowl of hot soup. Maybe a *Murder, She Wrote*. She inhaled, flipped her directional, and dialed Georgia.

"Hi. It's Helen. Am I getting you at a bad time?"

"Not at all. Any news for me?"

Helen started. "I need to explain..." She hesitated. She could hear the tension in Georgia's voice and thought of Tammi's reminder. Meet in person. In person was always best. "I thought I'd stop in for a few minutes on my way home if you don't mind."

"Why not come now?"

Wearily, Helen drove back toward town.

* * *

Georgia was at her door. "Can I offer you coffee or a glass of wine?" She led her into the family room.

Helen shook off her coat. "I'd love hot tea if you have it." She ran her cold hands through her hair.

"I'll join you. I appreciate the company."

"How's Matthew doing?"

"He's sad, but he's managing. I just picked him up from practice. Keeping him busy. He's upstairs doing homework." Georgia set out their mugs. "You must have something on your mind to come so late in the day."

"I do. I'm afraid I owe you an apology. I came from your father's house. Todd found me there and was really upset. I'd forgotten my gloves on your dad's desk and came back to get them."

"How did you get inside?"

"Your dad gave me a key the first time we met at his house. It wasn't until today that I remembered it was in my glove compartment. I should have called you first before I went to the house. I gave the key to Todd."

Georgia said. "I can't imagine why Todd was there."

"Maybe he wanted to check the heat. In this cold, it's a good idea to make sure the furnace is working. I should have thought of it myself."

"You're probably right. Other than at work, we haven't talked."

Helen drew her eyebrows together and waited.

"I asked Todd to move out, at least temporarily. We've been struggling for over a year. Since my dad died, working together has become nearly impossible." Georgia's voice quivered. She gripped her mug. "He's unhappy. He hates Bayworks. He lashes out at anyone."

Helen put her arms around her. "I'm so sorry. This is all too much for you. My dad and I were estranged years ago. Now he's gone. It wasn't the same kind of shock you've endured."

"I heard about your husband. How you lost someone you loved in a terrible way." Georgia lifted her eyes to Helen. "Why do I sense you have more on your mind?"

"Can you tell me anything about Todd's boat fire last summer?"

She looked surprised. "Oh, gosh. Must have been last June. He was trying

190

to sell it. There was a diesel leak, and the engine caught fire. Thank God for Vince. He made sure the insurance was up to date."

"Vince certainly is a good friend."

"They'd do anything for each other. I worry about Vince. He resents how life is turning out. Todd is as bad. They fuel each other's discontent."

"Tell me about the second million-dollar insurance policy Todd wanted Bill to sign. I heard they had a big argument in the office."

Georgia twisted a paper napkin between her fingers. "Vince and Todd thought Bill's first policy wasn't sufficient. Vince wrote a second policy application, but Dad refused to sign. He thought it was completely unnecessary, and I agreed with him. Given Dad's age, it was outrageously expensive. Todd offered to pay the premium." She stumbled. "He was furious when I insisted we couldn't afford it. He says I don't support him enough." She choked on a rueful laugh. "I run Bayworks, and he antagonizes our customers."

Helen grasped her hand. "You concentrate on taking care of yourself and Matthew. We're going to catch your dad's killer. It won't bring him back, but we owe it to him and you. He'd want you to have a good life."

"Mom?" Matthew's voice called out.

"Down here, honey. Need me?"

"I'm hungry. What's for dinner?"

"Dinner in ten minutes!" She winked at Helen.

"I'll get out of your way. Thanks for filling me in." Helen picked up her coat. She spotted a long line of wines on Georgia's wall cabinet. "Your dad wasn't the only one who drank Blue Heron wines. I recognize the label."

Georgia chuckled. "He made checking on our cleaning staff at the vineyard an excuse to chat with Oscar. He loved reading about wines and where they came from."

"Definitely a fan. There's a pile of books about wine in his study. He collected true crime stories, too, didn't he?"

"He had subscriptions for years. He'd donate some to Rupert's after he read them. You're welcome to take them if you want." Georgia hesitated. "A couple months ago, he told me he found a crime he thought might be close to home."

"That's interesting. Did he mention it to anyone else?"

"I haven't any idea. I never asked. I'm not into all those stories. I'm a Hallmark girl."

Helen laughed. "I'm a sucker for their mystery channel. Any chance your dad had a safe in the house?"

"He did. I should have told the police."

"Would you mind if I had the password? Maybe he tucked something inside that will help us identify his killer. Unless you rather we tell the police."

Georgia shook her head. "I rather you check first. I'd go with you, but I can't handle seeing his house. It's too soon."

She got up, walked to her desk, and came back with a slip of paper.

"Here. Don't tell Todd. He doesn't have the code. Take my key to the house." She grasped Helen's arm. "How is Rupert, by the way?"

"I saw him today. He had a rough time, but doctors say he's turned the corner." Helen gave her a hug. "Good night. Try not to worry."

Chapter Thirty

"Good morning!" Helen stepped through the door of Safe Harbor. "The sun is out, and the temperature is over twenty degrees. Hallelujah! How is everyone today?"

Stella looked up and grinned. Tag stepped out from his desk and followed her.

"You're certainly in a good mood this morning," he said. "McAlister catch your stalker?"

"Working on it. I'm attempting a mental reset. Any calls for me?" Helen tossed her bag on the floor next to her desk and opened her laptop.

"Nope, been quiet." He claimed a chair. "I have an appointment this afternoon at one."

"Terrific. Tell me if I can help you prepare." She sat back. "Talk to Tammi?"

"We've got a Zoom call today at ten. Sounds as if she's liking Texas."

"I'm glad. Marcus arrives any day."

"How's Rupert doing?"

"Much better. He's frail but feisty as ever. He suggested you pick out any of those true crime magazines you like and keep them. He's grateful you're covering the store."

"I'm trying to piece together the missing issues. It's kind of fun."

"Sounds like he and Bill Elison swapped them all the time. When his daughter gets ready to empty his house, I'll ask her about them. Are they important?"

"Consecutive years can double and triple their value for collectors. Maybe I'll hit the jackpot, and Rupert and I can split the winnings." Tag grinned.

"I flipped through the couple Rupert gave me last week. I forgot how depressing they can be. I have a hard enough time getting to sleep." She stopped. "Do you remember when Rupert told us Bill thought he'd found a local cold case? Any chance you've come across what Bill was talking about?"

Todd made a little smirk. "Not yet. Sounds like a real longshot for little Port Anne. I'll admit, when you read this stuff, your imagination starts to go wild."

"Exactly what I thought." Helen peered at her calendar. "I'm expecting a call from a client by the name of Harrison. He might call on Tammi's line."

"I'll let you know." He rubbed his hands over his knees.

"Is that paint on your hands?" Helen asked.

He glanced down, embarrassed. "I decided the front door at Five and Dime needed a touch-up."

"I noticed that too. That's very nice of you." Helen made a little smile.

"I'm training Tammi today." He flexed his biceps as he closed her door behind him.

She closed her eyes, her annoyance bubbling up. Jane commented in her ear, 'Clever young men know so little of life.' 'Jane, I'm listening to my gut. He's not going to work out.'

She reached for her phone. "Good morning, this is Helen Morrisey. Is Vince Caffrey in?"

"Vince is at the Kent Sports Arena this morning. Do you want to leave a message?"

"No, thank you. We'll catch up later."

She stared at her screen. I can't sit here. Let's go chat with Vince. 'Good idea,' Nancy spoke up.

* * *

The Kent County Sports Arena wasn't nearly as large as its name might suggest. A one-story building on six acres of parkland, it offered Port Anne area residents an indoor turf field year-round. Different sports teams reserved the field for practices. In the winter, it proved a life saver for antsy kids and grateful adults.

Helen traipsed past a closed concession stand and an empty party room to the field. Inside the arena, it was cool and dry. Vince Caffrey was leaning on a wire fence, waiting to be called up to bat. He spotted Helen. "Hi, what brings you in here? Planning on joining our men's league?"

Helen laughed and patted his arm. "You wouldn't want me. I was horrible in high school. I'd be worse now. How's your team doing?" She tilted her chin toward the bench.

"They're not the Orioles, that's for sure."

"I need to ask you a question. Georgia mentioned that Todd and you were upset with Bill before he died. Todd wanted him to purchase another insurance policy, and Bill refused. Why did Todd want it?"

The ex-pro chewed on a wad of gum and studied Helen. "Todd wanted the extra protection, and I thought it a good idea." He tossed her a cute, boyish grin. "After all, I am in the insurance business."

Helen looked him in the eye. "Given what's happened, it would have been quite the windfall."

"Bill should have taken my advice." Vince spat his gum into a trash container. "I'm up." He trotted to the plate, his shoulders stiff and his face red. Helen stuck her fingers through the wire fence and watched.

A strike, a second, two balls. He leaned into the plate. "You're out!" the catcher shouted.

Vince threw down his bat and stormed off the field. His eyes met Helen's.

"You're becoming a pain in the ass with your questions." Spittle hit Helen as he leaned into her face. He may have been soft compared to his pro days, but she could feel his physical power.

* * *

Outside, she dialed Joe. "Vince Caffrey's got a temper, a very short fuse."

"Stay away from him. What do you say we have dinner with Emma tomorrow night? Toss around some ideas."

"Excuse me? I'm not interested in hearing her opinions."

"Don't get so defensive. You sound like Agatha Raisin. Jessica would never turn down a nice dinner invitation. Crime is crime. You might find out you and Emma have a lot in common."

"Other than you? Let me think about it." She pouted. "Nope. I have plans to wash my hair."

"You are so stubborn. Call me tomorrow morning if you change your mind."

Helen grunted. She opened her car door and stared down at her feet. Her boots had tracked dirt into the car. Was this the same grit we found in Bill's house? She retraced her steps to the arena. A coach was leaning on the fence.

"Excuse me, I noticed this grit stuck onto my boots. Is this unique to this field?"

"It's all over here. It's called silica sand. The turf has beads of rubber mixed with sand. It helps the artificial grass stand up." He lifted his baseball shoes. "My wife hates it. I have to take off my shoes before I step inside our house."

Helen studied the ground, then the young man. "Any chance you know Todd Myers?"

"Oh, sure. Todd plays in my league, and he's here for his kid."

"Thank you. You've been helpful. Enjoy the game."

* * *

Helen got into her Mini, reached for her stash of clear baggies in the glove compartment, and scraped some grit from the sole of her boots into the bag. She dialed Joe.

"Any news on the sand analysis? I just left Kent Sports Arena, and they use silica sand. It's dark and gritty. Either Vince or Todd could have dragged silica sand into Bill's kitchen."

"Drop off a sample. We'll get forensics to compare it ASAP. I'll call you if we have any news."

Back through town, she decided to stop in at Taylor Lumber.

"Hi, Rachel. Dottie in?"

"In the paint section."

Helen knocked on a shelf behind Dottie. "Excuse me, but I'm trying to find a Pepto Bismol pink and Kermit green. Can you help me?"

Dottie whirled around, chuckling.

"Thought I'd stop by and make sure our wall artist hasn't shown up again."

"No sign of him, thank goodness. I'm short-staffed as it is; I don't need to be wasting time cleaning up after him. Any news?"

"Not yet. The creep is busy. Hit two more of my houses in the past week." Dottie shook her head.

"Keep your ears to the ground for me."

"Will do." She hesitated. "I heard an off comment about your club, though."

"Tell me."

"A contractor was complaining he lost a bid on the new roof. Someone else got the job and charged a lot more."

"How did he find out what they charged?"

"A member of the club told him the budget number was listed in the club's monthly report."

"Maybe the member misunderstood. I'll check it out."

* * *

The next morning, Watson and Trixie were climbing around her ears, demanding breakfast. Rocky's tail thumped on her carpet. She dragged herself out of bed and opened a slider so he could run out among the trees. A few minutes later, he was back.

Helen had already decided she was due for a slow day. Her coffee pot made a steady drip, drip, drip into her mug while she scrolled through her phone to check her calendar. Another appointment had canceled. 'Ladies, I'll be selling my first editions of your cases if we don't turn this situation around.'

'Let's not exaggerate.' Nora complained. 'For the record, we better solve this case soon. I have no intention of selling my fur coats or my silk shoes to help pay your bills.'

'Thanks for your help. I wish I could spend most of my days in lingerie.' Helen stroked her Costco robe. 'You're also independently wealthy.'

Back on her bed and sitting cross-legged with a steaming coffee mug in one hand, she clicked on her bedroom television and scrolled through the news. Disgusted, she flipped over to the latest True Crimes show. Rocky watched the introduction, then covered his eyes with his paws. She stroked his ears. "This is depressing, isn't it? I'm getting in the shower." She lowered the sound. The television screen flashed in the background while she traipsed back and forth from the bathroom to her closet.

A text popped up from Joe.

Change your mind about dinner with Emma?

Not happening. Have a nice time. Hope she's treating.

Not likely. Going to Beacon House.

Dirty play. Still a no.

The next *True Crime* episode flashed on the TV screen while she dug through her sweaters. A headshot caught her eye. She grabbed her remote and raised the volume. She hit reverse. Rocky whined at the foreboding narrator's voice. A crime in 1997 caught her eye. She stopped and played it back to the beginning. "Shush," she chastised Rocky as she plopped onto the edge of her bed.

The story headline read *Twenty-six years later, the FBI continue to seek elusive California bank robbers*. A stream of photos filled the screen as a retired special agent recited the details. "On Friday, May 14, 1997, two Sacramento California tellers entered First Federal Bank's vault, quietly stuffed $320,000 in a bag, and walked away from their old life. Not until Monday was their robbery discovered, giving them a two-day head start. Months became decades. Their haul is now valued at over three million dollars. Neither of the two men has been found."

'Ladies, what is it that feels familiar about this crime,' she declared. Helen googled the bank robbery on her laptop. Two head shots and the First Federal Bank building popped up on her screen. Another ten or so articles followed. She blew up the photos and printed them out. Her heart began to race. Next, she googled the recent headlines about Oscar Banyon's murder and printed his photo. She held the robbery photos from years ago next to Oscar today. She stared. "I'll be darned," she declared. She paced back and forth in her bare feet as she reached for her cell.

Dinner on with Wonder Woman. Digging through my closet. Between Agatha and Nora, we'll find an outfit.

You're impossible. What changed your mind?

Explain tonight.

???

Keeping you in suspense.

My life with Helen. Are they both coming with you?

Just Nora tonight. Agatha has a cold.

Pick you up at 6:30.

Helen stared at the television screen, mesmerized. "Am I crazy? Or brilliant?"

'Or lucky,' chimed Jessica. 'It's the basis of every case solved.'

Chapter Thirty-One

Beacon House was one of Helen's favorite restaurants. She knew Joe chose it to help entice her to come. The historic building sat on the edge of the C&D Canal, bridging the top of the Chesapeake with the Delaware River leading north thirty-five miles to Philadelphia's port. The two-story restaurant opened as a tavern and inn in 1829. Its centuries-old claim to fame was the 'Hole in the Wall Bar' with its entrance well below ground and lined with original brick. The name stemmed from a hole in the back of the bar where African Americans were served by reaching their hands inside to receive a drink. From May through October, visitors sat outside in the sun with the inn's famous Bloody Marys and took in the view. More than twenty-five thousand ships from around the world passed by Beacon House every year. Helen never got tired of it.

Emma was already seated with an Old Fashioned in her hand at a white-clothed table tucked along muntin-framed windows lining the enclosed second-floor porch. Joe pulled out a chair for Helen and sat down beside her.

"This is charming," Emma admired, glancing around at the candlelit tables.

"Keep your eyes on the cargo ships as they slide underneath the town bridge. You'll swear they're going to scrape their top deck as they pass under it. It's quite the optical illusion. I hold my breath every time," Helen said. "If you're on a sailboat, you flinch. You're sure your mast is going to be snapped in half."

A server handed them menus. "I'll have an extra dirty vodka martini, please," said Helen.

"Expecting a tough night?" asked Joe.

Helen made a sly smile. "We have a lot to talk about. Besides, it reminds me of Nora Charles. She loves a dirty martini."

"Joe told me you're a sailor."

"I am. I'm counting the months until I pull *Persuasion* off the hard and back in the water."

"I have a few D.C. friends who invite me on their boats each summer. I can't say I'm much help unless you count serving drinks from the galley."

"At least you've got the terminology right. And the most important job."

"Did Joe tell you why he suggested we get together?" Emma gave Joe a fond wink.

"I thought perhaps you wanted to elaborate on your dating history," Helen responded sweetly.

"I guess I deserved that," Emma said.

"The key word is history." Joe set down his menu.

Emma gave him a pained look of resignation. "From what I've heard, you've got yourself a stalker."

"I'm not sure what you'd call him, or her. Someone is out for revenge, although I don't know why. He's on a tear. I'm counting nine houses, one car keyed, and a horsewoman client hurt."

"Crimes without motive are some of the hardest ones to solve," Emma offered.

"Agatha Christie's Jane Marple would say there's always a motive, we just haven't found it yet."

Emma shot a quick glance at Joe. "I'll keep that in mind," she dryly responded.

Helen sounded disgusted. "Since January, the Sheriff's Office has been knocking on doors all over Kent County trying to catch my graffiti artist. I had my assistant, Tammi, comb through my sales records. We even went over my mailing list of people I know socially. Nothing."

"All because you can't figure out a motive," Emma reached for her drink.

"Jane's opinion exactly," Helen said. "Add Bill Elison and Oscar Banyon's murders, also my clients, and we've got a crime spree."

"Where's this leading?" asked Emma.

"I still believe Bill's death was probably accidental and covered up by someone in a panic."

"Or Bill's death ties into Oscar's," Joe insisted.

"We've been see-sawing the last two and a half weeks. We have no connection other than Bill stopping at the vineyard for their wine talks. The two murders appear completely unrelated."

"Except they were both your clients. It doesn't give you any motive for your slanderer either," Emma responded.

"Maybe I've been fooled. Maybe Oscar's killer planned this since January," Helen said. "Tammi made an interesting comment. She suggested I might be thinking about this all wrong. Oscar's killer knew Oscar had hired me to sell some of his land. He also knew I had a reputation for sleuthing when a client is in danger."

"So?"

"What if this person wanted to be sure I didn't have the time to get involved in solving his murder? I'm kept busy racing from house to house, client to client, trying to salvage my business."

"Seems like a lot of work to keep you off their trail." Joe looked doubtful.

"Planning a murder is a lot of work," Helen reasoned. "Remember what my Pro Con list is about? What my Detection Club taught me? Murder is based on greed, revenge, passion, envy. We have one killer, if not two, plus the vandal."

Their server arrived with their dishes. Emma ordered a bottle of red and three glasses.

Joe looked at Emma. "We've confirmed Bill, Georgia, and Todd increased their personal life insurance policies in December. Georgia and Todd's policies are $500,000 each. Bill increased his policy to one million."

"Those aren't crazy amounts, especially for business owners. They have families to protect," Helen responded.

"Agreed. I don't believe his million-dollar policy would make Bill feel threatened," Emma said.

"I still don't consider his daughter a suspect," said Helen. "Todd is a different story. He's unhappy, resentful. Hoping to find ways to make a quick buck."

"Find anything at the murder site to tie them in?" Emma asked.

"Tough to tell," Joe said. "They're family, so their DNA is all over his house. They're sticking to their stories. We also had our accountant go over Georgia and Todd's personal accounts. Nothing there."

They ate in silence, mulling over the details.

"Georgia told me Bill was in Oscar's house and vineyard at least once a week," Helen offered. "He checked on his staff's work. Apparently, the vineyard was one of Bayworks' largest accounts. When I met with Michele, I asked her about the tasting room's cleaning schedule. She told me Bill stopped by the Monday before he died and met with Oscar."

Emma chuckled. "Didn't she think it was an odd question coming from you?"

Helen glanced at Joe. "Do you remember the advice Calli from Tomes and Treasures gave me when Bill died? She said Bill's job gave him a lot of opportunity to see private, even damaging, information while he went through people's houses."

"You have a similar job," Emma acknowledged.

Helen nodded. "I made a bizarre discovery this morning. Bill might have learned a secret of Oscar's that could threaten his lifestyle, even his freedom. If it got out, Oscar would be done."

"I wondered when you were going to tell us why you came tonight," Joe said. "Here I was hoping it was my scintillating personality."

"You can always hope," Helen quipped. She turned to Emma. "I assume Joe told you I study old mysteries."

"I've heard about your Detection Club. A novel way to approach solving crimes. He told me you're a little obsessed."

"I consult with the best on all sorts of problems, not only crimes." Helen lifted her chin in defense. "Doctors and lawyers consult other experts every day. You've got yours, I've got mine."

Joe cleared his throat. "Now that you've explained your unusual fascination for women sleuths, what's this bizarre discovery?"

She eyed Emma. "I'm a restless sleeper. If I can't sleep and my eyes are too tired to read, I'll turn on a true crime program as a fallback. Or a classic British detective show."

Emma laughed. "An odd choice when you can't sleep. I'd be up all night. I'm more the Ambien or melatonin type."

"I'm particular about the true crime shows I watch. They can't be gruesome. I like to follow clues, not watch gore."

Emma stared at her. "You don't consider a vineyard owner sliced by his own wine bottle and a local businessman shoved down a set of stairs gruesome?" She raised her professionally shaped eyebrows.

Helen waved Emma away. "This morning, while I was getting dressed, I had a True Crime episode playing in the background. After the show ended, I searched online about the crime they aired." Helen reached into her bag and unfolded four sheets of black and white copy paper. She laid them out like a blackjack dealer with his fresh set of cards. "It took place in Sacramento, California, in 1997. Two young bank tellers, Oliver Epps and Warren Jackson, stole three hundred and twenty thousand dollars from the safe. In today's money, it's worth over three million. Have you ever heard of this bank robbery?"

Emma's eyes ran down the pages one by one. She passed them to Joe. She was quiet, eventually raising her head. "Yes, I have. We follow each other's cases, especially when they're interesting. About ten years ago, the FBI contacted the Baltimore police because a U.S. Marshal got a tip that one of these bank robbers might be hiding in the area. Joe and I started working together. But the lead went cold." She handed the sheets back to Helen.

"Why are you interested?" Joe asked.

Helen took her time pouring herself a glass of wine.

Joe narrowed his eyes. "You're stretching my patience. Not that it's the first time." He picked up the wine bottle and his empty wine glass.

"Patience makes the heart grow fonder," she volleyed.

The detective gritted his teeth. "I think the expression is 'absence makes the heart grow fonder.'"

"Close enough."

Chapter Thirty-Two

Helen drew another printout from her purse. "This is the first *Kent Whig* article about Oscar Banyon's murder, his vineyard, and me the day after he died."

Emma raised her eyes. "You *are* a local celebrity sleuth."

"See these articles about Oliver Epps and Warren Jackson and First Federal. Notice any similarities?"

The two cops studied each sheet.

"I believe Oscar Banyon was one of your Sacramento bank robbers," Helen continued, her voice earnest. "I believe Oscar was actually Oliver Epps."

Emma snorted. "Why in the world would you think that?"

"Don't be so anxious to discredit my theory." She ran an index finger from Oliver's face to the recent photo of Oscar. "In both photos, the men's ears tend to turn out a bit. Their noses are long and narrow. Compare the arch of Oscar's eyebrows behind his glasses."

Helen held the two photos up to the candlelight on their table, the photos turning translucent in the light. "This thief's eyebrows are shaped the same as Oscar's. His eyes slant down at the corners, same as Oscar's. Oscar was sixty-four when he was killed. The right age for an older Oliver." Helen handed them another photo. "I zoomed in and printed it. Look closely at Oliver Epp's neck above the collar of his dress shirt. There's a vague tattoo showing the outline of a grape."

"I'll be damned," Joe said. "Our coroner found a light grape tattoo below Banyon's left ear."

Helen set aside her glass. "It explains a lot about Oscar. He always wore a beret over his forehead, covering his left ear. Shawl sweaters and turtlenecks were his favorites, even in summer. He had a propensity for his over-the-top Frenchman act. You noticed it yourself, the Friday night you met him at the club. His wife told us he refused to travel outside the United States. I'm not a gambler, but I'll bet fifty dollars he never had a passport." She opened her phone and scrolled through her voicemail. "Listen to this message. It's from a friend of mine, Sarah Howard. She owns a local travel agency in town."

She held the phone up to Joe and Emma and hit play.

"Helen, I made a few calls and sent out a couple emails to some of my French contacts. One got back to me. Jean Paul's family goes back generations. They own a mammoth vineyard in the northern region, Oscar described as his homeland, and they know their competitors' history. Jean Paul says he's never heard of a vineyard owner by the name of Banyon. He also never heard of a vineyard owner whose son left them for the U.S. Not sure if this info is helpful but passing it along. Good luck. I'll call you if I hear more." Sarah hung up.

Joe narrowed his eyes. "Sounds like a stretch. I would imagine there's dozens of vineyards in northern France."

"I'm sure there are, but Jane Marple would never let it deter her," Helen retorted.

Emma made a face. "If there was a family split, Banyon may have decided to use a new name."

"True," Helen said. "Any honest guy with nothing to hide would use his respected family name when he opens his own vineyard. It opens doors. Why would Oscar pass up such an advantage?"

"It may be shortsighted, but many a family rift is never forgiven." Emma opened her phone and scanned Helen's articles.

"Okay, consider this," Helen said. "Oscar had an entire collection of photos and prints of French vineyards, churches, and old buildings covering his tasting room walls. When I asked him to tell me more about them, he changed the subject. I asked him about his French accent. He said he'd been in the States so long, his accent had altered. I don't believe it. I think he taught himself enough French to support his disguise. Want to bet he's not from France? Never been to any of those places?"

Helen's face flushed. "Another idea. I admired his tasting room bar wood. He told me it was a rare redwood he saw in a west coast restaurant and ordered through Dottie Taylor. This redwood species is indigenous to the west coast, specifically the Sacramento area, and the location of the robbery. My bet, he saw this redwood while working for First Federal?"

Emma looked doubtful.

Helen held up her hand. "Paula Banyon told me Oscar had never taken a trip to California in all the years they were married. If she's right, when did Oscar, I mean Oliver, see this redwood?"

Helen took a last bite and opened a copy of *Wine Gourmet*. "This is a magazine with international distribution I ordered from our library." She flipped to a full-color article on vineyard owners, state by state. "This was published last year. The only photo of Oscar Banyon is this tiny chance shot at a meeting. I tracked down the writer of this article and asked why Oscar wasn't interviewed with the other vintners in Maryland. He told me Oscar refused. You tell me, why would Oscar, who had an enormous ego, avoid such great publicity? Was he afraid he'd be recognized?"

Emma leaned closer.

"Don't believe me? Isn't this a perfect example of why true crime stories and tip lines are popular?" Helen pressed. "Is it possible someone around here discovered Oscar was an imposter? Bill read a magazine called *Unsolved Crimes* for years and sold the used copies to Rupert. He told his daughter one of the cases reminded him of a local crime. Before he died, he mentioned it to Rupert, too. Maybe Bill wasn't referring to a *crime* but a *criminal* because he recognized Oscar."

She paused. "Picture this. Bill's watching a true crime story on television. He's got a copy of *Wine Gourmet* magazine sitting on his coffee table. Later, he flips through an article about Maryland vineyards. Professional headshots of owners are lined up across the page. Oscar's photo is a casual shot, poorly lit and blurry, because he avoided the press. Bill notices a resemblance. He starts to wonder. He can't believe his eyes. After all, I had no reason to connect Oscar to a twenty-seven-year-old bank robbery either. Not until I happened across a television rerun featuring this robbery.

"If Bill threatened Oscar, Oscar may be his killer," Joe said.

"That's my bet."

"What about the partner?" Joe asked.

"They both went underground," Emma offered. "Law enforcement agencies never knew if the two men stayed together after the robbery."

Helen laughed. "You mean like Butch Cassidy and the Sundance Kid? Bank robbers and life-long partners?"

"From what I've seen, neither of these two resembles Robert Redford or Paul Newman," Emma lamented.

"Who does?" Helen asked. The two women laughed. "Did the two men split up? Maybe they thought it was safer if they each took their share and built separate lives."

"Definitely made it harder for law enforcement to track them," Emma replied.

A five-deck cargo ship entered their line of sight, its lights lining its hull under a cold, dark sky. It glided north past the Beacon House and up the narrow canal. They all went quiet, wincing as the ship glided under the bridge.

Joe caught their server's eye. "Coffee, please." He fingered the photos. "Until now we thought Oscar's killer was a local with some kind of grudge."

"That may still be the answer," Helen said. "My instinct is, whoever he is, Oscar's killer recognized him as a fraud and a criminal. He or she, don't forget, likely threatened to expose him unless they were paid to keep quiet."

Emma objected. "The blackmailer could have turned Oscar in to the authorities and claimed the fifty-thousand-dollar reward instead? A hell of a lot easier."

"You know as well as I do, greed can overrule logic. In today's world, fifty thousand is chump change. Why not go for the bigger payoff, a piece of Oscar's business? Oscar's lots alone could go for as much as four million. As a matter of fact," she paused, "maybe that's the real reason Oscar wanted to sell his lots. He never showed any serious interest until the last few months. Was a blackmailer bleeding him dry? Sorry, bleeding is probably a poor choice of words."

"I'll admit, this theory is tough on my ego," she said. "Now I wonder why he hired me. Did he hire me because I was the best Realtor? Or did he hire me because he was afraid a national broker's marketing might increase his chance of being recognized. He was between a rock and a hard place. He needed to stay incognito, but he needed to raise money?"

"Maybe Oscar decided he had to eliminate his blackmailer and planned their meeting in the barn. He misjudged their strength, they fought back, and he was killed instead," Helen said.

"I think it's likely his blackmailer never intended to kill him," Joe added. "I wonder how much Paula Banyon knows about Oscar's previous life of crime."

"I guess I've complicated your entire investigation, Detective," Helen smiled at Joe.

"And I don't see any connection to the vandalism of your other clients' properties." Joe reached for their check. "Bill's murder has to be tied into problems with Todd or Vince."

"I agree. My stalker is too amateurish, as if they're playing a stupid game. I'm feeling helpless, and helpless is not in *my* DNA."

Emma faced Helen. "Joe told me your deduction skills were unique. I underestimated you. If Oscar Banyon is Oliver Epps, we'll need to proceed with this investigation very, very carefully. Law enforcement agencies across the country have been watching for Epps and Jackson for years." Emma scanned the news articles. "Oliver Epps A.K.A. Oscar Banyon. This could be a major breakthrough," she whispered, glancing around the dining room.

She snatched the bill out of Joe's hand. "Given this conversation, the Bureau is covering dinner. I'll call my supervisor early tomorrow morning. He's not going to believe this development."

* * *

Helen spent the following morning at Safe Harbor working with Tammi by phone. By late afternoon, they'd created a newsletter update on the local market and double-checked client lists. Tag took over getting it downloaded and emailed out. Helen called all her graffitied clients to check on them.

She scheduled a meeting with Paula at five o'clock. Joe had texted earlier suggesting they meet at The Blue Crab in town at six o'clock. She felt more like her old self. At least it felt like a more normal day. Notes out to all her clients, and no phone calls coming in reporting more properties damaged. She flipped through her calendar. Not one new client appointment. Scary.

The temperature at four-thirty was hovering at eighteen degrees. The low February sun was boxing it out with the clouds. The clouds were winning. She scraped the frost off all her windows to give her Mini a head start, then started south.

The Blue Heron Vineyard sign seemed neglected and out of season. Maybe it's my frame of mind, Helen chastised herself. Her blue coupe, coated in salt and dirty snow, was grey and barely visible. It struggled past the bare trees lining the drive. She eased to a stop, her headlights exposing the dark house's first floor. She could pick out lights through closed draperies on the second floor. Her dashboard read four-forty.

She rang Paula's doorbell and listened to it echo through the house. One of those expensive chimes. Paula knew she was coming, so where was she now? Helen stomped around the side of the house and back. She peeked through a row of decorative glass along the four-car garage doors. IMSPECL was tucked inside, Paula's car beside it. She rang the front doorbell again. Footsteps. The lamp flipped on, and Paula leaned on the doorframe, her arms crossed.

"Helen, I've decided meeting isn't a good idea." She tugged on a beige cashmere sweater.

"I realize it's getting late, and you've had a difficult day. I wanted to drop off your paperwork on the lots and fill you in on a client who's showing interest."

Paula's eyes traveled to the folder in her hand. "What kind of interest?"

"Fairly serious." Helen tucked the folder back in her tote. "Why don't I call your attorney and go over the details with him? You don't need to be bothered."

Paula made an exaggerated groan. "You're already here. I might as well save on those greedy attorney fees." She whipped the folder from Helen's grasp and led her into her living room.

Questions finished, Paula set the file aside.

"Wine?"

"I'd love to, but it's getting dark, and these roads are hairy." Helen sat back. "Lizzie tells me Billie started at ShopTV. Congratulations."

"Thank you. My daughter is excited." Paula shrugged. "Who knows how long it lasts?"

"You've lived through so much tragedy. The death of three husbands is inconceivable."

Paula's arched eyebrows jumped another inch. "How did you hear?"

Helen tilted her head in sympathy. "This town doesn't hold many secrets. Tell me what happened."

"It hasn't been easy." Paula took a healthy dose of her wine. "My first husband died of a heart attack. He was only thirty-eight, and I was completely devastated. He was fit, ran every day, careful about his diet. We were a perfect match." She made a dramatic sweep of her hands.

"Was he Billie's father?"

"No, no. Billie's father was Martin. She was about four years old when he died. We'd decided to take a trip to tour the Grand Canyon. It was a beautiful, hot day, and we hiked to the southern rim." Paula's voice quivered. "Martin insisted on taking a couple pictures beyond the park barrier. I tried to warn him, but he was so stubborn. He lost his balance and fell off the rim. It was horrible. He was gone in seconds." She held her head in her hands. She sniffed and wiped her cheeks of non-existent tears. "And now, dear Oscar."

"More than any one woman should live through. I'm so sorry." Helen patted her knee. Here we go, she warned herself. Let's see how she reacts to my next questions.

"I've worked with people with all kinds of personalities over the years. There's an aura about Oscar that never felt right. It struck me as odd. We had a man born into a French winery family who never returned to his roots.

It's as if he was afraid to leave the U.S. Do you know why?"

Paula's glass stopped in midair. "Oscar was afraid of flying."

"Really?" Helen deliberately acted doubtful. "It's odd for a wine connoisseur, especially Oscar, a man of the world. With his money, his fear of flying could have been treated. I'm surprised you couldn't at least talk him into a cruise."

Paula pressed her lips together. "We all have our idiosyncrasies." She twisted her watch.

"I found the cover article in *Wine Connoisseur* magazine last fall fascinating. You remember, don't you? It covered all the top vineyards in the Mid-Atlantic region, including Blue Heron Vineyard. Yet not one good photo of Oscar. It's almost as if he avoided publicity."

Paula stiffened. "What are you insinuating?"

Helen made a poker face. "I keep wondering if he had a reason to avoid the press."

Paula flushed scarlet. "I'll talk to his publicist," she declared, rising to her feet. "It's nothing you need to worry about."

* * *

The bright coach lanterns at the barn door glowed an invitation like a siren calling as Helen walked to her car. 'Might be your last chance to walk around the casks,' whispered Nancy.

'You're a real estate agent. You've got a license to pry,' Nora urged.

'If I'm not careful, my license will get revoked,' Helen snapped back. 'I'm already on the public's Enemy Number One list.' Shifting gears, she parked in front of the barn.

The front door was locked. Hmm. She hustled back to the Mini and drove around to the rear of the building, and a door facing the water. She parked in the shadows under the overhang, flipped off the dome lights, then opened her door. From her glove compartment, she dug out her flashlight. She tapped in the digital password Oscar had given to her. The lock moved easily, and she stepped inside, grateful to be out of the cold. She shivered, keeping her gloves on. She flipped on the tasting room overhead lights and entered a different code to disarm the alarm system. She eyed Oscar's prints of France over the bar.

In the next room, hundreds of bottles of wine, stored in temperature-controlled areas, lined the perimeter. The concrete path toward the stainless-steel casks was open until she reached the rear, not far from where she'd found Oscar. The rows of containers stood like regimental soldiers waiting for their orders. She ran her hands lightly over them. Her flashlight stroked the gleaming steel hulks as they pointed upward. Smooth as a baby's butt. What was Michele talking about? There was no way she could have scraped her arm here.

A bit further along, yellow crime tape ran across the area and blocked her access. The scent of wine and blood hung in the air. She held her breath. She knew until Joe gave the go-ahead, Paula and Michele couldn't sanitize the crime area. Just as well it was taped off. She sure didn't want to contaminate any sand samples forensics might want. Turning off all the lights as she trotted toward the entry, she stopped to reset the alarm, then locked the rear door behind her.

Brrr. It's almost five-thirty. I should head into Port Anne to meet Joe, she told herself. 'All work and no play,' encouraged Nora. 'You're done here. Go warm yourself with a good glass of wine.'

Helen pictured all the racks and racks of wine inside, reaching to the ceiling. Water, water everywhere, and not a drop to drink. Who wrote that? 'Samuel Coleridge in his poem "The Rime of the Ancient Mariner",' said Jane Marple.

'You would be the one to remember that poem. It's too depressing,' Helen replied. She stepped out into the frosty air.

Helen's eyes roved down toward the frozen water's edge and Michele's carriage house apartment. A cluster of storage buildings was in the distance. She studied the sun. Holding her palm along the horizon, her sailor eyes told her she had less than thirty minutes of daylight. 'Let's hurry.'

'We're right behind you,' declared Nancy and Jessica.

"Yeah, right," Helen retorted out loud. "Curiosity killed the cat, remember?"

A carriage house lantern guided her down the winding, crusty drive. She knocked. A single-car garage attached to the house was empty. A bicycle leaned on one wall. Nice setup, she thought. Michele's wine master position came with a million-dollar view.

The next closest structure was only a hundred feet or so further along the fields. Four windows faced away from the tasting room barn. The door was locked. Standing on her tiptoes, her boots stiff, Helen scraped clean a spot of glass with her gloves. She cupped her hands around her eyes and peeked inside. Stacked along one wall in neat rows were eight-foot round tables and at least forty or so white folding chairs. Glass vases, hurricane lamps, and votives of various sizes filled another wall of wooden shelves. Event supplies, Helen surmised. This is fruitless. I've no idea what I'm trying to find, and my feet are blocks of ice.

'I say turn back,' Nora advised.

'There's only one more building,' Nancy coaxed. 'It can't be another fifty feet away.'

'You know I don't do cold,' Helen chastised her. She tipped her hand to the waning sun again. The sun might give her ten minutes before disappearing into the bay completely. A sliver of light from the moon barely cut through the night clouds, and a flock of snow geese plodded along the water edge, baying to each other.

'Go on, check it out. What do you have to lose?' Agatha urged. 'Can't take ten minutes.'

Helen marched across the spiky grass and snow, her flashlight pointing the way. "Wow. It's an icehouse," she breathed as she drew closer. She swore her words froze in the open air. Oscar never mentioned this. Three windowless walls, each about fifteen feet long by ten feet high and built with local blue-gray fieldstone, were buried into a natural earth berm. It mirrored the shape of a long lean-to, its rounded roofline shaped from stone set under a snow-covered mound. An ancient arched wooden door, originally hunter green, was worn to grey and fastened into the stone by heavy iron hinges. A glistening new padlock hung open from a latch in stark contrast to the hammered, rusted metal of the early Victorian era. Long dagger-like icicles draped off the roof and formed a glass curtain.

She pressed down on the door handle and swung the door outward, ducking inside. Someone had oiled the hinges. Her jaw dropped open as she reverently turned slowly around the room, illuminating the inside and four ice-coated stone walls. Pinholes in between the mortar and stone of the roof offered a meager scrap of light. A ceiling of wooden planks stuffed with straw had helped insulate the inside from the sun. Garden rakes, shovels, a gas leaf blower, and two plastic barrels filled the space. Three empty beer bottles were tossed on the floor. The summer lawn crew must use this place for afternoon breaks, she mused. Grabbing a rusted shovel, she propped open the door. She loosened her gloves and curved her fingers into her palms. I won't find clues for Oscar's killer in here. I sure pick the oddest places to search.

'Can't catch a killer from the comfort of your bedroom,' Nancy encouraged her.

The temperature can't be ten degrees in here. There's a reason this is called an ice house. She shivered. She took another spin around the wedge-shaped room, her flashlight poking into the corners. She stopped short at a large round well in the far corner, forming the ice storage pit. Her light picked up an iron grate near the bottom, which used to drain water away from the blocks of ice. She carefully backed away.

Hesitating, she reached down and ran her gloves across the stone floor. Bits of sand and mulch spilled from a couple bags of fertilizer. Could this be the grit we found in Bill's house? She kneeled, scooping a handful and dumping it into her coat pocket, zipping it shut.

A few slivers of light eked through the mortar cracks in the ceiling. Helen opened her phone. Five-forty. Let's go enjoy that hot meal Joe promised. The door creaked behind her, and she jumped up. A hooded figure, a black scarf covering their face, reached in and shoved her down onto the dirt floor along the pit's edge. Her flashlight went flying.

"Hey! What the hell!" Helen cried out. She dragged herself to her feet to hear the door slam shut. The padlock snapped.

She pounded her fists on the door. "Hey! Let me out! Let me out!"

'Snakes and bastards,' Agatha cursed for her.

Helen stood still, immersed in utter darkness, her heart pounding, grateful she hadn't fallen into the pit. She flipped on her cell light and ran her hands across the gritty floor to find her flashlight. Her cell picked up a gleam of stainless steel. She grabbed up the flashlight and pushed its switch. Nothing. She gave it a shake and heard the rattle of its lightbulb. Damn. Damn, damn, damn. Her phone read five fifty-eight.

The red-light indicator told her the battery was on its last leg. She hit Joe's number, but it failed to connect. You're on the water's edge in a building buried underground. Do you really expect to get cell service? Helen, how can you be so stupid? No one but her Detection Club was listening.

The winter sun disappeared from the cracks. The last visage of any light was gone, and the wind whistled in between the missing chinks of mortar. The snow geese bayed like hounds.

I swear, it's got to be another five degrees colder since I stepped inside. The dampness seeped through her leather boots and socks. She stomped her feet and tucked her hands under her armpits. Her breath hung in the chill. It's a refrigerator in here, she muttered to herself.

'Of course it is,' Nora spoke up. 'We're locked inside an ice house!'

Calm down, be logical, she chastised herself.

Maybe Joe will wonder where she is. She told him she was meeting with Paula. He'll never spot her car tucked against the rear of the barn in the dark. She paced in a circle as her cell light grew weaker. The battery gauge grew narrower. She was already feeling drowsy. She dropped to the floor and wrapped her arms around her knees.

You got into this God-forsaken mess, you'll have to get yourself out. Even if Joe wonders where you are, he could search for hours. You'll never live through the night in these temperatures. It was dropping by the minute.

Helen shook her head, trying to fight off her mental fog. "This ice house is a tomb. I'll be dammed if it's mine," she shouted. Carefully, she ran her hands along the rough stone around the perimeter of the room. She touched a round wooden handle. Her heart leaped. Grabbing it, she ran her fingers to the end, a set of long iron tines. That won't help. She felt for another tool, a rake. Worthless. Her hands ran down a shovel to a pointed tip. Gotcha!

"Here goes," she declared to the empty room. Only her Detection Club heard her. She ran her hands along the door, seeking the edge with the iron latch. Aiming the end of the shovel, she inhaled and lunged at the door. The shovel reverberated off the old wood planks, and her shoulder muscles protested in shock waves. The impact forced her to catch her breath, and the cold seared her throat. It left her gasping in pain. She lunged at the door latch again. It repelled her backwards, this time onto the floor and towards the pit.

This is one way to warm up, Helen thought. She got back onto her numb feet and felt around for the shovel. This time, she tried to make a running start. The door only creaked. She stood back and hesitated, catching her breath. Where's a wimpy hollow-core door from a cheap builder when you want one? She inhaled and charged at the door, the impact traveling up her arms to her shoulder sockets. She attacked again and again. The door creaked. She pulled her right glove off and felt along the latch. The wood was starting to splinter.

She hammered again and again until she heard the wood giving way, separating from the lock. She sweated in the cold.

Hope inspired her. She stepped back, then hurtled forward. "Give me liberty or give me death!" she cried. This time, the screws in the old hinge started to give way. She shoved again and again, and the door widened about twelve inches. She squeezed through, tearing her parka, and tumbled out onto the snow. She steadied her breathing, her hands on her knees. Gratefully, she stared up at the stars. Thank you, Lord.

She took off for her car, her heavy feet like clods. Her Mini was untouched. Panting, she climbed in and engaged the ignition. She locked all the doors, put her head back, and breathed in relief as the heat blasted. Her face hurt as it sensed the warmth. Her fingers and toes tingled. The time on her dashboard read a few minutes before eight, and the temperature read seventeen degrees. Joe must wonder where in the world she'd gone. She plugged in her cell charger, crawled down the lane with her headlights off, and dialed.

Chapter Thirty-Three

W here the hell have you been? I have three cars patrolling the streets for you. I drove out to Banyon's, but no one was there. Not one car in the lot. Your kids are calling me every twenty minutes."

Helen wasn't sure if he was furious or frantic. "I met with Paula, then I decided to check the outbuildings. I lost track of time."

"You lost track of time! In this weather? That's the worst excuse I've ever heard. Why are you panting? What in the world did you expect to find? My squad already searched every outbuilding the night Oscar was found dead."

"It was stupid, but I did. Besides, your squad was focused on murder clues, not old papers or stolen money. Where are you now?"

"At the station," he grumbled.

"Have you eaten, because I'm so hungry."

"You are unbelievable. Meet me at The Blue Crab. Their kitchen is open until nine. And don't get lost!" Joe shouted.

Helen gave him a meek "I won't. Be there in ten minutes."

* * *

Joe was already seated in a rear booth, beer in hand.

"Hi. I need to run to the restroom," Helen said, raking her fingers through her hair.

Joe took in her muddy jacket and her streaked makeup. "Your jacket is torn. What in the world were you doing for the past three hours, Miss Drew?

219

Digging ditches? And don't tell me it wasn't her who got you into this."

"I'll explain, but you're not far off. Can you order for me? A sirloin burger medium rare and fries. And a glass of Cabernet." Five minutes later, she was back. She tossed her tote onto the bench seat and collapsed across from Joe. She picked up the glass of wine and winced.

The detective studied her face and body movements. "Tell me right now. What were you doing, and why are you sore? You're breathing like your chest hurts. I have a feeling I'm not going to like your answers."

She lifted her chin.

"Don't try to give me a cocky Nora expression. I'm not falling for it." He glared as he emptied his glass. "Start at the beginning with why you're hoarse. I want details." His face was still bright with fury.

"Calm down. I'm fine." Helen inhaled. "I met with Paula to discuss a possible offer, then asked her about how her first two husbands died. She was obviously surprised I knew. Her explanations would sound suspicious to anyone with half a brain. When I asked her about Oscar and his past, she told me to leave. I think she knows about his bank robbery."

He shook his head. "You teased her like a bullfighter waving a red cape."

"After I left her, I decided to take another walk around the tasting room."

"Why?"

She raised her chin another indignant inch. "I thought I might notice a detail I'd missed. I stopped when I reached your yellow crime scene tape. I knew you were sending out forensics to get sand samples off the floor where I found Oscar."

"How thoughtful. Go on."

"I ran my hands across a couple of stainless-steel casks. They're perfectly smooth. Michelle lied to us."

"I know that. We already checked." Joe ordered another beer.

"Oh." Helen looked chastened.

"Then what?" Joe prodded.

"It was about five o'clock and still light out."

"Barely," he growled. "Sunset was at five thirty-two."

Helen reached for the ketchup and flinched.

Joe raised an eyebrow. "You can't even bend your fingers."

"Michele lives in the carriage house about a hundred yards from the barn. No answer. I spotted another small building and decided to check it out." She salted her French fries.

"Haven't you seen those buildings before?"

"No. Never needed to."

"This story is taking *far* too long."

Helen tried to ignore him. "I could see a tiny building closer to the water. An ice house. Did you know that in the eighteen and nineteen hundreds, ice was cut from the river and stored inside? There's a park near Ferry Point called Ice House Park. "

"Spare me the history lesson," Joe shot back.

"It was freezing inside. As I was poking around, the door opened and someone wearing a hood shoved me to the ground and locked me in. I shouted and shouted. No one came. I had no cell service, so I couldn't call you."

"How long were you shut inside?"

"About two and a half hours. I tried to keep warm by moving, but after the first hour, I was getting sleepy."

Joe's face was livid. "Do you realize people can die of a heart attack when their body temperature keeps dropping?" He finished off his beer and thumped the empty glass on the table.

She ignored him. "I found a shovel with a pointed end and beat at the door." She gave Joe a sweet smile. "The latch finally gave way, and I was able to push open the door."

"You are lucky you didn't freeze to death, which I assume was your attacker's objective. It's why your shoulders hurt, isn't it?"

She avoided his eyes.

Joe reached for her hands. "Your fingers are stiff. Where did you get the scrape on your cheek?"

Helen touched it. "Must have been the fall. Lucky my down jacket had so much padding." She popped the last of her fries into her mouth and reached for her wine. "This wine is doing a good job of taking off the edge. Let's talk

221

about who might have locked me in."

"My bets are on Paula or Michele. Either one could have followed you."

"I agree." She dug out her journal. "Can we revise my Pro Con list?"

Joe stood up. "Only if you come back to my house and get into a hot bath."

She smiled. "Only if you send out someone from your squad to check inside the ice house. If we're lucky, they'll spot some footprints other than mine or prints on the door lock."

"I'm sure they wore gloves."

"I do feel pretty achy."

Joe signaled for their check and helped her into her coat. When they reached the front door of the restaurant, he wrapped his arms around her. "Let's go home," he breathed into her damp hair.

* * *

Joe's cell rang about ten o'clock. "Emma, what's up? I have Helen here on speaker. Mind if she listens in?"

Emma hesitated. "As long as she knows this is between the three of us."

"Absolutely," Helen spoke up from his couch. He'd wrapped a wool blanket around her. His fireplace was stoked.

"The FBI and State Police plan to knock on Paula Banyon's door late tomorrow afternoon with a warrant to search the property for any information Oscar hid concerning the Sacramento bank robbery. We need your squad covering the perimeter. At this stage, we can't bring Paula or her daughter in for questioning. I'm sure they'll act shocked and claim they knew nothing about Oscar's past. I want to prove Paula is an accessory to hiding a fugitive, but that's down the road."

"We'll be there." Joe glanced at Helen, her chin buried under his purple and black Ravens sweatshirt, the cuffs pulled down over her fingers. "Someone locked Helen in the Banyons' ice house down near the water. They might be sniffing around tomorrow morning, hoping she's dead from hypothermia. We'll check early tomorrow in case they left any trace."

"My God. How did she get out?"

222

"She beat at an old wooden door with a shovel. Took her about three hours to break through."

Helen was giving him downcast eyes and pouting lips. He shook his head. "She's sulking because she can't be with us when the warrant is served."

"I realize she's the one who helped break open this case, but we can't have civilians there. We'd both be hung."

"Agreed."

"I'll text you tomorrow to confirm our exact warrant time," Emma said.

"I'll line up our people. Good night."

Joe set down his phone. "You still look cold. Can I help?"

Helen pulled him down onto the couch. "You most certainly can."

* * *

Tammi called Safe Harbor early the next morning. "Thought I'd check in. How's Tag doing?"

"He's feeling his oats. Agatha Raisin would never put up with him. Jane Marple probably would. She'd be a lot more patient with trainees. Right now I'm eating a day-old donut from the office kitchen." She tossed the crumbs into her wastebasket. "I heard back from his former broker. Tag said his parents owned a farm, and he sold it after they died. His boss said Tag's dad never owned it. He worked as a field hand. Thought they always struggled. Tag got his license but was restless and decided to move east. Kind of bothers me, Tag's story didn't exactly match up."

"Sounds to me as if his family led a hard life, and Tag would rather keep it to himself. Can't blame him for that," Tammi said.

"You're probably right. It takes guts to build a new life. Still…" she went silent.

"Still? Out with it."

"Jane Marple wouldn't agree. She always advises me against being too trusting."

"Let's talk about Monday night. It's a lot more fun."

Helen laughed. "I met the FBI's answer to Cat Woman for dinner at the

223

Beacon House. With Joe."

"Must have been cozy," Tammi said dryly. "The three of you."

"Dinner went better than I expected, although she dressed for action, and I don't mean SWAT gear."

"Did you?"

"I wore my new black knit dress, long silver earrings, and borrowed Agatha's four-inch red heels. I think I blew her socks off. Or more accurately, leggings. Of course, I was miserable since I hate heels. I kicked them off as soon as we sat down."

"Good job. That's why I wear big earrings instead of heels. Always fit perfectly."

"Is this phone tapped?"

"Yes," replied Tammi. "I'm recording our conversation. The U.S. Army Intelligence believes you're hiding Russian plans to infiltrate the Chesapeake Bay." Tammi chuckled. "Come on, tell me all the juicy details."

Helen lowered her voice to a whisper. "I hit paydirt. I believe Oscar was a fraud, a total fake."

"What!"

"Shush. People can hear you from Texas." Helen glanced up. "I'll have to fill you in later. Someone's at my door."

"You're leaving me hanging?" Tammi protested.

"It's your fault for moving out of Port Anne. Talk later."

Chapter Thirty-Four

At ten a.m., she met Joe at the top of the drive to the vineyard. Together, they drove his Explorer down the hill to Michele's carriage house.

"She's home. Let's see her reaction to you being alive and well." Joe gave Michele's front door a loud knock.

"Coming!" Feet padded from inside. "Oh! Hello, Detective. Can I help you?" She tussled her dark hair off her brow with a sexy little gesture. Her hand stopped in midair as Helen stepped out from behind Joe. She blinked. "Helen, I'm surprised to see you."

"Hi, Michele." Helen made a big smile.

"Can we come in?" Joe asked, his tone telling her she had no choice.

"Um. Of course. I'm getting ready to leave for the barn. I have a staff meeting to run." Michele stepped back and gestured them into the tiny hall. "Any news on Oscar's killer?"

"Not yet, although we're getting closer. I'm surprised you aren't keeping your doors locked."

Joe and Helen's eyes traveled down to her stockinged feet and two pairs of wet boots placed on a mat.

Michele caught their glance. "I'm glad you're here, Detective," she said, crossing her arms. "I took a walk down to the water this morning. Someone broke into our ice house. I can't imagine why. Did a real hatchet job."

Helen spoke up. "It was me. I met Paula yesterday afternoon. I decided to see your outbuildings. Do you use them often?"

"We use them for storage. Come in handy when we have outdoor events.

Our fieldworkers store fertilizer and tools in the ice house. Why did you break in?"

"I was admiring it. The door was unlocked, so I stepped inside."

"Must be awfully cold in there. Bad enough in July," Michele said. She fidgeted with her watch.

"Worse if someone locks you in," Joe glared.

Michele's head shot up. "Are you saying someone locked you inside? In this weather?"

Helen stepped closer. "Someone shoved me to the ground and locked the door. Left me to freeze to death."

The young woman's face flushed. "That's horrible."

"Michele, where were you last evening between five thirty and six?" Joe studied her, his voice calm and cool.

"I met a friend in town."

He opened his pad. "I need their name and contact information."

"You're not suggesting I locked her inside, are you? I wasn't around."

The detective ignored her question. "The name, please."

She stuttered. "Tag Stolz. You've met him. Detective, why in the world would I want to lock Helen inside our ice house? That's insane."

"Her attacker wore a hood and black scarf across their face. Did you notice anyone near the ice house before you left here or after you returned?"

Michele shook her head. "I came home about nine-thirty and went straight to bed. Are you sure it wasn't a prank?" She turned to Helen. "I'm relieved you're okay. I'll have one of our workers padlock the door today. You shouldn't have gone by yourself."

"Thanks for the advice," Helen replied dryly. "I heard you have a history of pulling pranks. You couldn't work on a Mancuso vineyard even if you wanted."

Michele took a step back. Her eyes narrowed. "Where did you hear that nasty piece of gossip?" she sputtered. "My disagreements with my father were strictly teenage growing pains. I'm here because I want to be and getting paid well for my efforts." She drew in a breath.

"Have you and Paula decided to run the vineyard together?"

"I'm now her general manager and winemaker." She brightened up. "We're sending out invitations to our March opening and the first tasting of our new red soon."

"Sounds exciting. I'm glad for you." Helen eyed the detective. "Should we check the ice house?"

"You bet." Joe lifted his eyes to the ceiling. Floorboards squeaked above their heads. He stared at Michele, his tone impatient. "I was waiting for you to tell me. Did you think I didn't know? Who's your visitor?"

Michele was indignant. "Tag. He stopped in this morning. Is that a problem?"

"Not at all. Keep your eyes out for someone who doesn't belong on the property. And lock your door."

"Thank you, officer." Michele plastered a sweet smile across her face.

* * *

"Let's peek inside her garage," Helen pointed.

Joe strode to the other side of the garage and peered through the glass. "A black Chevy truck."

"Tag. I guess their trip to Baltimore wasn't a one-off."

"Not against the law. Let's get to this ice house."

"Just ahead," she pointed. "The door is hanging on one hinge."

Joe chuckled. "You sure beat the hell out of it."

"Desperate times call for desperate measures."

"No trace of your assailant. We had a dusting of snow overnight. I can bring out forensics, but chances are in this cold the person was wearing gloves."

She kicked at the frozen dirt floor. "Check this out. I put a handful in my pocket last night. Does it remind you of anything?" She tugged on a bag of fertilizer stacked in a corner and reached for the iron pick. "Punch this open for me."

Joe stabbed the tines through the heavy plastic, and silt leaked onto the floor.

VILLAIN IN THE VINEYARD

"Is this the same sand we saw at Bill's house?"

The detective sifted the silt through his fingers. "Hard to tell. Let's make it official." He removed a plastic bag from his jacket pocket and filled it. "No need to stand in the cold." He tugged on the broken door.

"Whoever locked me in knew it was a death sentence. Ten bucks, it was Paula after our conversation. But how would a killer track this grit onto their shoes?" She rubbed at her sore arm and took in the room one more time. "Question. Michele said she's continuing to work with Paula and getting paid well. That's quite an attitude adjustment. What if Paula is our killer and Michele made it easier for her to meet Oscar in the fermentation area?"

"Couldn't Paula follow Oscar there on her own?"

"I don't think Oscar's whereabouts were easy to track. Michele might have turned off the security system and acted as Paula's lookout. In this weather, visitors are scant, but there's always delivery trucks in and out. If one of her crew walked toward the building, she could deflect them from entering."

"Which would make Michele an accessory to murder," Joe said. "Let's hope our interview with Paula and Billie helps us prove Oscar's true identity. I'll take this sample back to forensics." A text buzzed. "Sand mix in Bill's house doesn't match silica sand at the sports arena."

"That doesn't eliminate Todd or Vince. They were both trying to force Bill into doubling his life insurance. Vince was losing his house. Couldn't make the payments. Todd needed money. Why else would he set fire to his own boat, and Vince file the false claim? I guarantee you, Todd paid Vince to smooth over an investigation."

Joe dropped her off in front of the main barn.

She unlocked her coupe. "Did I tell you a contractor complained to a club member about our bidding process? He underbid our roof job and still didn't get it. Oscar was right. Vince padded club bills and pocketed the difference. They could have argued at the vineyard. Vince lost his temper and killed him."

Joe started to pull away, stopped, and threw the Explorer into reverse. He lowered his car window next to Helen's. "Emma texted me. The search is delayed. Scheduled for tomorrow, four o'clock. Please, do us both a huge favor. Stay at your office or go home. We don't want you within five miles of the vineyard." He took off down the lane.

She made a half-hearted salute, sat back, and stared out to the bay. No way I'm sitting home and sucking my thumb, she swore to herself. 'Let's go, chums. Let's check out Bill's safe.'

'Darn right,' they chorused.

The Mini crept down Lara Cove Road toward the water and Bill's. Helen didn't want to run into Todd. "The coast is clear." She said it out loud, smiling to herself. She'd always wanted to say that phrase. Inside, she locked the door behind her and moved through the house with her flashlight. She went directly to his office, closed all the shades, and switched his desk lamp on low. If Todd came by, she didn't want him to see any light.

Photo albums, bowling team certificates, and more family pictures sat on decorative shelves. In the opposite corner, Bill had Rupert's *Unsolved Crimes* magazines stacked inside a wooden box. 'Never realized how popular these were,' she breathed to her chums. One by one, she opened each cover and ran her finger down the list of articles. She stopped to chastise herself. Don't make this more complicated than it is. Concentrate on the missing issue. March 2014 is not in this pile. Maybe Bill never had it.

Four cabinet doors ran beneath his bookshelves. She opened each one. The door at the far corner exposed a safe about two feet wide and two and a half feet high with a digital dial. Helen dug into a zippered pocket and read Georgia's slip of paper. Twenty-seven, fourteen, eight, nineteen. She inputted the numbers, hit Enter, and the door swung open. Helen's heart raced.

Three yellow envelopes, four jewelry boxes, and a plastic box holding about twenty gold coins. Bill's handwriting in black marker labeled the first envelope 'Copy, Will 2023'. The next one was labeled 'To Georgia'. The third was blank. She opened the metal tab. Her hands began to shake. Slowly, she slid out a copy of *Unsolved Crimes* magazine. It was dated March 2014. Oh my God! She'd found the missing magazine. She sat back on her heels and stared.

The cover story read, "Where Are They Now?" It was a summary of famous unsolved cases from across the U.S. with excerpts from the original stories produced over the years. Two-inch square photos ran down the outside of the page. Oscar's face stared back at her. The same photo she'd seen on the *True Crimes* TV show about the Sacramento bank robbery and Oliver Epps. The narrow chin, the long-shaped ears, the hint of a tattoo of grapes under the shirt collar. His partner in crime, Warren Jackson, was pictured next to him dressed in a dark suit jacket. He had a broad forehead, a rounder nose and full mouth,.

Now she knew. Bill wasn't visiting Oscar because of his love of wine. He was visiting to study him. To learn more. He suspected Oscar was Oliver Epps. Once Bill was sure, did he threaten Oscar? Press him for money? Oh, Bill. You should have known better. You were tangling with a desperate criminal. He'd built his own kingdom over the years, and he wasn't going to let you bring it down.

Hastily, Helen returned the rest of Bill's belongings to the safe and clicked it shut. She slid the magazine into the envelope, buried it at the bottom of her bag before checking the room one last time. Was everything back as she'd found it? She turned on her cell light, switched off the desk lamp, and opened the blinds. In the kitchen, she peeked between louvered blinds to the drive. She was alone. She let herself out the door, locking it behind her, and scuttled toward the car in the dark.

Chapter Thirty-Five

A snow plow was cleaning up Safe Harbor's driveway when she arrived about eleven. Helen collapsed behind her desk and stared at the envelope and her Pro Con list. She opened her door.

"Tag, are you working at Five and Dime today?"

"Going there now. Thought I'd move some shelves, but I've got to close the shop early. How was your visit with Rupert?"

"Good. He's feeble but hasn't lost his spunk."

"Does he know who hit him?"

"Not a clue. I've got a question for you. When you're reading those *Unsolved Crimes* magazines, have you ever come across a story about two bank robbers in California named Jackson and Epps?"

"Bank robbers? You mean Bonnie and Clyde types?"

Helen raised her eyebrows. "Not that old, or that violent. I'm trying to find any information on them. They disappeared after the robbery back in 2002. The Feds never caught them."

He looked puzzled. "Why do you care?"

"Bill Elison told Rupert he thought a fugitive might be here in the area. I saw a TV show, and it made me wonder if Bill was talking about one of the bank robbers."

"That would be bizarre, don't you think?"

"They had to hide somewhere."

He shrugged. "It's a big country. I think your imagination is getting away from you."

"I guess all my unhappy clients are pushing me over the edge. By the way, how'd you do with the seller you met yesterday?"

"Great. The house is in good condition and should sell fast."

"Nice. Congratulations. Isn't that your third agreement in the past five weeks? Pretty good for a new guy. You're on a roll."

"This last one was pure luck. The seller called in looking for an agent."

* * *

A little after two, her door opened. Joe set a brown paper carton on her desk.

"I wasn't expecting you here." She smiled. "Aren't you getting ready for the big reveal tomorrow?"

"I was hungry. Stopped at Prime and Claw. Rib eyes with horseradish on toasted subs."

"Exactly what the doctor ordered." Helen laid out the sandwiches and inhaled. "I've got a present for you and Emma too." She slid the *Unsolved Crimes* article across the desk. "We already know Oscar was one of the FBI's missing bank robbers. Now I'm convinced Bill recognized Oscar. It's what got him in trouble. This is the missing magazine with an article about the California bank robbery."

"Where did you find it?" Joe's eyes darkened.

"It was locked inside Bill's home safe. Don't get mad. Georgia gave me permission to look. I may have watched an old rerun of the crime, but Bill discovered it months ago in his magazine collection. That's how he recognized Oscar as Oliver. We can't prove it yet, but I think he accused Oscar. Maybe he even tried to blackmail him. Oscar decided to come to Bill's house and shut him up."

"Bill tangled with the wrong man."

"Absolutely. A desperate man. He'd kept his crime hidden for over twenty-seven years, and now Bill was threatening him with exposure. Emma learn anything new?"

"It's FBI business."

"Don't be so tight-mouthed. I deserve more details. Without me, Emma and every law enforcement agency would still be wandering around the countryside trying to solve a cold case. If I'm right, you and she will be national heroes."

He chuckled. "Let's not get ahead of ourselves."

"You're such a sweetheart, Detective."

"And you're so annoying." He inhaled an onion ring. "I have information on your sand. I think you'll like it."

"Is it as good as this steak sandwich?" she mumbled.

"Depends upon your priorities. The sandy mixture in Bill's house matches the bag of soil from your favorite ice house."

Helen almost choked. "How did you find out?"

"Forensics sent the sand sample out to a viticulturist."

"A what?"

"They're experts in the nutritional needs of vineyards. The sample from Bill's floor is silt loam. It's a mix to imitate soil from the Bordeaux region of France."

"Perfect for growing Michele's new red blend and not a substance other people would have. Someone tracked silt loam from the vineyard to Bill's kitchen." Her voice rose. "Hard to believe it was carried all the way from the ice house."

"My bet, it's all over the property. In this weather, we're all wearing boots with grips on the soles."

"Can you check the soles of Oscar's boots?"

"Already at the lab. I'm betting that silt was in your cut."

"Two problems with your theory. If Oscar killed Bill, why was Vince there?"

"As much as I don't like Vince, I don't think he killed Bill. He was at the house, argued with Bill, but left him alive. Oscar arrived later." Joe rubbed his chin. "The second problem remains. Who killed Oscar and why?"

Helen tapped on her Pro Con journal. "We're back to motivation. Is it fear, anger, envy, greed? In my mind, Paula fits any of these perfectly."

"Any chance Todd knew Oscar killed Bill and wanted revenge?"

"Doesn't fit. There was no love between Todd and his father-in-law. With

Bill dead, Todd gets his share of the insurance a lot sooner. Oscar did Todd a favor. I'm betting on Paula or Michele or the two together. Paula could lose Oscar's money if they divorced. Michele, if she were seeing Oscar, was afraid he wouldn't divorce Paula. Maybe they decided to team up. Let's face it, Paula eliminated husband one and two. Talk about a black widow. Jane would say a third coincidence is pointing to a truth."

Joe balled up his napkin and tossed it into her wastebasket. "Let's hope Emma gets Paula to talk when she delivers that warrant."

"It's a long shot. Paula's tough. If she can talk her way past two dead husbands, she'll keep her mouth shut now. Could she lose the vineyard?"

"The Statute of Limitations on the robbery has run out as a federal crime, but she's got plenty to worry about. She harbored a fugitive, and the state can file charges for possession of stolen property and money laundering. That means jail time. The IRS, along with First Federal, can file for late fees and interest earned from the original stolen funds. After all these years, it's a pot full of money."

"Wish I could be there to witness the shock on her snotty face when you knock on her door," Helen grumbled.

Joe chuckled. "No begging. I'll call you when it's over." He grabbed his coat and leaned over to give her a kiss.

"I'll walk you out."

Joe took in the Valentine decorations strung around the front door. "You realize Valentine's Day was yesterday."

Helen grimaced. "We've been busy."

"You're the only woman I know who would excuse forgetting Valentine's Day."

"I promise. Payback will be hell."

* * *

Stella was in the lobby. It was close to four.

"Stella, you working the front desk? Where's your help?"

"I sent everyone home early. The roads are icing up."

234

Helen studied Stella's pale face. "You look worried. What's on your mind?" She leaned over the front desk. "Come on, you've never held back on me before."

"Okay. Call me crazy, but I've been in this business a long time. I can't help but notice Tag's business has picked up a lot since December. He had another new buyer in here early this morning."

"I'm glad he's doing well. Is it a problem?"

"I'm surprised he scooped you on the cute Bayside ranch. You've worked in that neighborhood for years."

"I've been a little distracted. Exactly which house did he list?"

Stella shifted her computer screen toward Helen. "It's number fifty-two. Owners' names are Philip and Julia Norton."

Helen raised an eyebrow. "I've worked with Julia's parents for years. I wonder why Julia didn't call me?"

"Let me show you another buyer contract he gave me last week." Stella clicked open a list of company transactions and scrolled down the clients' names. "Teresa and Ronald Schluter."

Helen sat back. "Are you serious? I called them about three weeks ago. They were on vacation, and we planned to meet when they got back." She tossed her bag onto the counter. "Well, I'll be darned. Can you pull up all Tag's sales for me?"

Stella opened four more transactions.

"Every single sale is connected to my repeat clients. I can't believe this." Helen stared at the computer screen.

"Coincidence, I think not," Stella declared primly.

"You're beginning to sound like Miss Marple."

"I knew you'd say that." She couldn't help but eke out a smile. "You're rubbing off on me." Worry lines took over. "I should have told you sooner. I wasn't sure until I overheard a call come in yesterday on Tammi's old number. He's picking calls up for you, isn't he?"

Helen's eyes snapped. "He sure is. The weasel. All while I'm fighting off alligators to keep my business afloat. What happened?"

"The caller asked for you. Tag told her you were tied up with the police because a serial vandal is targeting your clients. The woman hadn't heard a word about them."

"Let me guess. He fills her in. He plays real coy and apologizes for letting my problems slip out. In a matter of minutes, she's asking if he can help her instead." Helen started to pace. She stopped, her arms tightly crossed. "Does this sound likely? Tag came into town and picked out his target, a busy agent with enough business that it takes a month or two for her to notice a downturn. The target happened to be me. When Tammi gave notice, his plan got even easier."

She flung her bag over her shoulder and straightened her stance. "I'm going home, pouring myself a large glass of cabernet, and writing his Letter of Termination. He's lucky I don't press charges."

She put an arm around Stella. "Thank you. Thank you very much. Come on, let's lock up together."

* * *

Her sailboat, *Persuasion*, sat up on high metal jacks in McFadden's boatyard. She swore it was shivering in the cold when she parked next to it. A heavy grey canvas cover from bow to stern kept off the snow. Helen dragged a ladder from underneath a neighboring boat and leaned it against *Persuasion's* stern. She climbed up into the cockpit, loosening the tarp and ducking underneath. The wind howled a bit less. Unlocking a padlock, she lifted up the three sections of glossy teak planks forming the hatch cover. She'd lovingly revarnished the teak last fall. Climbing down the narrow companionway stairs inside, her heavy boots were clumsy compared to her summer Crocs. She dropped into the cabin and flipped on the boat's battery power for lights.

"Hello, old friend." She ran her hands along the chart box before collapsing onto one of the couches. She needed to think, alone. She was desperate for a safe place. No Tammi, no Joe, no Shawn, and Lizzie. She'd had business conned from her by an unscrupulous agent or two over the years. Thankfully, it was rare. Never had she been taken in by someone working at her elbow.

Tag had systematically used his access to her personal records and client calls to steal her business. He'd acted without guilt. And as someone who too often laid guilt at her own feet if anything went wrong, Helen was devastated. She'd been so busy contending with graffitied houses and violated clients, she'd been played. She'd lost her confidence. She'd ignored her instincts.

Persuasion's cabin was bone-chilling, its walls of thick fiberglass made for cutting through water, not insulating her from a cold world. She opened a cabinet and pulled out a Coleman aluminum coffee pot and flipped on the two-burner propane stove. It was the only source of heat in an otherwise winterized boat. A Maxwell House can held three last scoops of coffee. Hot water percolating through a glass top sent a small plume of comfort into the cabin.

Helen dug inside a cubbyhole and found Andy's old wool blanket with a Navy insignia. She wrapped herself into a cocoon with her insulated mug. Was stealing clients all Tag did? A vision of paint splashes stuck to his hands flashed before her. Darn you, Helen. You've fixed up a zillion houses. You know better. No one can paint an outside door in weather like this. Her mind traveled over the past three months of warned-off clients and nasty online gossip. She couldn't count the number of sleepless nights. Tag fit the police profile. He was wiry and lithe, easily able to slip in and out of strangers' houses to leave torn cards and slander behind. His tech skills made it easier to disrupt security cameras and post embarrassing comments on chat sites and online local news.

"I was an easy target," she shouted to the empty cabin. He left her to scurry around town, trying to salvage her reputation while he coerced her buyers and sellers.

Helen dialed Tammi. "I don't have time to explain, but Tag is our stalker."

"That can't be possible!" Tammi sputtered.

"It definitely is. I need for you to go into our business accounts and software programs and change all our passwords. We have to shut him down."

"Where are you?"

"I'm sitting inside *Persuasion*."

"It has to be a meat locker in there."

"Pretty much," she agreed. "Can you change our passwords right now? I'm about to fire him. He's vindictive enough to make one last stab at accessing our client information, maybe even delete all our data."

"I'll start right this minute. There's at least twelve or fifteen sites. I'd better change passwords on your Instagram and Facebook, too. Take me at least an hour. Did you tell Joe?"

"I can't bother him today," Helen said. "Emma and Joe are preparing to serve a search warrant to Paula Banyon tomorrow."

"You need to stay away from Blue Heron."

"Joe sidelined me and all my sleuths."

"I'm glad. I'll text you after Tag's completely blocked."

Chapter Thirty-Six

A t ten a.m. the next morning, Helen sent Tag his Letter of Termination with copies to Stella and Tammi. *"You've been caught. I want you out of Safe Harbor. Collect your personal belongings in the office no later than eleven o'clock. I've filed a complaint with our Board of Realtors and the state real estate commission. Leave your keys to the office and Five and Dime with Stella. I'll inform Rupert. The Sheriff's Office will be knocking on your door as a person of interest for vandalizing houses."*

Tag sauntered in about twenty minutes later. He filled a backpack as Stella glared over his shoulder. He flashed Helen an insolent glare on the way out, slamming the door.

Helen called Rupert's floor nurse. "Can I ask you to contact me if a young man, medium height, slim with longish hair, stops in to visit Rupert? I'm afraid he may want to hurt him." The nurse agreed to make a note for his chart. "Thank you very much."

She texted Joe.

Fired Tag this morning. Nervous about Rupert's safety. Can a deputy watch his room? Explain later.

Between Stella and Tammi, they put together a list of Helen's clients who might be working with Tag. She started making phone calls explaining her suspicions. Time crawled by. About two-thirty, she decided to call it a day and wait to hear from Joe.

"Stella, you can catch me at home if you need me."

* * *

239

But she couldn't stay away from the vineyard. Her chums wouldn't let her. When she reached the lane leading toward the Banyon property, two Sheriff's Office black and gold SUVs flanked the entrance. A deputy approached her coupe.

"I'm sorry, ma'am. You can't enter now. You need to leave the area."

"Oh! Of course, Officer. I'll turn around." Helen made a three-point turn and considered her options. She'd lived and worked on these private roads her entire life. A hundred yards south, she spotted a pull off into the park and prayed the Mini wouldn't get stuck in a snowbank when she tucked the car among the evergreens. It was after three. She reached for some stale Twizzlers from her glovebox to calm her nerves. Three unidentified sedans drove past her, followed by two black Ford Explorers. She recognized Joe as he climbed out and spoke with his deputies. He didn't look in her direction. He continued through the gates and down the Banyon private lane.

More activity, more vehicles silently crept forward. Helen slunk down behind the wheel and held her breath, praying no one would notice her. She opened her journal and paged through her notes. Her title *Motive plus Opportunity equals Murder* ran across the page. She had two lists, one for Bill and one for Oscar. Under Bill's name, she'd written Oscar, Vince, Todd. She added Paula. She circled Oscar's name. She was sure Bill had accosted him with the truth. Joe was right all along. Bill's death wasn't accidental. Oscar knew he had to eliminate Bill. Did anyone else know? Under Oscar's name, she'd written Paula, alone or with Michele, Billie, Todd, Vince.

Her mind traveled back over the past three months. Firing anyone never came easily to Helen. She was all about believing in second chances, but firing Tag was easy. She should have followed her first instincts. Realtors enjoyed being with people. They chatted around the office coffee pot. They brought in donuts for the sales team. They shared information. Tag did none of that. He was always friendly but kept anything personal close to the vest. She'd written him off as new to Port Anne and new to the office, shy.

Why was Tag so determined to steal her clients? So much work. Such a complicated effort sneaking in and out of neighborhoods and dodging the police. All to discourage clients from using her. He turned it into a game of cat and mouse. It worked, she thought bitterly. She tapped on the cold, dark window glass, her face reflecting in the dark. Some clients went elsewhere. He didn't get all her business, but what was his end game? It had to be bigger.

Tag must have known she'd catch up with him. It was only a matter of time. She opened the envelope from Bill's safe with the *Unsolved Crimes* issue and ran her cell phone flashlight up and down the pages. The words March 2014 leaped out.

Four o'clock ticked by. Her teeth chattered. She stamped her feet and curled her toes. She took a chance, started her car, and threw on a blast of heat. She studied the faces of Oliver Epps and Warren Jackson again. Two men, appearing young and innocent in their First Federal banking suits. Oscar, with his grapevine creeping barely an inch above his collar, his narrow chin. Warren Jackson, with a broad forehead, full lips, and square jawline.

Helen only had one bar of service. She pulled up the photos of all the Safe Harbor agents on the company website. Her search crawled through Google. She opened Tag's photo and held the phone screen next to Warren's photo in the magazine. Helen's hands began to shake. She remembered Tammi's comment about Tag's appearance. "He's cute. Thin. Has a kind of Elvis mouth and jawline." Tag's broad forehead, square jaw line, and full mouth were a mirror image of Warren's.

She sat back. I'll be darned. Tag searched for months to find this one missing issue, March 2014, the one Bill had in his safe. He'd been more than curious; he was relentless for one reason. He was Warren Jackson's son. All the pieces finally fit together. Tag had been determined to confront Oliver Epps, Oscar, face to face, and to keep anyone else from recognizing either of them.

A dark car pulled up behind her. Their headlights flashed. A cop. Joe is going to be furious if he spots me here. She watched the figure walk from behind and approach her passenger door. She lowered the window. "I'm sorry, Officer. I'll move my car."

The words barely left her lips when the door flew open.

She jumped. "Tag, why are you here?" She swallowed hard.

Tag shut the door and hit the locks. "I saw your car. Thought you might be stuck in the snow. It's really icy."

"No, you didn't." She reeled back. "You're stalking me."

Tag stared down at the photos of Oliver and Warren on her lap. "You found the missing issue."

"I did. Want it for your collection?"

"Such a smart mouth." His eyes narrowed into slits. "You know, don't you? You could never play poker."

"I know you're Warren Jackson's son and you killed Oscar."

Tag smirked. "I came to make Oscar pay what he owed my father. He ruined my father. Ruined his life. My father risked his future in that robbery, and Oscar never split the money. Not a penny. He disappeared on my dad. My father died working in the fields of a Washington vineyard for peanuts."

"Oliver became Oscar. He bought the vineyard they planned to buy together, didn't he? Your dad couldn't turn Oliver in to the police without exposing himself. It must have eaten him alive."

Wearily, Tag rested his head on the headrest. "My father spent years searching for him. Online, magazines, newspapers, anything that might help him find Oscar. My mother and I never knew why."

"When did he tell you about the robbery?"

"On his deathbed. He was obsessed."

"Now, you're obsessed."

"I had no choice." Even in the bitter cold, Tag's hurt and anger radiated from his every pore.

"You took over his search after he died," Helen said, trying to sound sympathetic. "It wasn't easy. Oscar dodged the national press for years. He made one little slip. A reporter snapped a chance photo and ran it in *Wine Gourmet* magazine. You found him."

"I jumped on a plane to Philadelphia. Joined Safe Harbor to give me a cover. A few weeks later, I started hearing about you. You, who thought you were Port Anne's answer to Jessica Fletcher. I didn't give you much thought until I met you in person. I knew then you'd be a problem."

"Why did you haunt my clients?"

"I thought if I kept you busy chasing a phantom vandal, you'd be too distracted to go after Oscar's killer. It was fun watching you scurry around."

"Why did you kill him? Money?"

"I visited the vineyard in early November. Used Michele to introduce me to Oscar. I knew Oscar was Oliver the minute we met. He didn't recognize me for Warren's son until I got him alone and told him who I was. He was shocked. Speechless." Tag made a sadistic chuckle. "Offered me a hundred thousand to go away." Tag threw back his head and laughed, his tone pure evil. "Can you imagine? Oscar was worth millions. He thought my father's life was worth a measly hundred thousand. Not even half the amount they stole years ago." Tag's eyes were cold and glossy. He clasped and unclasped his hands.

"Did Oscar kill Bill Elison?"

"I did. Oscar told me Bill knew who he was and threatened him for a payoff. I decided to get rid of him. Who was he, trying to get a share of my father's money? Pushing Bill down the stairs was a piece of cake. Paula knew Oscar's killer was tied to the robbery the moment she heard he was dead. That's when I went to her and demanded my share. She promised to pay me but needed time. I decided to stick around. I've been trailing Paula and waiting to make my next move. When I saw the cops lining up tonight, I knew they were on to Oscar. I knew you'd be here. Too nosy to stay away."

"Why did you attack Rupert and Calli?"

"Rupert started searching through old crime magazines because of the conversation he had with Bill about a local fugitive. I was afraid he'd help the police. He was supposed to die. Calli was a mistake. She caught me defacing the inside of her store, so I knocked her out."

Tag drew a gun from his jacket pocket. "Let's get out of here."

Helen jerked away. "Put down the gun, Tag. You don't want to kill me. It won't help you get your money."

"I don't care about the money anymore. I wanted Oscar to suffer, and he did." He shifted in his seat and pressed the pistol against her right cheek. "Pull out and turn around. Now."

Helen jumped, flipped on her headlights, and eased her car into reverse.

Her tires spun, then caught. She turned south toward Osprey Point and deeper into the park.

"What are you going to do?" she cried.

"There's plenty of cliffs along this coast. The cops will blame your crash on the storm. You lost control. I'll hike back to my truck. Take a flight out tonight. They'll never find you before morning."

Helen crept down the lane. Her wipers strained to scrape the glaze off her windshield. Her blower struggled to defog the glass.

"These roads are too bad. We won't get far," she protested. "Just let me go."

Her mind reverted to Joe. He'd warned her before. Never, ever, get into a car with your assailant. You'll never get out. If you're hostage, find a way out. Fight, bite, kick, run. Don't ever believe they'll let you go.

His cold gun grazed her face.

She gritted her teeth. She knew she had one advantage over Tag. She knew these roads, every twist and turn.

The Mini's headlights washed over the ice in front of them, its sheen coating the surface. It was a skating rink. Ahead, a neon yellow sign warned her of a sharp curve. She neared the familiar bend, held her breath, and jammed on her brakes. The yellow warning symbol for slippery conditions flashed onto her dashboard. The coupe fishtailed back and forth across the road, nearing the cliff and the water's edge a hundred feet below.

"Stop the car!" Tag shouted, grabbing at the wheel.

Helen yanked it back and stepped on the gas. The Mini slid, scraping metal against metal along the guardrail, crushing its passenger door. Her seatbelt caught, her neck jerked back against her headrest. She was too terrified to feel any pain. Without a seatbelt, Tag had swung to his right, slamming his head against his window and the door jam. He dropped the gun to the floor. Holding her breath, she fishtailed again. Her coupe crunched across the road into another bank and the next guardrail.

He grabbed his head in agony with both hands, then scrambled in the dark for his gun. He was a caged lion. "Stop the damn car!" he roared. He reached out for her, his hands digging deep into her throat.

She was choking. Panic pressed on her chest. Clawing at his hands, she struggled to pull his fingers off her windpipe. Desperately, she groped for the Mini's gear shift with her right hand and jammed it from second into reverse. The engine whined, and Tag lost his grip. Spinning the wheel, she shoved into first, praying the coupe was still mobile. One tire found a patch of pavement, and she tore back up Osprey Point, bobbing and weaving like a linebacker at the twenty-yard line. She spun onto the lane toward the vineyard. Her car shuddered, careening over the ruts. Lights at the entrance ahead shone brighter and closer through the pitch dark. She could barely see the iron gates. Her windshield was cracked, and her wipers gave up. Headlights from police cars and vans flooded the courtyard beyond. Blindly, she stomped on the gas and skated across the cobblestones. Officers leaped for cover as the Mini slid sideways into the rear of a sheriff's car and jerked to a halt.

Seven officers surrounded her car, guns raised. "Hands up! Out of the car! Out of the car!"

Gasping, Helen slowly released her vise grip on the steering wheel and fumbled for her door release. She stepped out, her hands held high above her head, her knees collapsing beneath her. Tag, groggy from the head slam, was trapped inside.

Chapter Thirty-Seven

Helen's house on the cliff never felt so comforting. It was after ten o'clock, and Lizzie was whipping up pasta when she came from the shower. Shawn handed her a glass of red. Joe tossed his gun and badge onto the mantel.

"Why did you come to the vineyard?" she asked Lizzie and Shawn.

Shawn, never a natural hugger, put his arms around his mother. "Joe told us the showdown with Paula was scheduled for four o'clock. I scrapped a meeting in Baltimore and got here about five. Lizzie was already waiting. When you didn't pick up your cell, we came looking for you."

"I was petrified when I saw your smashed-up car surrounded by all the police," Lizzie said. "Thank God, we spotted Joe holding you." Her voice trembled. She held back tears. "Oh, Mom. I was so scared."

Helen smiled. "Don't cry. Your mom has nine lives." She leaned down and patted Rocky while he poked his nose into her thigh. Watson and Trixie blinked their support.

Lizzie squared her shoulders. "Pasta and sauce and Italian bread is on the table. Serve yourselves. I want to hear all the details."

Helen took a deep breath. "Stella, our admin, overheard Tag sabotaging my business while he was answering my client calls on Tammi's line. We checked his sales. It wasn't much of a leap to deduce he was our serial stalker."

"When you and I found the silt sand, we thought Oscar had killed Bill," Joe said.

"It was logical. When Bill tried to blackmail Oscar, Oscar had to eliminate him. But Tag was determined to beat him to it. He wanted complete control over Oscar. He must have picked up that grit on his shoes while visiting Michele. I'll bet Oscar was stunned when he heard Bill was killed. He knew Tag did it. My guess, Tag showed up at the vineyard late morning on Saturday, and their argument escalated. Any negotiating was over. Tag wanted revenge for his father. He no longer cared about the money."

"Why did you go to the vineyard?" Shawn asked.

"I found the missing *Unsolved Crimes* magazine about the First Federal robbery in Bill's safe with the photo of Warren Jackson in his early thirties. Tag's facial features were an obvious match. That's when I knew his motive for stalking my houses had to go far beyond sabotaging my business. He was determined to send me off in other directions. It worked. All those torn cards and warnings kept me focused on my clients. That's why there were no warnings near Bill and Oscar's bodies."

"Was Michele helping Tag?"

"Not really. I think Joe will prove Tag used her as a handy alibi. He was the one who insisted on a selfie the weekend they were together, not her."

"Who do you think locked you in the ice house?" Joe asked.

The twins frowned at each other. "What ice house?" Shawn asked.

Helen waved it away. "Not important. After I probed her about Oscar's past, I think Paula panicked and followed me down the hill."

"I'm surprised Bill tried to blackmail Oscar," Shawn commented.

"That's sad. Bill was a good man, and it was very out of character. People get embroiled in stupid decisions and can't get out of them. He should have gone to the police instead of pressing Oscar."

"Tag admitted he watched Bill's house," explained Joe. "He wanted Oscar all to himself. He heard Todd and Vince arguing with Bill about ordering extra life insurance. After they left, Tag walked in. He shoved Bill down the stairs."

Helen walked over to her bookcase and ran her hands across her Detection Club's cases. "I know some people think my attachment to famous sleuths is a bit odd. But I wouldn't have gotten through these last few weeks without these women. It's their insight into human nature. Their razor-sharp logic and determination. Justice had to prevail. They kept me going. I've helped some friends out of legal problems and nasty gossip but never appreciated the terrible strain they felt because their actions were questioned. Not until the past few months. I was watching my integrity, my very reputation, be destroyed, day by day, by unfounded rumors. It was death by a thousand cuts."

"You asked me why I was at the vineyard. I didn't have a choice. If I had a chance to face my enemy, I had to be there." She smiled. "Nancy would never have allowed me to sit home, even if my Mini had to be donated to the cause."

Chapter Thirty-Eight

The Morrisey crew scattered by nine o'clock the following morning. Joe was long gone.

Maggie caught her as she unlocked her door at Safe Harbor.

"Last night we were getting tips on police activity, including the FBI, at Blue Heron. The Sheriff's Office scheduled a press conference for today at noon. Are you going to tell me what it's about? McAlister is ignoring my calls."

Helen chuckled. "I'd tell you if I could. We're both going to have to wait until noon."

"Hmmm. I expect an interview afterwards." Maggie dashed out.

Stella tapped on her door. "Do I have to worry Tag might show up?"

"I can guarantee you, neither of us will see Tag ever again."

Stella gave her a thumbs-up.

"Until I hire myself another assistant, you'll need to field my calls on Tammi's line."

"Not a problem. We'll come up with someone good."

"From your lips to God's ears." Her cell rang.

"Helen?" It was her builder, Alex Jordan.

"Alex, how are you?"

"Doing well. Two more deposits taken at Baywood. I'm wondering if we can walk a property for sale off Susquehanna Road. Any idea when you have the time?"

"How's tomorrow at one? I'll meet you there." She paused. "If you're near a computer or TV, you should watch Baltimore news at noon. The Sheriff has a major announcement to make."

"Got your vandal?"

"Much, much more."

She dialed Maureen Nagley. "Good morning. Ready to get your house on the market? We're in the clear." Maureen sounded pleased. "Let's make it Tuesday at ten. Thanks for sticking by me. I'll never forget it."

Next, Tammi.

"Hi, ready for news?"

"Until you texted 'all okay' in the middle of the night, I couldn't sleep."

"Tag Stolz was arrested last night for the death of Bill Elison and Oscar Banyon. He's also accused of the attempted murder of Rupert Weber and the assault of Calli James."

"You can't be serious!" Tammi's voice jumped three octaves.

"Twenty-seven years ago, Oliver Epps and his partner, Warren Jackson, robbed a California bank. Afterwards, they went completely underground. Oliver took the entire bundle, changed his identity to Oscar Banyon, and purchased his vineyard. Jackson never got a dime. Law enforcement has been searching for them ever since. Jackson spent his life trying to track down Oscar. He died a year ago. Tag is his son, and he's been seeking revenge ever since."

"I don't believe this. I encouraged you to hire him."

"But you, my friend, were key. You suggested days ago that someone was trying to keep me from discovering Bill and Oscar's killer. I should have listened to you."

"Not the first time. Sounds like you're back to work."

"Yes, yes, I am." Helen let out a deep sigh of relief.

"You'll need to hire a new assistant."

"Can you start posting ads? Try not to hire another murderer, please."

"I actually found a perfect candidate."

"Really? Who do you have in mind?"

"Let me describe her for you. She's extremely attractive. Wears jewelry to reflect her mood, which is usually sunny. A bit of a drill sergeant."

"Why does this person sound vaguely familiar? Got a sister I've never met?"

Tammi broke out into a lengthy laugh. "Marcus was approved for what the Army calls compassionate reassignment due to the age of my mother and my grandfather's nursing care needs."

Helen stood up and started shouting. "Leave it to you to move the United States Army! You are a miracle worker! When are you back?"

"Paperwork is processing now. Most likely about two weeks."

"I'm breaking out the champagne!"

* * *

Joe walked in about five o'clock, one hand behind his back. "I thought I'd stop in. Stella says your phone's been ringing off the hook."

Helen flashed a big smile. "I'm back in the saddle."

"Another catch phrase?"

"I thought you'd be tied up until midnight."

"I am. I've got to go back to the office. But I wanted to bring you a present."

"A present?"

"We completely missed Valentine's Day, and I wanted to make it up to you."

"Who says Valentine's Day has to be on February fourteenth?" She cocked her head. "What are you hiding?"

Joe brought his arm around. "Flowers."

"Flowers?" She untied a big red ribbon wrapped around a short white florist box. She slowly pulled back layers of sparkling red and white tissue. Her eyes opened wide, and she began to laugh. "These look like red Twizzlers in a vase with a Valentine card."

"To be accurate, there's at least sixty. Don't forget the red bow around them. I tied it myself."

"They're perfect. They don't need water and will never wilt." She leaned in and gave him a warm kiss. "Actually, Detective McAlister, you're not the only romantic. I have a present for *you*."

Joe looked stunned.

She pulled a fat blue and white envelope wrapped in red ribbon from inside her desk. "Howard Travel rushed this over to me about an hour ago. The morning you called me about Bill, I had made a momentous decision." She blushed. "At least, it was momentous for me."

"Yes?" He offered his signature upside-down smile.

"Sarah wangled us onto the trip to Italy you wanted. We leave May fifth."

"Seriously? Oh, baby!" Joe picked her up and twirled her around the room.

He stopped, dropping her to the ground. "Do you promise to leave your sleuths at home? I'd like to have you all to myself."

Helen wrapped her arms around his neck and kissed him. "I'm sure that can be arranged."

Acknowledgments

Wineries and vineyards attract so many enthusiasts, and the state of Maryland is fortunate to have over eighty to choose from. About two years ago I visited a vineyard a few miles from my home on the eastern shore of the Chesapeake. It was a blustery February afternoon. Bohemia Overlook inspired me with its unique history going back to the Revolutionary War. I'm grateful to the owners who gave me an extensive tour of all its beautiful buildings and grounds. I assure you, dear readers, the murder of my vineyard owner stems only from my imagination. You never know how a person or location might be fodder for one of my mysteries! Hope you'll keep your suggestions coming.

Family always support my long hours hiding away in my upstairs study. My husband John is resigned to rarely seeing me except for irregular meal times or a cup of hot tea. Wine is a treat, especially when I'm writing a mystery centered on a vineyard. My twins, John and Meghan, are my strongest critics when it comes to beta reading my manuscripts. Their comments are usually right on point. Thank you and much love.

Special thanks to my editor Shawn Reilly Simmons and the patient Deborah Well at Level Best Books. Thank you to Blackstone Publishing who offers my audios of the Chesapeake Bay Mystery Series. I'm grateful to all your attention to detail. Thank you to Peter Senftleben for your wise advice on my storylines.

The staff of Cecil County Public Library are the dearest professionals. Giving me a quiet harbor to work when I need a change from my own four walls is a Godsend.

Huge thank you to book clubs who invite me to meet my readers in person. Sharing Helen's favorite wine and Twizzlers and talking about characters, clues, twists, and of course, laughter, is an absolute pleasure.

Join me through my website or on social media. Thank you for all your wonderful reviews. They inspire me.

All the best, Judy L. Murray

About the Author

Judy L. Murray is winner of the Silver Falchion Award, Independent Publisher Gold Medals, PenCraft International First Place Awards, and an Agatha Award Nominee. A former Philadelphia real estate broker and restoration addict, Judy worked with enough delusional sellers, jittery buyers, testy contractors, and diva agents to fill her head with back-office insight and truth versus gossip. She is a graduate in newspaper journalism from the S.I. Newhouse School at Syracuse University and began her professional writing career as a newspaper reporter and magazine columnist. She holds a master's degree in business from Penn State University. She lives atop a cliff on the Chesapeake Bay with her husband. They're buffeted by winds in winter and invaded by family and dogs in summer. Judy is a member of Sisters in Crime and Mystery Writers of America. Sign up for her newsletter at www.judylmurraymysteries.com. She would love to hear from you.

AUTHOR WEBSITE:
  https://www.judylmurraymysteries.com/

SOCIAL MEDIA HANDLES:
  https://www.facebook.com/judymurray4

https://twitter.com/judylmurray
https://www.instagram.com/judylmurraymysterywriter/
https://www.tiktok.com/@judylmurraymysteries

Also by Judy L. Murray

Murder in the Master

Killer in the Kitchen

Peril in the Pool House

www.ingramcontent.com/pod-product-compliance
Lightning Source LLC
Chambersburg PA
CBHW032030040625
27716CB00032B/393